SURVIVE THE NIGHT
Harmony Grove Series, Book 4
Copyright © 2014, 2021 by Carol J. Post

Note to readers: An earlier, shorter version of this book was published through Love Inspired Suspense in June 2014 under the title Out for Justice.

ISBN: 978-0-9863802-9-7 (ebook)
ISBN: 978-1-7368200-0-1 (print)

Cover Design and Interior Format
© KILLION
THE
GROUP INC.

SURVIVE THE NIGHT

Harmony Grove Series

CAROL J. POST

ONE

———

" WE'VE FOUND ANOTHER victim."

Lexi Simmons tensed at Sergeant Tomlinson's words flowing through her Bluetooth headset. *Not again.* She eased to a stop at a red light and gripped the Explorer's steering wheel more tightly. "Where this time?"

"A couple miles outside Harmony Grove."

Harmony Grove. *Home.* She closed her eyes, her insides drawing into a painful knot.

Tomlinson continued. "You're from there, so you might know the victim. If you need to be excused from this one, all you've got to do is say the word."

She swallowed back the bile rising in her throat. This made number five. Lexi had worked each case, two of them as the lead detective. Except now it had gotten personal. Tomlinson was right. She probably *did* know the victim. Harmony Grove was a tiny town.

"No, I'm all right. I can handle it. Give me what you've got."

A horn sounded behind her and she stepped on the gas. She had left Polk County Sheriff's Office five minutes earlier, looking forward to a girls' night out with her cousin Kayla. Dinner and a movie.

Her plans had just changed.

Tomlinson relayed the details of the case in that impersonal monotone that underscored the subject's status as yet another statistic. Her age fell in the middle of the range of the other victims, which spanned from early twenties to mid-thirties, but that was where the similarities ended. All the women had different builds, different hair colors and styles, different occupations—nothing linking them except that broad age range and how they were killed.

When Tomlinson had finished, Lexi disconnected the call. There was one more person she needed to speak with before heading into what was going to be a long night. She pressed a button on her Bluetooth. "Call Kayla."

After four rings, her cousin's voicemail came on and she left a message. The cancellation was going to be last-minute, but her cousin would understand. Lexi's job came first. There was a reason she had changed her major from business to law enforcement, and that girl lying in the woods, cold and alone, was it.

Three miles before reaching the outskirts of Harmony Grove, the road ahead disappeared under a flashing display of red and blue. Other law-enforcement officers were already on site, securing the scene, keeping away the curious. So were the Polk County Sheriff's Office crime scene investigators.

Lexi slipped between two Harmony Grove Police Department vehicles and ground to a halt. This was the county's jurisdiction, but it was so close to the city limits that Harmony Grove P.D. had responded, too. Chief Willis was there. His car was prominently labeled Chief of Police. If she was lucky, Shane Dalton was the other officer who'd responded. At least her chances were fifty-fifty.

As she stepped from her vehicle, she shifted her gaze upward. A blanket of steel gray wrapped the western sky and a musty-scented breeze whipped the ends of her ponytail into her face. The storm had been building for the past couple of hours, an ever-increasing threat. Now it was more of a promise.

She smoothed her jacket and swung the door shut. They had their work cut out for them without being hampered by one of Central Florida's early spring thundershowers. Of course, if this case was like the other four, there wouldn't be anything to gather. The killer had a knack for leaving behind no evidence except a body.

She glanced around the area. Up ahead, ribbons of yellow interrupted the solid green of the woods. Crime scene tape. She headed in that direction with frequent glances at the leaf-covered ground, always on the lookout for snakes. During her eight months in homicide, she'd trudged through worse.

She stopped at a section of the tape stretched between two trees. A few feet away Tommy Willis, Harmony Grove's chief of police, stood with his back to her. In front of him, two Polk County crime scene investigators took photos. Her colleagues. They would be there for the next several hours, scouring every square inch of the area, combing the body for clothing fibers, strands of hair, and bits of skin under the fingernails, anything that might bring them one step closer to linking a person to the crime.

As she reached for the tape, ready to duck under it,

rustling drew her attention to the left. A dark-haired, muscular figure wove between the trees with sure steps. Alan White. She frowned. Yep, fifty-fifty. She'd never been good with odds.

When he looked up, that sure step faltered. He held a roll of the yellow plastic tape in one hand. Apparently, he'd been the one cordoning off the area.

"Hello, Alan." She greeted him with the same stiffness that had characterized their interactions for the past seven years.

"Lexi." The stiffness was as pronounced on his end as hers.

He moved closer. He looked sharp in his midnight blue Harmony Grove Police uniform. Of course, he looked sharp in whatever he wore. Maybe someday that unwanted tug of attraction would fade.

He stopped a couple feet away from her. "Did you just arrive?"

"About two minutes ago."

"How much information have you gotten?"

"White female, about twenty-five years of age. Punched in the face several times, then strangled."

Same as the others. The pictures hadn't arrived yet. But they would. They always did. The creep got a sick thrill out of photographing his crime, step by step, and sending the pictures to the *Ledger*. Fortunately, the newspaper had turned them over to Lakeland P.D. right from the start, without a single one going to print.

She frowned at Alan. Something wasn't right with him. It wasn't just the customary stiffness. Deep creases of concern marked the bridge of his nose and anguish had settled in his blue eyes. "It's someone we know, isn't it?"

"I'm afraid it is."

As she ducked under the tape, Alan grabbed her arm. "Wait."

She pulled from his grasp. He was trying to protect her. It wasn't necessary. She was a professional. She wouldn't let her personal feelings get in the way of doing her job. Right now, that job entailed performing the best investigation she could. Maybe, for once, the killer had gotten careless or bold or stupid and left behind some inconspicuous shred of evidence that would ultimately lead to his capture.

Summoning strength she didn't feel, she moved past Tommy. Alan followed, once again grasping her arm, trying to hold her back. "Lexi, wait. Let me talk to you."

She spun on him, her words a harsh whisper. "Let me do my job."

Straight ahead, not more than fifteen feet away, lay a body, partially obstructed by a downed limb. Crime scene investigator Vickers squatted, sitting on one heel to shoot another photo, further blocking her view. She ignored Alan's pleas and moved closer, heart pounding.

The victim was definitely a woman, judging from the baby-blue silk sleepwear. Bare feet extended from the hem of the pajama bottoms, toenails painted hot pink.

Then Vickers straightened and moved aside, offering her an unobstructed view of their newest victim. Lexi's brain shut down. Alan said something, but the words didn't register.

Matted auburn hair flowed over a blanket of dying

leaves. Green eyes, one swollen almost shut, stared unseeing at the leafy canopy overhead. Blood had trickled from a cut on one cheek, but had long since dried. A piece of neatly-applied duct tape hid the mouth, and a blackish-red ring circled the creamy white neck.

No.

Lexi shook her head. The ground seemed to tilt beneath her and she took a stumbling step backward to steady herself. A scream of protest clawed its way up her throat, followed by a wave of nausea that almost brought her to her knees.

Alan's words finally penetrated her befuddled brain, several seconds too late.

"Lexi, it's Kayla."

———————

Alan reached for her, his heart twisting in his chest. The confident air she'd had just moments earlier had evaporated like drops of water on a hot tin roof, and her complexion had grown pasty white above the dark charcoal gray of her jacket. Suddenly she seemed broken and vulnerable. And much younger than her twenty-six years.

A sense of protectiveness surged through him, but she backed away from his advance. He didn't expect any different. She would stand alone before she would accept comfort from him.

He'd known there was a possibility that Lexi might show up. The body was found outside the city limits of Harmony Grove. In fact, the CSI van had arrived right after he had. But with ten homicide detectives working for Polk County, the odds of Lexi being the one to respond were only ten percent.

"Lexi, I'm sorry." He stepped toward her again, wishing he could wrap her in a comforting hug. Just like old times. He settled instead for a steadying hand under her elbow. But that gesture wasn't any more welcome than the hug would have been. She jerked away, as if touched by something vile, then spun and walked back the way they had come. The younger of the two investigators started to follow her—Wayne Blanchard, if he remembered the introduction correctly.

Alan held up a hand. "Let me talk to her."

He hurried after her. He should have warned her. That was what he'd intended, at least once he'd recovered his wits. Even though he'd known she might be the one assigned to the case, actually seeing her had caught him off guard. Seeing Lexi always caught him off guard.

He'd wanted to talk to her alone, to give her the bad news in private. It would have allowed her to compose herself before she had to face the other law enforcement personnel. She hadn't given him the opportunity.

That was no excuse. He should have stopped her, physically tackled her if he had to. Or told her before she even crossed under the crime scene tape that Kayla was the victim. Instead, she hadn't learned the truth until the moment she'd viewed her cousin's battered body.

Now he was kicking himself. Hard. Actually, he hadn't stopped kicking himself since she'd jerked away from him and stepped around his chief. Of course, this wasn't the first time he'd kicked himself where Lexi was concerned.

When he caught up to her, they'd almost reached the vehicles. A growing rumble followed them, and as he stepped into the clearing, he cast a glance skyward. Heavy black clouds rolled ever closer, the wall of rain already visible in the distance.

"Lexi, where are you going?" She shouldn't be driving in her state of mind.

"I'm getting some things I need out of my vehicle."

She couldn't be serious. "You're not really thinking of investigating that back there, are you?"

"I'm not *thinking* about it." She pressed a button on her key fob, then opened the back door of her Explorer. "I'm *doing* it."

"Lexi, you don't have to do this. Let someone else work this one."

She spun to face him, eyes blazing. Her anger wasn't aimed at him, but he still had to stifle a grimace.

"This is *my* case." She jabbed an index finger at her chest. "I'm making it my number-one priority to catch this guy."

Stubborn, as always. He opened his mouth to object, then caught movement in his peripheral vision. Detective Vickers had emerged from the woods and was moving toward them.

Lexi cast a glance at Vickers, some thirty feet away, then turned suddenly and grasped both of Alan's upper arms. "Don't say anything." Her voice was a hoarse whisper. "They'll take me off the case."

"Maybe that would be best."

"No." Her eyes flicked to Vickers again and she lowered her voice even more. "This case is important to me. This creep is preying on women."

His jaw tightened. She was right. Kayla wasn't the first. Although the other murders hadn't happened near Harmony Grove, the sheriff's office had disseminated the information to all the agencies.

Lexi continued, her gaze imploring. "You of all people understand what that means to me."

Yes, he did understand. That passion had begun long before this current killing spree. He'd been there for her then, had worried with her when her best friend Abby had become the target of a stalker and had comforted her when they'd later found her body. At the time, they'd all recently graduated from high school, and Lexi was heading to Florida State in the fall. Alan had encouraged her new passion to try to make the world safer for at-risk women and supported her decision to change her major from business to law enforcement.

His days of offering any kind of support or encouragement were long past.

She dropped her arms to rest a slender hand on his forearm. "He's taken Kayla now. Let me bring him to justice. Please, Alan."

She stared up at him with those pleading green eyes, tears pooled at their lower lashes, and all his arguments dissipated, drifting away on the rain-scented breeze. Somehow, being within ten feet of Lexi always turned his will to mush. He'd never been able to deny her anything. Even her freedom.

He released his breath in a heavy sigh. "All right. I'll leave it be. But if you need to talk, I'm here. I cared for Kayla, too."

All he got from her was a brusque nod. Detective Vickers strode past them and stopped next to the crime scene van.

Alan watched him and then returned his attention to Lexi. "Is there anything I can do?"

She started to shake her head, then drew her brows together. "Have Aunt Sharon and Uncle George been told yet?"

"I doubt it. No one had an ID until crime scene arrived right before you did. Would you like me to talk to them?"

Relief flooded her features. "I'd really appreciate it."

He nodded slowly, hesitant to leave her. But she would be all right. She wouldn't be alone, and she'd have the distraction of work. She'd throw herself into it with a vengeance and make it through the next few hours.

Then she would drive back to Auburndale, to her empty house. And there'd be nothing to distract her. Those quiet, lonely hours would be the hardest. He understood. And he'd give anything to be there for her.

But she had made her choice. Seven years ago. They'd been young, both nineteen. He'd had hope in his heart, a ring in his pocket and a love that he'd thought would last for eternity. But she'd had dollar signs in her eyes. She'd figured out that if she wanted to have the life she'd envisioned for herself, being saddled with a small-town cop wasn't going to cut it.

He made his way to his patrol car and slid into the driver's seat. As he shut the door, the sky opened up and dumped its burden. Fat raindrops plopped onto the windshield, combining to form a steady stream down the sloped glass. After cranking the car, he put the wiper lever in the *high* position. Between swipes, he watched Lexi shrug into a raincoat and pull its hood over her head. It was going to be a long night for her.

He had often wondered if she had regrets. Things obviously hadn't turned out as she had hoped because she was still single. But during all of their chance meetings over the past seven years, she'd never hinted at any interest in reigniting old sparks. She always eyed him with a sort of uneasy coldness, coupled with underlying hurt and anger.

As if *he* was the one who had dumped *her*.

He pulled onto the road, the roar of the downpour and the swish-swish of the windshield wipers a backdrop to his thoughts. A knot of dread had settled in the pit of his stomach. Kayla was George and Sharon's only child. They wouldn't handle the news well. Neither would the class of second-graders who would return from spring break next week to find their beloved Miss Douglas gone. Kayla's absence would leave a hole in a lot of lives.

When he pulled into the Douglases' driveway, the garage door was up. The white Escort sat on the right, but the spot reserved for George's Silverado was vacant. That meant Sharon was home alone.

He got out of the car, the knot in his stomach growing larger. He would stay with Sharon until George arrived. Then maybe he'd go have dinner at Pappy's. Not that he would feel like eating. But the hometown pizzeria was always hopping.

In Harmony Grove, news traveled fast. And the more shocking the news, the faster it spread. Maybe Kayla had said something. Or maybe someone had seen something. He would look for any shred of evidence that might help them find whoever had done this to her.

Lord, help us catch this guy before anyone else gets hurt.

Lexi was probably at that moment working on the investigation, doing her best to hold it together, the rain masking tears she would try so hard not to shed. A pang of tenderness shot through him.

And Lord, please give Lexi the strength to do what she feels she needs to do.

TWO

———

L EXI STRAIGHTENED HER spine and tried not to fidget. A couple dozen other detectives sat at tables around the room and Tomlinson stood at the front ready to bring everyone up to speed on the latest developments in the case.

The weekend had been a blur and hadn't included nearly enough sleep. By the time she'd gotten home and crawled into bed in the wee hours of Saturday morning, it had been almost dawn. But even then, sleep had eluded her. Every time she got just on the brink, the image of Kayla—bound, gagged and strangled—shot through her mind and jolted her instantly awake.

Saturday and Sunday hadn't offered any opportunities for rest, either. Family had occupied all the daylight hours and a fair share of the nighttime ones. Aunt Sharon and Uncle George were a wreck, so Lexi had jumped in with making phone calls, helping with funeral arrangements and securing lodging for those who would be traveling to attend the service.

Now she was beyond exhausted. If she sat still for long, she'd probably fall asleep. Hopefully, Tomlinson would keep it short.

When the sergeant stepped up to the podium, his expression was grave. "Thursday night, our killer struck again. The newest victim was Kayla Douglas, a twenty-six-year-old teacher at Harmony Grove Elementary. Friday afternoon, a couple of teenagers were walking their dog in the woods about three miles north of town and found her body."

Tomlinson's gaze shifted to Lexi and lingered. If he was looking for a reaction, he wasn't going to get one. No way was she going to give him a reason to pull her off the case.

Finally, he continued. "The photos arrived at the *Ledger* in Saturday's mail. They're being processed now, along with the envelope."

Just like the others. Lexi sighed. It almost seemed a pointless waste of time. The killer had never left behind any prints. No DNA on the envelope seal or the back of the stamp. He used one of the well-known brands of envelope sealers. He was too smart to lick them. Or to touch anything without gloves.

But as long as he kept killing, they would keep investigating each case as if it was the first. Eventually they would get a break. If someone killed long enough and frequently enough, no matter how meticulous and methodical, he would make a mistake sooner or later.

Tomlinson moved out from behind the podium to pace slowly back and forth across the front of the room. "We've checked out her house and lifted some prints from the entry area. But just as with the other women, there was no sign of a struggle, and the neighbors didn't hear a thing. If she disappeared from home, she went willingly. Or at least opened the door willingly. It'll be a while till we get the toxicology report back, but my guess is they'll find chloroform in her system, too."

Lexi struggled against the churning in her gut. How could Kayla have fallen prey? She was smart, always cautious. According to friends and family members, the other victims were, too. These weren't women who hung out in bars and went home with strange men. They were careful, responsible girls who disappeared from their own locked homes after settling in for the night.

"As you know, this is the fifth one. The killer's M.O. is always the same. He shows up at the homes of his victims, convinces them to open the door, then puts them out with chloroform. And before he leaves with his unconscious victim, he twists the lock and pulls the door shut behind him."

He stopped his pacing and faced them fully. "We've already been working with several of the local agencies, and we've got the FBI assisting with behavioral analysis and searching for any links to cases in their database. We still have no fingerprints or other forensic evidence. Since this latest murder, Harmony Grove will be coming on board. Simmons, coordinate your efforts with them. I'm guessing you know the chief of police and the two officers."

She nodded. Yes, she knew them. One better than the others.

Seven years ago, on Thanksgiving night, Alan had offered her a ring. She had panicked. Instead of asking for time, she'd broken it off completely. Her reaction had been partly due to youth, but mostly a result of having spent seventeen years observing her parents' miserable relationship. She'd returned to school, hoping deep down that Alan loved her enough to wait for her. He'd waited, all right. Maybe a week. She'd come home during Christmas break, ready to tell him she'd made a mistake. He'd met her at the door...with his new fiancée. *Pregnant* fiancée, if the rumors were to be believed.

Since then, even though her mom still lived in Harmony Grove, she and Alan had managed to avoid each other most of the time. The first three years, she'd been away at school. Then, instead of returning to Harmony Grove, she'd settled in nearby Auburndale. Up until Friday, they'd seen little of each other.

That was about to change.

Tomlinson resumed his pacing. "The Harmony Grove officers likely know everyone in town. They should be able to help us. I want the names of every person Kayla Douglas came in contact with for the past month, and every possible lead followed. There's got to be some connection between these five women, someone they each knew and trusted enough to open the door for late at night."

"Yes, sir." She wouldn't leave any stone unturned. Even if it meant working side by side with Alan.

Tomlinson returned to the podium and rested both hands on its top edges. "The story has already hit the papers, and at some point, the Sheriff will call another press conference. We have to be careful. There's a fine line between warning the public and giving this guy the fame and recognition he wants."

He inhaled slowly. "A lot of killers like to keep trophies, but this guy is different. Maybe he *is* keeping pictures, mementos to savor, but it's more than that. He wants his crimes on display for the world to see. Right now, he's killing at the rate of once a month. Seeing his actions publicized could spur him to kill more. Fortunately, the publisher has promised to continue to keep the photos they receive out of the hands of the public and turn them immediately over to law enforcement." Tomlinson's gaze circled the room. "All right, then. Let's get out there and get this thing solved."

Lexi dropped her pen into her purse and gathered her notepad. So she was going to have to work with Alan. She could handle it. At least Tomlinson hadn't taken her off the case.

She moved across the room and as she reached the open door, Tomlinson's voice stopped her.

"Simmons, hold up. I need to talk to you."

She paused outside the open doorway, tension creeping through her shoulders. Maybe she was premature in her assessment that he wasn't going to pull her. "Yes, sir?"

He stepped out to stand next to her. "Are you okay working this case? I heard you almost lost it out there."

Heat crept up her neck and settled in her cheeks. Blanchard or Vickers. One of them had squealed on her. Either that, or Alan had broken his promise and made a call to her supervisor.

"I'm fine, sir." She looked past Tomlinson to where one of the deputies was making his way toward them from the restrooms. Greg something, in patrol. She'd talked to him once or twice. She didn't want him knowing her business. Nothing against Greg. He seemed like a nice enough guy. But she didn't want *anybody* knowing her business.

She waited till he passed, then turned her attention back to Tomlinson.

"Sir, Harmony Grove is a small town, and I grew up there. So I knew the victim." That was all she would tell him.

"I suspected as much. I can assign someone else."

"No, sir, that won't be necessary."

He studied her, and she fought the urge to squirm under his gentle scrutiny. Brent Tomlinson was like a father to everyone in the division. "Is there something you're not telling me?"

She shook her head. "I can handle it, sir."

He hesitated for only a moment longer. "Then get out there."

"Yes, sir. I'll do that."

"Maybe with a lot of luck and some really great detective work, we'll catch this guy." He smiled, crinkling the skin at the corners of his eyes. "A little prayer wouldn't hurt, either."

She nodded. The really great detective work—she was all over that. But the prayer would have to be someone else's department. She and God weren't on speaking terms. Hadn't been for quite some time. Eight years, to be exact. Not that they'd been all that close before.

When God took her best friend, that had cemented it. Okay, maybe God hadn't taken Abby. He just hadn't done anything to stop what had happened, even though it had supposedly been in His power to do so.

The same with her dad a year earlier. After spending

his entire adult life catering to an impossible-to-please woman, he'd come home from work, sat down to read the newspaper and keeled over with a massive heart attack. No warning.

Now it was her cousin Kayla. Kayla was the kindest, most generous person Lexi had ever known. She poured her life into her students, never missed a church service and tithed her ten percent.

But God had silently watched while a ruthless killer had snuffed out a beautiful soul.

No, if that was the kind of God people served, someone else would have to do the praying.

———

A dismal, gray sky hung low over the manicured lawns of Peace Memorial Gardens, and a light mist rained down on those gathered around the freshly dug grave. The weather fit the mood.

Alan had joined the others who had made the short trip from Hope Community Church to the cemetery at the edge of town. Most of Harmony Grove had come out for the funeral, and the small brick church had been filled to capacity and beyond. He'd arrived ten minutes before the start of the service and had had no choice but to squeeze in along the back wall. Lexi, he'd assumed, had been seated at the front with the family.

The group attending the simple graveside service was much smaller than what had been packed into the church. Currently, Pastor Tom was positioned in front of the casket, in the center of the elongated semicircle of mourners, reading the 23rd Psalm. Alan stood with about three dozen of Kayla's closest friends and family members. Many of them were his friends, too, people both he and Kayla had grown up with. Over the past couple of years, several had married. At twenty-six, he and Kayla had been some of the last holdouts.

Melissa Langston had started it off by reuniting with her ex after a seven-year separation. That was a path he and Lexi weren't likely to follow. A few months later, the director of the abused women's shelter and her beau had tied the knot. Then, in the most unlikely match of the century, Alan's fellow officer, Shane Dalton, had married Harmony Grove's bad girl. Three weddings over the span of less than a year. Three happy couples.

Though his friends still included him in their gatherings, he often walked away with a hollowness inside. His own marriage hadn't lasted long enough to even glimpse happily-ever-after on the horizon.

As the pastor finished the reading, Alan cast a glance at Lexi several feet away. The simple black dress she wore emphasized the paleness of her skin, and crystalline mini-droplets coated her blond hair, giving her an almost ethereal quality.

She stared straight ahead, her shoulders stiff and her jaw rigid. He understood. He felt it too—anger at whoever had done this to Kayla.

But Lexi's anger was also directed at God. At least it had been before, when Abby had been killed. Back then he hadn't had any answers for her. He hadn't shared any godly wisdom, because he'd had no faith of his own.

Now he did. He had that faith. Kayla had, too, so he knew where she'd gone. But he still didn't have any answers.

After Pastor Tom gave the closing prayer, the small crowd began to disperse. Alan fell in beside Lexi as she walked toward her car.

"Are you doing all right?"

She shrugged. "As well as can be expected."

"Anything I can do?"

"Help us put this monster behind bars."

"I'll give it my best shot." He'd already talked to Chief Willis. Harmony Grove was working with the other agencies, helping in the investigation. He'd been talking to people, even on his own time, trying to uncover any information that might lead to a break in the case.

Lexi stopped next to her car and turned to face him. "Get in."

He hurried around to the passenger's side of the gold Mazda before she could change her mind. By the time he slipped inside, she was already sitting at the wheel, her gaze fixed on some point beyond the spotted front windshield.

"It looks like you and I are going to be working together. Instructions from my supervisor." She spoke without looking at him. "We'll at least be coordinating our efforts." She didn't sound thrilled. But she didn't seem miffed, either.

"Are you okay with that?"

Now she looked at him. "We both want to see Kayla's killer caught. I think we're mature enough to set aside our past differences and work toward the same end."

He nodded. "The sheriff's office has filled us in on each of the cases. But give me everything you've got."

"The women's ages range from twenty-two to thirty-one. The oldest one looked young for her age, so I'm thinking our guy wants girls in their twenties. Two of the victims were from Lakeland, one was from Bartow and one was from Winter Haven. Kayla was number five."

She rested a hand on the steering wheel. "The perp feeds on recognition. He takes photos of his victims and sends them to the *Ledger*, likely hoping they'll be printed."

"Have they been?"

"No. They've turned them over to Lakeland P.D., who has turned them over to us."

"I guess responsible journalism exists after all."

He gave her a wry smile. She might have even returned it. Just a little.

She continued, expression again somber. "Sometimes we get the photo before we find the body. Sometimes we find the body first."

"Kayla?"

"The photos arrived Saturday."

He clenched his fists. It wasn't enough he had to kill her. He'd furthered his thrill by photographing his work. Whatever it took, Alan was going to catch this guy.

He drew in a deep breath, then released it in a controlled exhale. "What can you tell me about these murders?"

"I don't know about Kayla, but with the other four, friends or family members have stated that they knew for a fact that the girls were home for the night and not planning to go back out."

"Kayla, too."

She looked at him sharply. "You're sure?"

"Positive. She was with me that evening. I dropped her off at her house at nine-thirty."

Her eyes raked over him. "You were dating Kayla, too? You get around."

The sarcasm in her tone stabbed at him. "No, it wasn't like that. She needed to buy a gift and conned me into driving her to Lakeland Square Mall."

"Uh-huh."

Her response was heavy with skepticism. So he dated a lot. Big deal. Some people claimed he was Harmony Grove's most eligible bachelor. He doubted it. Or maybe he held the title by default. After all, there were only a handful of single guys his age.

At least he kept it casual. He wasn't out to break any hearts. His dates were more friendship than anything.

"Is there any link between the victims? Jobs, friends, places they frequent?"

Lexi shook her head. "None that we've been able to find. The first four had no friends in common, didn't hang out at the same places and had totally unrelated careers. One was an administrative assistant and one was a dental hygienist. The other two were students at two different colleges. One went to Florida Southern and the other to Polk State."

"How about physical description? Any particular body type or hair color he's targeting?"

"Nope, they go all the way from a petite one hundred eight pounds to a hefty two-thirty. And we've got a platinum blonde, a dishwater blonde and two brunettes. And now, with Kayla, a redhead."

Lexi heaved a sigh and continued. "The only similarities are the age group and the way they're killed. He chloroforms them and takes them into the woods. After they wake up, he bloodies them up a little, then strangles them." Sadness filled her gaze and she lowered her voice. "We know they're awake because of the pictures."

Alan closed his eyes, a vise squeezing down on his stomach. These weren't nameless girls she was talking about. This was Kayla.

Lexi stared out the windshield. "Our best clue at this point—our *only* clue—is that the killer is someone each of the victims knew well enough to feel comfortable unlocking and opening their door late at night. But it has to be a newer acquaintance, or their friends and family members would be aware of him. So far we haven't gotten a single match."

Alan thought for a moment. Who could each of these women have met recently who would be unknown to friends and family members? "What about workers—cable or phone techs, carpet cleaners, plumbers, electricians, anything like that?"

Lexi frowned. "Nothing that matches. One of the Lakeland girls had Stanley Steemer clean her carpets three weeks before she was killed. The one in Winter Haven had cable installed two months before she died. The other two didn't have any kind of work done, at least nothing that shows up on receipts, credit card statements or banking records."

Alan nodded. "What now?"

"Talk to everyone we know in Harmony Grove who might have any information."

"I've already talked to her neighbors. No one saw or heard anything that night. Well, I take that back. Old Mrs. Thayer saw me pull up, get out and walk

Kayla to the door."

She cocked a brow at him. "That just might make you our only suspect. Have you ever met Meagan Bowers, Stephanie Wilson, Donna Jackson or Sylvia Stephens?"

"Nope, never heard of them."

She gave him a quirky grin. "Okay, then you're probably not the killer."

"I hope your interrogations aren't always that easy."

"No, they're not. Usually, I'm a tough interrogator." She grew serious again. "Look, keep everything I've told you under wraps. Tomlinson is afraid if we give him the publicity he wants, it'll just encourage him to kill again."

"Will do."

"We need to exchange cell numbers, too."

He pulled out his phone and tapped to add her name and number. He'd deleted her from his contacts long ago. Unfortunately, he'd never quite been able to delete her from his heart.

Seven years ago, he'd been ready to commit his life to her. She'd turned him down flat. He should have seen the writing on the wall. When she'd insisted she didn't want to tie him down while she finished school, he'd believed her. And even though he'd been willing to wait, when she'd suggested they date other people, he had reluctantly agreed.

It hadn't taken long for her to find someone else. Her mother had been the one to break the bad news to him. Lexi hadn't had the guts to do it herself. The message had been clear—this bright, young medical student was worthy of her, and Alan somehow wasn't. Her rejection had set him up for a whole series of bad choices of his own.

But this wasn't the time to dwell on past mistakes. They had a murder to solve. He climbed from the car, then poked his head back inside. "Lexi, be careful. You're in that age group."

"Don't worry, I'm not the type to open my door to anyone in the middle of the night."

"Neither was Kayla."

THREE

——◆——

LEXI WALKED DOWN the hall of Harmony Grove Elementary School, the click of her boots against the vinyl tile floor drowned out by a cacophony of excited voices. The release bell had just rung and teachers were herding their unruly charges toward the pickup area.

She moved against the current, dressed in her standard business attire—leather boots, dark suit and coordinating blouse, weapon hidden under the blazer. She'd arranged to meet with two of the teachers who'd been close to Kayla. Maybe they would remember something she'd said before she died, something that had seemed insignificant at the time but could be important in solving the case.

She hadn't been thrilled about having to work closely with Alan, but as they'd sat in her car yesterday after the funeral, his diligence had impressed her. He'd already taken the initiative to talk to at least a dozen people who knew and were close to Kayla. Definitely not a slacker. Maybe it was because of the relationship he'd had with Kayla, whatever that had been. Not likely, though. Alan had always given 110 percent to whatever he was involved in, whether school, job, friendships or physical training. He was going to make a good partner.

Lexi slowed as she approached the third door on the left. Until the beginning of spring break, it had been Kayla's classroom. This week, someone else would have taken charge of her students.

She stopped at the locked door and peered through the glass in the top. Before meeting with her cousin's teacher friends, she had one other task to handle. Someone needed to clear out Kayla's personal items, and Aunt Sharon was in no shape to deal with it.

Lexi crossed her arms and leaned back against the wall. The room was empty, but since she'd scheduled her visit in advance, someone would be back soon.

Less than five minutes later, a young woman rounded the corner and approached, lifting a hand in greeting. "You must be Detective Simmons."

She slid a key into the lock, then swung open the door. "I'm Terri, the substitute filling in until they get someone permanent. The whole situation is so tragic."

Lexi nodded and followed her inside where small wooden desks were lined up in five neat rows. Two plastic crates sat atop the larger desk at the front reserved for the teacher.

Terri led her up one of the center aisles. "They told me you were going to be coming, so I gathered up Ms. Douglas's things." She motioned toward the two crates filled to overflowing with books and various items.

Lexi removed a box from one of the crates. The words "Cuisenaire Rods" stretched across the upper portion, pictures of narrow, rectangular blocks in various lengths and colors beneath.

Terri tilted her head toward what Lexi held. "They're math manipulatives."

Lexi nodded and pulled out the other items—flash cards and a variety of children's books. "Are these things you or the other teachers could use with the students?"

"You betcha."

"How about if I leave them here?" Better than letting them collect dust in a closet. Aunt Sharon would probably agree.

Lexi emptied the other box, then repacked everything, keeping out three framed photos and several objects that had most likely been gifts from students. Those items Aunt Sharon would treasure.

Terri flashed her an appreciative smile. "Thank you for donating all the educational things. I know the students will enjoy them."

"No problem. I'm glad they'll get some use out of them."

The young substitute opened a desk drawer and pulled out a plastic grocery bag. "This will make what you're taking a little easier to carry."

Lexi thanked her and packed the items into the bag. "How well did you know Kayla?"

"I'm afraid I didn't. This is my first time subbing at Harmony Grove. But everyone says she was a special lady. Well loved. She's going to be a hard one to follow."

Lexi walked toward the door, Terri next to her. She was young, probably not more than twenty-two or twenty-three, with dark brown eyes that still held a touch of youthful innocence. If the lack of a wedding band was any indication, she was probably single, which meant she was as likely as anyone to be the killer's next victim.

And she was completely oblivious to the danger.

Lexi stopped at the door. "Do you live alone?"

Terri raised her brows in question. "Yes, why?"

"Be careful. Don't ever open the door to anyone at night without calling the police first."

Terri nodded slowly. "O-kay."

Lexi wished her farewell, then headed toward the teacher's lounge, leaving the young substitute to ponder the warning. If Kayla had fallen prey to the killer, no one was safe.

As soon as she stepped into the teacher's lounge, both Evie and Miranda hurried toward her. They each wrapped her in a hug, then stepped back.

Lexi flashed Kayla's two best friends a sad smile. She knew them well. The four of them had enjoyed more than one girls' night out. "Thanks for staying to talk to me." If anyone had little-known information that could help solve the case, it would be these two teachers.

Miranda sank into a chair at one of the four round tables. "You know we're happy to help in any way we can. We want this monster caught as much as anyone."

Evie sat opposite Miranda and Lexi settled in next to her.

"Do you know of anyone who would have wanted to hurt her?"

Evie clasped her hands together on the table. "Everyone loved Kayla. I don't think she ever made an enemy."

"Had she mentioned being afraid? Anyone

following her or taking an unusual interest in her?"

Miranda shook her head. "If there was, she never mentioned it."

"Did she say anything about meeting anyone new recently?"

"Kayla was always meeting someone new." Evie smiled wryly.

Evie was right. Kayla had been outgoing and bubbly, the kind who struck up conversations with cashiers and gas station attendants. She'd never met a stranger.

"Anyone specific that she mentioned?"

Evie answered immediately. "Not that I know of."

"Wait." Miranda held up a finger. "There was the water guy."

Lexi raised her brows. "Water guy?"

"Oh, yeah." Evie leaned forward in her chair. "How could I forget? Some guy trying to sell her one of those whole house water-filtration systems. He kept checking back. Didn't want to take no for an answer."

Lexi's pulse picked up speed. Was this the link between all the victims? It was possible. Nothing had turned up, but if they hadn't purchased a system and had thrown away the guy's card, there would be no trail. "Did she mention a name, or a company that he was with?"

"I don't think so." Miranda looked at Evie, who shook her head.

Lexi scribbled her cell number on the backs of two of her cards. "If anything else comes to mind, call me."

As soon as she reached the parking lot, she pulled Alan up in her contacts. He answered on the third ring.

She pressed the key fob. "What are you doing?"

"Getting ready to mow the lawn. Why?"

"You're off duty?"

"I can put myself back on duty. What's up?"

"I'm headed to Kayla's. I've got a lead."

"I'll meet you there in ten minutes."

She dropped her phone into her purse and climbed into the County-assigned Explorer. She would turn her cousin's house upside down if necessary. Kayla wasn't a pack rat, but she wasn't a total neat freak, either. Hopefully she'd left behind some kind of clue. An estimate. A business card. Anything that could help them find this mystery water-filter salesman, because it was the only lead they had.

When she pulled into Kayla's driveway, Alan hadn't arrived yet. She stepped from the SUV and moved up the sidewalk that bordered a bed overflowing with day lilies and blooming spring annuals. Grief stabbed through her. Kayla loved her flowers. Every Saturday, she would spend two or three hours piddling in the yard, weeding, watering, fertilizing and pruning. All the tender loving care showed.

But Lexi wasn't there to admire the landscaping or to concern herself with what would happen to the delicate plants Kayla had spent so much time nourishing. She took the key she had gotten from Aunt Sharon and pushed it into the lock. If she was lucky, the break they were hoping for waited somewhere inside the small two-bedroom house.

When she swung the door open and stepped inside, the cold and empty feel of the place took her aback. It had always seemed warm, cozy and full of life, qualities that obviously came from Kayla's presence. She closed the door and looked around. The crime scene investigators had finished with their work. Fine black powder still coated the door and jambs. They hadn't found anything of note but were still waiting for lab results.

She took in a deep breath and headed toward the spare bedroom. A soft knock on the front door interrupted her halfway there. Good. Alan had arrived. The thought of having company sent an unexpected sense of relief whooshing through her. It didn't matter that the company came in the form of one local cop she'd spent the better part of seven years trying to avoid.

She backtracked to the front door, and when she swung it open, Alan stood on her cousin's front porch, clad in worn jeans and a light gray T-shirt. Black letters across his chest proclaimed, "If you see me talking to myself, I'm just getting expert advice."

Lexi smiled. His yard work attire. The shirt molded itself to his muscular torso, ending just past the waistband of his snugly fitting jeans. Definitely the body of a sworn protector of the innocent.

But she wasn't going to notice that. She snapped her gaze back to his face and stepped aside. "Come on in."

She worked with buff, athletic cops every day and didn't give them more than a casual glance. Alan was no exception. As quickly as he had moved on, whatever they'd had in the past, it had obviously meant more to her than it had to him.

Giving Alan his freedom had initially been her mother's suggestion. Florida State was a long way from home. It wasn't fair to make Alan wait three years for her to complete her criminal justice degree. Lexi had absorbed enough of those gentle arguments that when Alan had floored her with his marriage proposal, those had been the first words out of her mouth. That was how her mom worked, her control techniques so subtle that her victims didn't know they'd been manipulated until it was too late.

By Christmas break, she had realized her mistake and come back to tell Alan. She'd known he was dating. Casually, he'd said. At his cool greeting, her stomach had tightened. When Lauren had appeared next to him and proudly displayed her sparkly new diamond, Lexi had almost gotten sick. Somehow, she'd made it through the congratulations without embarrassing herself by losing her lunch or dissolving into a weeping puddle on the porch.

Her mom had gotten her wish. Lexi hadn't married a cop. Instead, she'd become one.

Alan stepped into the house and closed the door. "What's our lead?"

"A salesman of water-filtration systems." She shook off the last remnants of regret and led him toward the second bedroom, which Kayla had set up as a combination guest room and den. "I talked to Miranda and Evie at the school today. Some guy tried to sell Kayla one of those whole house water-filtration systems. According to Miranda and Evie, he was pretty persistent, kept contacting her."

"So we're looking for something with this guy's information."

"A card, a proposal, a contract—anything that might lead us to him."

Alan pulled the trash can from under the desk and peered inside. "Empty."

Lexi approached the desk. A business card holder sat near the back. She removed the cards and thumbed through them. There were about a dozen, mostly from establishments around town. None had anything to do with water-filtration systems.

After almost an hour of searching, she heaved a sigh. "The kitchen is the only room left. If we don't find anything there, we'll contact the companies in the area that sell those things and see if any of them had her down as a potential customer. If Kayla had this guy's information at one point, I'm guessing she threw it away. According to Evie and Miranda, she'd been trying to get rid of the guy."

Alan followed her into the kitchen and opened the narrow pantry door. A vague odor of garbage hit her nostrils when he took the lid off the trash can. It wasn't very full. Kayla must have taken the trash out the day before she was killed.

He poured the contents of the can into the sink. "I'll do the honors."

A haphazard stack of papers sat amid salad and other food scraps. Most of the discarded sheets appeared to be junk mail. Alan inspected them one by one, then dropped them back into the can. Finally, he looked over at her. "Unless there are clues on the backs of these cucumber peels, I'd say we've struck out."

After returning the rest of the garbage to its place and rinsing out the sink, he tied up the top of the bag and lifted it from the can. "I'm going to take this out before it gets really ripe."

"Good idea." Lexi grasped the can to slide it back

into the pantry, then hesitated. A small piece of paper lay in the bottom. Something must have fallen in beside the trash bag or was thrown away before the bag was inserted.

She took the item from the can and turned it over. A half-inch band of blue ran across the top, water ripples inside. Italicized print below spelled out *Martin Jeffries, All-Pure Water Treatment*.

She held up the business card. "Bingo."

They finally had a potential suspect.

Alan opened the door to warehouse number seven in Thompson Commercial Park and let Lexi go in ahead of him. All-Pure Water Treatment was a bare-necessities-no-frills kind of place. Fabric-covered office partitions segregated an area on one side of the room and a metal desk stood near the opposite wall. Except for a photo frame on the desk, a clock on the wall and one of those fake Ficus trees in the corner, the space was devoid of any decorative touches.

A young woman sat at the desk, a phone propped against her shoulder. Her gaze flicked over him, and her eyes widened, but she continued speaking. Unlike when he'd met Lexi at Kayla's house yesterday, he was on duty, sporting his Harmony Grove Police uniform, his pistol at his side. Lexi was armed, too, but her jacket hid her weapon.

Alan pulled the door shut behind them and waited for the woman to finish her conversation. Maybe *conversation* wasn't the right word. *Pitch* was more accurate. Apparently, All-Pure had gotten back the results of the free water test, and there were some serious issues with the quality. But she, of course, had a specialist she could send to explain the details and present some options. Why drink tainted water when a person could have all the pure water he would ever need for just pennies a day?

The pitch must have been successful because she jotted a name in the appointment calendar that lay open in front of her, then hung up the phone, smiling.

"How can I help you?"

Lexi stepped forward. It was her case. Things would go more smoothly if he let her lead.

"Do you have a Martin Jeffries who works here?"

Concern flashed across her features. "Is he in some kind of trouble?"

"No, we just need to ask a few questions." She indicated the badge clipped to her belt. "I'm Lexi Simmons with Polk County Sheriff's Office, and this is Alan White with Harmony Grove P.D. Do you keep an appointment list for him?"

"We do." The woman cast an uneasy glance at the cubicle on the other side of the room. "But I'm not sure what information I'm allowed to share."

As if on cue, a man stepped out of the makeshift office. "Hi, I'm Buddy Jacobs, the owner of All-Pure." He extended his hand, that salesman air even more pronounced than it had been with the girl securing the appointment. "How can I help you?"

After they each accepted the handshake, Lexi continued. "We need a list of Martin Jeffries's appointments going back, say, six months. Is that something you keep?"

"Of course we do. We don't have anything to hide." He nodded toward the girl. "Kimmie, go ahead and print out his weekly calls going back to the beginning of October. If the boy's up to no good, I want to know about it."

After several clicks of the mouse, pages began to spill into the printer.

Lexi continued. "How long has he worked for All-Pure?"

"Since the beginning of September. About seven months. Moved here from out of state."

"Have any of his customers ever complained about him?"

"A couple of times."

"What kind of complaints?"

Buddy laughed. "He's a salesman. Some people think he comes off a little too…high pressure. But I can't argue with his sales figures. He's good at what he does."

"Where can we find him?"

"He's off today and tomorrow. Won't be back in until Saturday."

Kimmie removed the small stack of pages from the printer and handed them to Lexi.

"Do you think Martin might be at home?"

"He might be. I'll have Kimmie get the address for you. It's new, as of about a month ago. I think he's living with a lady friend."

Kimmie jotted an Auburndale address onto a Post-It note, which Lexi pressed to the front of the other pages.

"Thank you. We'll let you know if we need anything else."

When he and Lexi had gotten back into her SUV, she handed him the list of customer appointments and programmed the address into the vehicle's GPS system. "See if you can find any of the victims' names on Jeffries's appointment list."

Alan picked up the file Lexi had slid between his seat and the console. It held her notes and duplicates of the information she needed quick and easy access to. While she drove, he read through the names Buddy Jacobs had provided, comparing them to the victim names in her folder. Halfway down the second page, anticipation surged through him. One name matched.

"In early November, he had an appointment with a Stephanie Wilson in Winter Haven."

"She was the third victim, killed about two months ago. What address?"

"Cypress Gardens Road."

Lexi frowned. "The victim lived in the Inwood area."

"Maybe she moved." He continued to search for the other names, scanning the single-spaced pages. The guy saw a lot of people. Finally, he slid the sheets into Lexi's folder. "That's it. Just Stephanie and Kayla. The others aren't here."

Lexi nodded. "If it's the same Stephanie Wilson, that's two out of five. He might have even deleted the other three names. I mean, if you were killing your customers, would you leave that kind of a paper trail?"

"You've got a point. That's assuming he has access to All-Pure's computer."

She turned into an upscale neighborhood and moved slowly down the road until reaching the number she sought. If the grand, two-story Colonial beyond the circle drive was any indication, Jeffries's lady friend had some bucks.

Chimes followed the ringing of the bell, then faded to silence. Apparently, no one was home.

Lexi turned to head back to the Explorer. "I'll try again this evening."

"I'll meet you. What time?"

"I live about a mile that way." She pointed over his shoulder. "It doesn't make sense for you to drive here from Harmony Grove."

"Let me come with you. You shouldn't do this alone."

She pursed her lips. "I don't plan to. I'll have one of the other detectives come with me."

What if no one was available? Would she then go alone? Was that even allowed? He didn't know Polk County's procedures for questioning suspects in cases like this.

As he watched her climb into the driver's seat, his chest tightened. It wouldn't do any good to take a stubborn stance with her. She would only dig in her heels harder. She hadn't always been that way. When they'd started dating their junior year of high school, she'd been happy and agreeable and perpetually optimistic. But life's knocks had stamped out that youthful innocence and left her with a hard edge. Something told him he'd unwittingly contributed to it.

"I don't mind the drive. Granted, I was looking forward to binge-watching reruns of *Fringe*, but you can make it up to me later."

She cranked the vehicle, the side of her mouth lifting in a smile. "I'd hate to interfere with that." She dropped the transmission into *drive* and guided the SUV around the circle toward the street. "You can meet me at my house at eight."

He jotted down the address she gave him, then slid his spiral mini-notepad back into his shirt pocket. Shortly after they drove from the subdivision, a gold Lexus moved toward them in the opposite lane, slowing as it approached. A male driver sat at the wheel. He appeared to be the only one in the car. His left signal came on, and Lexi slowed, casting several glances in her rearview mirror.

"He just turned into Somerset." She pulled onto a side street to turn around. "He might be our Mr. Jeffries."

When they arrived at the house they had just left, the Lexus sat in the driveway. The occupant had exited and was leaning into the car through the open back door. Lexi braked to a stop a short distance behind him. As Alan stepped from the SUV, the man straightened, several shopping bags dangling from each hand. His head swiveled toward them, and his eyes widened. A split second later, he dropped the bags in the driveway and shot toward the right side of the house at a full run, disappearing through a wrought-iron gate that led into the back yard.

"Stop! Police!" Alan tore off after him, Lexi right on his heels. Jeffries was guilty of something. If it was murder, maybe they could end this thing more quickly than he'd anticipated.

When they slipped through the open gate, Alan slowed to a stop. The lavishly landscaped backyard offered numerous places to hide, and Jeffries was nowhere to be seen.

Alan tilted his head to the left. Lexi gave a slight nod and moved across the back of the house with sure, silent steps, weapon drawn. He moved deeper into the yard, his own pistol raised. Manicured hedges wrapped around curved walks, and a figure of some Greek goddess stood framed on three sides by walls of vine-covered lattice. Somewhere nearby, the gurgle of a fountain masked the sound of their steps.

He'd almost reached the back boundary of the yard when Lexi's shout came from somewhere to his left. He tore along the back perimeter at a full run. Jeffries had climbed a tree in the corner and was shimmying along a lower branch. Lexi wasn't far away. As Jeffries dropped to disappear behind the wall, she slid her weapon back into its holster and hoisted herself up.

Alan closed the remaining yards, heart pounding in his chest. Jeffries had had too much of a head start. And Lexi was confronting him alone.

Once he'd secured his weapon, he followed the path Jeffries and Lexi had taken. When he dropped to the ground, Jeffries was limping toward the front of the adjoining yard. He'd evidently sprained his left ankle, which was giving Lexi a distinct advantage. She was only about fifteen feet behind.

Suddenly, Jeffries skidded to a stop, and so did Lexi. Alan moved cautiously closer. A low growl came from somewhere out of sight. It increased in volume, then erupted into angry barking. Seconds later, a Doberman sprang from behind a tree, then stopped, two humans and canine forming a wary triangle. The dog alternated between barks and growls, razor-sharp teeth glistening in the afternoon sunlight.

Jeffries crept backward, feeling for the side fence.

"Good dog." But all he managed to do was attract the Doberman's full attention. The stance grew more threatening, the growls deeper. The dog inched closer, muscles tight, ready to spring.

In a sudden burst of panic, Jeffries spun and lunged for the fence. He was half over when those lethal teeth sank into one calf. Alan cringed at Jeffries's agonized shriek. When the dog pulled, Jeffries lost his grip and fell to the ground with a cry of fear-tinged pain. For several moments, the dog stood over him, stance threatening, low growls rumbling through the strong chest.

"Boomer, heel!"

The command rang out from the front yard, holding undeniable authority. The dog froze but didn't relax his posture. A man rounded the corner of the house at a jog.

"Thank you." Lexi unhooked a set of handcuffs from her belt. "Is it okay to cuff the suspect?"

The homeowner smiled. "Absolutely." He stopped next to the Doberman. "Boomer, sit."

Boomer obeyed the order, and Lexi stepped forward to restrain Jeffries. He lay rolling back and forth on the ground, clutching his lower leg.

Once Lexi had cuffed him and read him his rights, she straightened and looked at Alan. "How about if you keep an eye on him while I bring the vehicle around. Although I don't think he's going to be climbing any fences anytime soon." She cast a disdainful glance at the man still writhing on the ground. "I suppose I'd better call an ambulance."

Alan watched her turn away from Jeffries with a coldness in her eyes that shocked him. He halfway expected her to kick the man first. Of course, if Jeffries had killed Kayla, Alan would be eager to do it himself.

The man seemed to be settling down. Maybe he was going into shock. They would get him some medical treatment. Then they would try to interrogate him.

Maybe by then he'd be ready to talk.

FOUR

———

LEXI BRAKED TO a stop at the Lakeland Regional Medical Center emergency entrance. Ahead of them, two paramedics lifted a gurney from the back of the ambulance and wheeled it toward the automatic glass doors. It was a good thing Martin Jeffries was getting speedy medical care. By the time the paramedics had arrived, he'd grown pasty white and had begun to shiver.

Lexi slanted a glance at Alan. "I'm leaving you to make sure our illustrious Mr. Jeffries doesn't take off."

Alan raised his brows. "Where are you going?"

"After I park, I'm going to stay in the vehicle and see what I can find out about this Stephanie Wilson. If Jeffries decides to start talking before I get back inside, take good notes."

"Aye, aye, Captain." He lifted his hand in a salute and stepped out.

As soon as the ambulance pulled away, Lexi circled around and chose a parking space. She opened her laptop and, within a few minutes, found five different listings for women named Stephanie Wilson. None of the addresses matched the one on All-Pure's paperwork.

When she did a search on the address All-Pure provided, the property appraiser listed a Lamar Deeson as the owner. The mailing address was different from the site address, so he apparently didn't live there. Stephanie was probably his tenant.

Since she had hit a dead end looking for Stephanie's contact information, she tried Lamar's. Apparently, there was only one Lamar Deeson in all of Winter Haven. The address matched the mailing address on the property appraiser's website.

A curt "hello" followed the third ring.

Once she had verified that the voice on the other end of the line belonged to Lamar Deeson, she identified herself.

"I'm a detective with the Polk County Sheriff's Office. We're looking for Stephanie Wilson. I understand she's a tenant of yours."

"*Used* to be a tenant of mine."

Her pulse kicked into high gear. "Used to be? What happened to her?"

"She left. She and her boyfriend split up, and she moved out. A couple of weeks ago, he did, too. Stuck me for two months' worth of rent."

"When was this? When did she move out?"

"It would have been in January."

January. A month before Stephanie Wilson was found murdered. Now, as for whether it was the same Stephanie Wilson...

"Do you know where she went?"

"I have no idea."

"How about a phone number?"

"I had a cell phone. Hold on." A minute or two later he came back on the line. "I don't know if it's any good. It just has one of those generic messages, and since I was hounding her for the rent, she never bothered to call me back."

Lexi jotted down the number. "One more thing. Do you get a date of birth or social security number on your tenants?"

"I don't bother with all that. I'm not some big property manager. This is my only one. Since I couldn't sell the place, I decided to rent it."

"How old would you say Stephanie is?"

"Young. Mid-twenties, maybe."

"Hair color? Height and weight?"

"Light brown or dark blond. Average height and weight."

Her heart beat faster. "Where did she work?"

"I think she worked part-time at a restaurant. But she was a student. I don't know what school."

Lexi tapped her pen against the steering wheel, excitement coursing through her. Everything fit, right down to her size and hair color. But there was only one way to know for sure. "I'd like to show you a couple of pictures, see if it's the Stephanie you know. Can I meet with you later this evening or tomorrow?"

"I'm headed out of town in about thirty minutes. But I can meet you when I get back next week." He hesitated. "Did something happen to her? I mean, I'm not identifying a dead body, am I?" He forced an uneasy laugh.

"We're not sure. A Stephanie Wilson was found murdered, but we don't know if it's *your* Stephanie Wilson."

"Oh." The single word was heavy with concern.

"She stiffed me for the rent, but I never wanted to see her dead."

Lexi ended the call with a promise to meet after he returned on Wednesday. Then she tried the cell number Deeson had given her, without success. It was no longer a working number.

She entered the emergency room lobby a few minutes later, and after a brief explanation of who she was and why she was there, the intake person allowed her to go back to the treatment area. Alan stood in the hall next to one of the triage rooms. An easy smile climbed up his cheeks when he saw her, creating an unexpected flutter in her stomach. She promptly tamped it down. He used to have that effect on her, but not anymore. All the butterflies had died a quick and sure death seven years earlier. At least she thought they had. Apparently, there were a few holdouts.

She returned his smile with a casual one of her own. "How's Jeffries?"

"The doctor's working on his leg now. Our friend Boomer did quite a number on it."

"Yeah, I gathered as much." Especially with the amount of blood that had soaked through his torn pant leg.

"What did you find out about Stephanie?"

"She's not there anymore, but I talked to her former landlord. Everything matches victim number three. I'm going to have him look at the photos and tell me if it's the same Stephanie."

Alan crossed his arms and leaned back against the wall. "What about the other three victims?"

"Maybe Jeffries knew them in some other way. If

we take his picture around to their friends and family members, someone might recognize him."

"Good thinking. We could split the list. You take half and I'll take half."

Before she could respond, a doctor stepped from the triage room and addressed Alan. "Okay, Officer, he's all yours. He'll need to have the stitches removed in another week or so, and he'll have to go through a course of antibiotics. After that, he should be fine."

Alan thanked him and walked into the room.

Lexi followed. "Looks like you dropped into the wrong yard." They both approached the bed that held a disgruntled Martin Jeffries. He responded with a deep scowl.

Alan continued. "We just wanted to ask you some questions. Why'd you run?"

"I didn't know what you wanted."

"It doesn't matter what we wanted. Honest, law-abiding citizens don't run from the police."

"Well, you can't arrest me. I didn't do anything wrong."

Lexi crossed her arms. "Actually, we can. It's called attempting to elude a law-enforcement officer. It happens to be a second-degree felony."

He shrugged off her threat, his attitude growing cockier by the minute. "Whatever. I know how the system works. I won't end up doing more than ninety days, if that."

Alan circled around to the other side of the bed, putting Jeffries between them. "We're doing a murder investigation, and you're looking guiltier by the minute."

The man's cockiness ratcheted back several degrees

and fear flashed in his dark eyes. He held up his hands and shook his head. "No way, man. I didn't kill anybody."

Lexi nailed him with an accusing stare. "Then why did you run?"

"Because I thought… I thought Tanya accused me of taking her money."

Lexi nodded. "We haven't talked to Tanya. Maybe we'll do that later."

Jeffries's gaze narrowed and a muscle twitched behind his jaw. He was probably kicking himself for even mentioning it. But he had more to worry about than some pilfered cash.

She leaned closer. "Did you try to sell a water-filtration system to a Kayla Douglas in Harmony Grove?"

"Yeah, I did."

"When did you last see her?"

"About two weeks ago." A flash of annoyance shot across his features. "What's that got to do with anything?"

Alan leaned in, too. The guy was probably feeling ganged-up-on. "A lot, considering she was found murdered a week ago."

"You can't pin that on me, man."

Lexi didn't acknowledge his protest. "How many times have you been to her house?"

Her question hung in the air for a brief span of time. Then Jeffries pinched his mouth shut. "I'm not saying any more without talking to a lawyer."

"Don't worry. You'll get one." She backed away from the hospital bed. "We'll find out what you're up to with or without your assistance."

A nurse rolled a wheelchair into the room. "Well, Mr. Jeffries, it looks like you're free to go."

"Not exactly free." Lexi watched Jeffries struggle into the chair, then stepped behind it to grip the handles. "You get to come with us."

Jeffries didn't respond. She didn't expect him to. He was done talking. But she wasn't finished with him. Not by a long shot. First, she'd call to have him transported. He'd be fingerprinted, and she'd see if there were any outstanding warrants for him. If everything went the way she hoped it would, they'd be able to come up with a valid reason to keep him.

Maybe he hadn't killed Kayla.

But he was guilty of something.

———

Lexi turned off the ignition and frowned over at Alan. "I hope this isn't as much of a bust as our other efforts."

Alan sighed. "I know. I was hoping Jeffries was going to be it." Over the past several days they'd shown his photo to at least sixty people. No one could say they'd ever seen him. If Martin Jeffries was the killer, he'd managed to keep his relationships with his victims secret from even their closest friends and family members.

Actually, his name wasn't even Jeffries. They'd run his prints through IAFIS and learned that Martin Jeffries was one of several aliases. His real name was Raymond Moore.

"I'm glad we got him anyway. He's not a good person."

No, he wasn't. He preyed on women, but not in the

way they had thought. His attacks were financial. He had a habit of taking up with well-to-do ladies and slowly draining their bank accounts.

He was still being held, but likely wouldn't be for long. Lexi had convinced the judge to hold off setting bond on the forgery and fraud charges since he was a possible serial murder suspect and a flight risk. Without evidence, though, they couldn't keep him indefinitely. Soon he'd be allowed to bond out.

His current lady friend wouldn't be helping him. Once the police had tipped her off, she'd done some checking. Raymond had forged a couple of her checks but hadn't had a chance yet to do too much damage.

Alan stepped from the Explorer. He and Lexi had just arrived at Lamar Deeson's house. It was late—the sun had set some time ago—but this was the earliest they could come. Deeson hadn't gotten in from his trip until six that afternoon.

As they made their way toward the house, the shades at the windows were drawn, but the glow of the porch light welcomed them up the front walk. Lexi was dressed in her usual tailored suit, this one navy, with a pale blue blouse under the jacket. A gold clip secured her shoulder-length hair. Everything about her screamed *professional*. It seemed like forever since he'd witnessed the relaxed side of Lexi.

She lifted one hand to ring the bell. The other held an envelope containing four photos. They probably wouldn't use the last one. The first three were sufficient for identification. They weren't going for shock value.

The door swung open, and a burly man with hair

graying at the temples stood inside.

"Lamar Deeson?" At his nod, she continued. "Alexis Simmons. And this is Alan White. Thanks for being willing to do this."

He stepped aside. "Come in."

After he'd closed the door behind them, Lexi pulled the small stack of photos from the manila envelope, then handed him the top one. "Can you tell me if this is the Stephanie Wilson you know?"

The woman in the photo lay on her right side, a bed of decaying leaves beneath her. Her arms were bound behind her and a piece of duct tape covered her mouth. Tangled dishwater-blond hair flowed over her shoulder. The picture had been shot from above.

"I—I'm not sure. Looking at her from the side like this, I can't tell."

Lexi handed him another photo. In that one, the victim sat upright, the trunk of a pine tree supporting her. An angry red splotch marked one cheek, the remnants of an open-handed blow. Above the tape, fear-filled eyes pled for mercy.

Deeson shook his head and turned away, mouth set in a grim line. "That's definitely not her."

Lexi took the photo from him. "You're sure?"

"Positive." He swallowed hard, his throat twitching with the action. "I'm sorry. I have a daughter that age. She even looks a little like the girl in the picture. I hope you catch the guy who did this."

Lexi nodded. "Believe me, we're trying our hardest."

Unfortunately, they couldn't promise him any more than that. They thanked him for his help, then walked to Lexi's SUV. Instead of starting the engine, she sat with her shoulders slumped. Discouragement radiated from her. "We're back to square one. Five girls dead and not a single lead. After four months of searching for this guy, I thought we finally had him."

The disappointment in her voice sent a pang of tenderness shooting through him. He rested a hand on her shoulder. "We'll catch him. Eventually we'll get a break. He'll get careless and make a mistake, and we'll nab him."

She turned weary eyes on him. "And how many girls will die in the meantime?"

He dropped his hand. She was right. They had exhausted the only lead they'd had. No mistakes were likely to happen unless he struck again. Their "break" would mean another young woman lost her life.

She cranked the SUV and backed from the drive. Alan let his head fall back against the seat. "I don't know about you, but I'm glad to be heading home. It's been a long day." It had been a long several days. It was draining, talking to person after person. Or maybe it was the fact that they didn't seem to be getting anywhere.

Lexi sighed. "Ditto."

Twenty minutes later, she pulled into her driveway and eased to a stop in the double carport. Her Mazda occupied the space next to them, his Mustang parked behind it. He'd left it there that afternoon. Shane Dalton had been the one on duty this evening and was using their shared cruiser.

Lexi turned off the ignition but didn't immediately get out. Since he was in no hurry to leave her, Alan didn't either.

She gave him a tired smile. "Thanks for your help today."

"No problem. I want this guy caught as badly as you do."

She pulled the key from the ignition but still sat, long enough that the headlights clicked off, plunging their surroundings into darkness. He looked out the window at a sky devoid of the moon, clouds hiding most of the stars. Lexi's porch light was off, and the nearest streetlight was too far away for its glow to reach her yard. Whenever she decided she was ready to go inside, he would walk her to the door. He'd even check the inside of her house if she'd let him.

She finally broke the silence. "I don't know about you, but that fast-food burger I had two hours ago really didn't do the trick."

He returned her smile. "Yeah, same here."

"I've got some nachos and killer bean dip if you'd like to come in for a snack."

"Killer bean dip?"

"Bad choice of words."

When they had climbed from the vehicle, Lexi clicked the key fob. The headlights came on long enough for them to make it to her door. On the small front porch, a rocking chair and a potted plant greeted them. Lexi lived in one of the older Auburndale neighborhoods, with moderate houses, well-kept yards and an obvious lack of bicycles and toys at a good number of them. He'd surveyed it when he'd arrived that afternoon. It was likely one of those neighborhoods where people had put down deep roots, raised their kids, then remained in their empty nests. It held a sense of quiet serenity. Under normal circumstances, that would be comforting.

But a killer on the loose targeting young women

wasn't normal circumstances.

Now that the headlights had clicked off, Alan navigated to the flashlight app on his phone and held the beam centered on her doorknob. When Lexi put the key into the lock, yowling commenced inside. She grinned up at him. "That would be Suki. She's not happy that dinner's late, and she's letting me know."

She twisted the key and opened the door. Just inside sat the source of all the racket—a sleek, blue-eyed cat, mouth open in that low, eerie cry that only Siamese make. Lexi bent to pick her up, and the yowls turned to purrs.

She headed through an open doorway into the kitchen. "I know I promised you nachos and bean dip, but Suki gets fed first. Otherwise, she'll drive us crazy."

As soon as she put Suki down, a black cat appeared in the doorway, sized Alan up with big gold eyes, then apparently decided he was okay.

"You have two?"

She gave him a sheepish smile before bending to pick up porcelain dishes with painted paw prints in the bottoms. "Actually three. After Suki showed up, I decided she needed company and adopted Midnight from the Humane Society. Two weeks later, Itsy appeared on my doorstep."

As if on cue, a third cat waddled into the kitchen. Alan eyed Lexi doubtfully. "This is Itsy?"

Lexi grinned. "Well, she *used* to be tiny. She's sort of gotten fat."

Alan laughed. Lexi had always had a soft spot for animals. With the toughness she had developed over the past seven years, it was good to see that the soft spot was still there.

While she spooned canned cat food into the three bowls, he settled into a chair at the small kitchen table. Soon, all three cats sat in a row, smacking happily. Lexi pulled a Pyrex dish from the fridge and placed it in the center of the table.

Alan leaned forward. "That looks good."

"It's a seven-layer dip. Although I think this one's actually eight." She put down two plates, dumped a bag of tortilla chips into a bowl and took a seat opposite him.

Sitting across the table from her in the warm, cozy kitchen, a sudden sense of intimacy wove through him. This was the way it was supposed to have turned out—a lifetime of sharing meals and dreaming dreams. Why had she thrown it all away? Maybe someday he would ask her. Just not tonight.

Whatever her reasons, he'd given up too quickly and turned to Lauren on the rebound. Of course, Lauren had made it easy. The instant she'd found out Lexi had dumped him, Lauren had been in hot pursuit. Several years earlier, long before Lexi, it would have been a dream come true. He'd had a crush on her all through ninth and tenth grade, a crush he'd kept secret. Cheerleaders didn't date science nerds.

For Lauren, though, things had changed. He was no longer the nerdy geek and she'd found herself in trouble—pregnant and recently dumped. Their relationship had been doomed from the start. Lauren had just been using him, and Lexi still had his heart.

His eyes met hers across the table. "I'm sorry for the way things turned out. I—"

She held up a hand to stop him. "It's in the past. Let's just leave it there."

He nodded and scooped a glob of dip onto a chip. He'd wanted to be involved in trying to find Kayla's killer. He still did. But maybe working with Lexi wasn't such a good idea.

He cleared his throat. "Where do we go next?"

"Except for a small handful of people we haven't shown Jeffries's photo to, we're done. If we had some idea of what draws this creep, I'd even be willing to be bait."

His chest clenched. He bit off the words of protest that were on the tip of his tongue and drew in a stabilizing breath. She was a trained law-enforcement officer. She was cautious and smart and armed.

And she was alone with her three cats. He'd feel better if Suki was a Rottweiler.

Before he had a chance to formulate a response, her cell phone rang. She rose to retrieve it from where she had left her purse on the counter, then cast a glance back at him. "It's Tomlinson."

Within moments of answering, her face brightened. "That's awesome!"

Alan straightened in his seat. It had to be good news, and it likely involved the case they were working on together.

He waited through a series of "Yes…uh-huh… okay," wishing she would have put Tomlinson on speaker. Finally, she tore a sheet of paper from the small notepad stuck to the fridge and picked up a pen. "Location?"

In the brief span of silence that followed, her pen moved across the paper in smooth strokes. "We'll be right there."

She disconnected the call and dropped the phone into her purse.

"We just got our big break." Her eyes shone with excitement and she shifted her weight from one foot to the other, unable to stand still.

"Victim number six got away."

FIVE

———

LEXI LIFTED THE curtain aside and stepped into the sectioned-off area, trying to ignore the ever-present scent of disinfectant. It was her second trip to the emergency room in less than a week, this time Heart of Florida. And she didn't even like hospitals.

The occupant of the bed lay with her head turned, facing the opposite wall where a male figure waited in a chair. The shape beneath the thin sheet looked tiny and frail. Matted brown curls flowed over the pillow, a dead leaf still trapped in the tangles.

As Alan stepped in behind Lexi, the curtain slid several inches on its metal track. The sound drew the patient's attention, and she slowly pivoted her head. Her lips were broken and misshapen, and one eye was swollen almost shut. A pinkish ring circled her neck, the beginnings of ligature marks. She was lucky to be alive. Her physical injuries would heal in a short time. The invisible scars would likely stay with her the rest of her life.

Her gaze traveled up Lexi's blouse and jacket and came to rest on her face. Her eyes were haunted, and she wore the trauma of her ordeal in her features. The next several minutes weren't going to be easy for either of them.

"Denise? I'm Lexi." She moved to the side enough for Alan to step into the space next to her. "This is Alan."

Terror flashed across the girl's face. She released a startled shriek and scooted away, sheet pulled up to her chin.

The visitor shot from his chair and circled the bed in four brisk steps. "Get him out of here."

Lexi glanced from the man to the girl to Alan, confusion rendering her speechless. But Alan didn't have to be told twice. He was already ducking from the room before she could gather her thoughts.

"I'm sorry." The man moved back to the other side of the bed and took the girl's hand. "It was a cop who did this to her."

Lexi's stomach did a sudden free fall. Their killer was a cop? "What?"

"At least, he was in an officer's uniform."

He was a cop or someone impersonating a cop. One small piece of the puzzle fell into place. He didn't know the victims. They opened their doors because they trusted the uniform.

She approached the bed, her mind still reeling. "You're her father, I assume?" At his nod she continued. "I need to ask her some questions."

She bent to touch the girl lightly on the shoulder. According to the report Tomlinson had, the girl's name was Denise Andrews, and she was twenty-one. Her small form and the fear on her face made her appear much younger. "I need you to tell me what happened. Can you do that?"

The girl's eyes filled with tears and she shook her

head. Lexi sympathized with her. But Denise had information that could help them solve the case. She was the only one to fall into the clutches of the killer and live to tell about it.

"Honey, I know it's hard." She squatted next to the bed, putting her at eye level with the terrified girl. Her tone was low and soothing. "Right now, you just want to forget about everything you went through tonight. But the killer is still out there, and he's going to strike again. We need you to help us stop him. Will you do that?"

After a prolonged silence, she nodded.

Lexi took a notepad and pen from her pocket. "Where do you live, Denise?"

She gave a Haines City address, her voice paper thin.

"And you were at home?"

"No."

Lexi's brows shot up. Their meticulous, methodical killer had deviated? "Where were you?"

"Coming home from a friend's house in Kissimmee."

"What happened?"

"My car broke down and I was on that stretch of 17–92 where I don't have any cell service. I locked my doors and waited, because I knew if I wasn't home in an hour, my dad would come looking for me."

The man nodded. "She always calls me when she's heading home. She's a good girl. She didn't deserve this."

"No, sir." None of them did. "What happened next?"

"After I had waited about ten minutes, a car drove past really slow, coming toward me. I looked in my rearview mirror and saw him turn around, come back and park behind me."

"Was it a police car?"

"No. I couldn't tell at the time, because it was dark. But no, it wasn't a police car."

So it probably wasn't a cop. Unless it was an undercover one. "Then what happened?"

"A guy got out of the car and came to my window. He was in uniform. When I saw it was a cop, I opened my door to talk to him. I asked if he could call my dad and let him know I had broken down. He told me not to bother my dad, that he would take me home. He even offered to call someone to have my car towed."

"What did you do?"

"I got out and went back to his car."

"Can you describe it?"

"It was a light color, like silver or white. I couldn't tell for sure, because it was really dark outside."

"Any idea what kind?"

"I'm not good with cars. It was a four-door. It didn't look new, but it wasn't an old clunker, either."

"You didn't happen to notice any part of the tag number, did you?"

"No, I never went around to the back of the car."

"That's all right. Tell me what happened next."

"I got into the front passenger's seat. There was one of those old-style gumball patrol lights sitting on the dashboard."

Lexi nodded. Yep, definitely an impersonator. Those gumball lights had been phased out years ago. All the vehicles now had the lights built in. "Did he get in the car then?"

"No, he said he had to get something out of the trunk."

"Then what happened?"

"I was just sitting there waiting. All of a sudden he opened the passenger door and held something over my face."

"What?"

"A cloth. It smelled sweet, and it made me light-headed and sick to my stomach. I fought to get away, but he was too strong."

While Lexi listened, misty images played across her imagination. But the face she kept seeing was Kayla's.

"What's the next thing you remember?"

"I woke up in the woods. My hands were tied behind my back and he had taped my mouth." A shudder shook her body.

Lexi squeezed her arm. "You're doing great, sweetie. What else can you tell me?"

"He hit me and took my picture."

"Did he say anything while he was doing this?"

"He kept calling me Jeanie. He said after ten long years, justice is finally being done."

Lexi scribbled some notes in her pad. The killings were retribution for some perceived wrong. Someone else's wrong. "Did he say anything else?"

"Just that it wasn't supposed to be my time yet, but how could he resist when I had fallen right in his path."

"What happened then?"

"He hit me again and took two more pictures. Then he put like a rubber strap or something around my neck and started to squeeze." She raised shaking fingers to her throat. "That's when the dog came."

"The dog?"

"I think it was a Lab. It came running through the woods, and when the cop guy heard it coming, he hid."

"What happened then?"

"The dog came up to me and was barking. I could hear his owner yelling at him to get back home, but the dog wouldn't listen. Finally, the owner found us. He had a flashlight. He untied me and walked me back to his house and called 911."

Saved by a Labrador retriever. Denise was one lucky girl.

"Can you describe him—the cop guy?"

"Not really. It was dark."

"Anything at all?"

She closed her eyes, trying to call up a memory she would probably rather forget. "When he went to the trunk, he left the driver's side door open, so the dome light was on. He opened my door, and when he leaned inside, I could see his face. His hair was really short, like a buzz cut, maybe brown, and he didn't have a beard or mustache. His arms were muscular. I don't know how tall he was, because I never stood close to him."

"Age?"

"Maybe thirties? I don't know."

"Anything else you can tell me that might help us catch this guy? What about the uniform?"

"It was a dark color, I think dark green. He had a badge on his pocket and some kind of patch on his sleeve. It looked so real." Her brows pulled together in concentration. "But he wasn't wearing it in the woods."

"What?"

"He had changed. I think he had on jeans and a T-shirt."

Lexi nodded. He probably hadn't wanted to dirty his needed prop. "Anything else?"

Denise shook her head. Lexi straightened and pulled a business card from her pocket.

"If you remember anything else, give me a call, even if it seems unimportant. A lot of times it's the seemingly insignificant details that help us solve crimes." She bent to squeeze her hand. "And thank you. You did good."

When Lexi stepped around the curtain, she almost bumped into Alan. She dropped her voice to a whisper. "Eavesdropping, are we?"

Alan grinned. "Nope, taking notes. And saving you from having to repeat all that in there."

She walked with him toward the emergency area entrance. "Now we know why Kayla and the other girls opened their doors."

"And we know this is all about something that happened ten years ago."

The automatic doors slid open and they stepped out into the balmy night air. At almost midnight, only a dozen cars dotted the emergency area parking lot, two of them hers and Alan's. She stopped next to the driver's door of her vehicle.

"The killer is evidently following a particular order in choosing his victims. He's been so methodical and planned everything out so well that he hasn't left behind a shred of evidence. Tonight, he deviated. I'm hoping he's going to live to regret it."

She leaned back against the Explorer and crossed

her arms. "Tomlinson's getting Crime Scene out there first thing in the morning. But he sent deputies tonight to secure everything so the killer can't go back and cover up any evidence. Of course, there's the span of time between when the neighbor found her and got her back to his house to call 911."

"Well, I'm praying he overlooked something. Since this one was spur-of-the-moment and not well thought out, there's always that chance."

She nodded, her mind stuck on his choice of words. *Praying?* What was it with him and Tomlinson? But she would take whatever help she could get. As much as they had learned tonight, they still didn't know who the killer was, what he drove or anything about him. Unless there was something really incriminating left behind in the woods, they may as well be looking for a needle in a haystack.

"Do you want me to follow you home?"

She looked up at him with a quirky grin. "Davenport to Harmony Grove, by way of Auburndale? That's a little out of the way, don't you think?"

He grinned back at her. "Maybe a little. But I don't mind. I'm worried about you."

His smile faded and warmth filled his eyes. In the dim glow of the parking lot lights, they had deepened to an almost midnight blue. He moved closer to rest a hand against her SUV. If he lifted the other one, he would have her hemmed in. Suddenly that didn't seem like such a bad place to be.

How different their lives would have been if he had waited for her. Would they still be together? What would their chances be if they gave it another shot? She dismissed the thought as soon as it entered her mind. Alan wasn't the "settling down" type. Neither was she.

She stepped aside while she still could and opened the driver's door. "We both need to go home and get some sleep. I'll be fine. I've got my weapon."

She slid into the seat and watched him walk away, a hollow emptiness filling her chest. She tamped it down and took in a cleansing breath. They had a killer to catch. She had no business thinking about captivating blue eyes.

Or second chances.

———◆———

Alan cruised slowly down Tranquility Way, driver's side window lowered and soft strains of a popular Third Day song streaming through the radio speakers. At eleven o'clock on a Thursday morning, there wasn't a lot of police work to do. But after more than a week of making himself scarce, it was time to take up some slack. Chief Willis had given him free rein to work on Kayla's case but Shane, the other Harmony Grove officer, needed some time off.

Now here he was, driving through quiet streets, past the sleepy neighborhoods of Harmony Grove, his greatest accomplishment of the morning helping old Mrs. English bring in her groceries. But that was all right. He loved his job. That was because he loved Harmony Grove and its residents.

He put his arm out the window to wave at Delores Griffin, who was halfway through taking Molly the schnauzer on her late-morning walk. The dog had stopped to sniff the base of some shrub that was covered in little blue flowers. Alan took in a breath himself, savoring the scents of spring. It was his favorite time of year, a time of new beginnings and the last chance to enjoy the mild weather before the onslaught of summer's brutal heat and humidity.

Currently, Lexi was probably hard at work on one of her other cases. Surely the string of murders he was helping her to investigate weren't the only open homicide cases in Polk County. As far as the search for Kayla's killer, there wasn't much they could do until the CSI team collected and analyzed their latest evidence. They were probably still at the scene, doing their tedious work, careful not to overlook anything that could possibly identify the killer. Maybe by tonight or tomorrow, they would have some good news.

The distant sound of a mower drifted in through his open window. Up ahead on the left, a riding mower disappeared around the opposite side of a ranch-style home that looked much like the others on the street. Peace House, the abused women's shelter, used to occupy the space but had since moved to a much larger facility outside of town. Now four girls lived in the home in front of him—students at Polk State. He'd met them shortly after they moved in. He made it a point to get to know all of Harmony Grove's residents, at least on a casual basis.

As he approached, the front door swung open, and two of the girls stepped out. Tori and Emma. Tori was the one talking, her gestures animated. Alan stepped on the gas, trying to get past while they were still engaged in their conversation. Both girls were nice enough—actually, all four of them were—but Tori's open flirting was bold enough to be uncomfortable.

He'd almost reached the end of the driveway when Tori suddenly looked up. A smile spread across her face, and she lifted a hand, waving enthusiastically. The gesture was a combination greeting and request that he stop. Maybe he could ignore the latter, return the greeting and keep going.

He hit the brake. He couldn't play dumb. She was already halfway to his car.

She stepped into the road and stopped at his open window. "Hi, Alan." She stretched out his name, her pitch rising on the last syllable. "What are you up to?"

"Just patrolling."

"Keeping the streets of Harmony Grove safe. It's such a comfort for us to know we have strong guys like you protecting us." She tilted her head to the side, even batted her eyelashes.

Alan stifled a groan. Although he went out frequently, his "dates" were just friends. Women like Kayla who he'd known all his life, more like a sister than a girlfriend. Tori had never been one of those dates. That was one good decision he'd made. Otherwise, he'd never get rid of her. Flighty, silly, a bit immature, she wasn't at all his type. Apparently, his type was women who wanted nothing to do with him. One woman in particular. He'd always been one for challenges.

Tori put a hand on his arm, as it rested on the window opening. "We're having a cookout tomorrow night."

Emma had joined her and now raised her brows. "We are?"

Tori elbowed her in the ribs. "Yes, we are, and we wanted to invite you to join us."

"Thanks for the invite, but I'll be working." At least, he hoped he would be. That would mean the crime scene folks uncovered something for Lexi and him to investigate. "Maybe another time."

"We're going to hold you to that."

"One more thing. Be careful. Don't open the door to anyone you don't know, and don't get in a stranger's car, even if you think he's a cop."

She gave him a sly smile. "I'd get in *your* car anytime."

He heaved a sigh. "Tori, I'm serious."

"So am I."

"There's someone out there killing young women, and we believe he's impersonating a cop." At barely nineteen, Tori and Emma were a little *too* young. But their roommates Autumn and Brittany were at the lower end of the victims' age range.

Tori's smile faded. "I heard. Autumn said the killer got someone from here last week, a teacher." All teasing had disappeared from her tone. "Autumn knew her. I didn't, but I was still sad to hear about it."

Alan released some of the pressure on the brake and allowed his cruiser to roll forward. Tori dropped her arm. "We'll be careful. I'll tell Autumn and Brittany, too."

A block later, he took a right on Main Street. As he drove past Pleasant Drive, his gaze traveled down the street. Patty Simmons still lived there, fifth house on the right. It was the same ranch-style home where Lexi had grown up. Even though seven years had passed since he'd made regular trips down the quiet street, it still drew his attention every time he passed. If he wasn't careful, his thoughts followed. That was never a good thing. It only led to what-ifs. And mental kicks in the rear.

Keeping the memories at bay was difficult when he was spending almost every day with her. Last night had been the hardest. Maybe he'd had fatigue to blame. It had been a long day and heading into the next by the time he'd walked her to her SUV in the emergency room parking lot. Seeing her standing there in the glow of the parking lot lights, and thinking about her driving back to Auburndale to her empty house, he'd wanted to wrap her in a protective hug and never let her go.

Fortunately, he hadn't acted on his impulses. Whatever he was feeling, it wasn't returned. He didn't measure up. He'd long ago had to accept that fact. Lexi had no intention of repeating her mother's mistakes. Patty Simmons had grown up privileged, her wealthy parents giving her anything she desired. She'd married beneath her, then had never gotten over the fact that her blue-collar husband couldn't keep her in the style she'd felt she deserved.

Alan pressed the brake as he neared Harmony Grove's only traffic light. Booming bass reached him first, reverberating in his chest. The light turned green, and the scream of peeling rubber followed. An ancient Impala approached from the opposite direction. The familiar face behind the wheel wore a can't-touch-this smirk. The car sped past, then skidded into a right turn, its two inner wheels almost leaving the pavement

Great. The Harmony Grove Hellion. Why wasn't he in school? Alan was getting ready to find out.

He brought the siren to life, turned the vehicle around and made his own peel-out turn. Thirty seconds later the Impala eased to a stop on the side of the road.

Alan stepped from the car and approached. The window lowered in front of the grinning face of Duncan Alcott.

"Why aren't you in school?"

"Because I was bored. I can get Cs and Ds without being there every day."

"Think what you could get if you applied yourself. Do your parents know you're not in school?"

"They don't care."

Unfortunately, the kid was right. With an alcoholic father and a mother who struggled to keep food on the table, sixteen-year-old Duncan's whereabouts were usually an afterthought.

"Let me see your driver's license and registration."

Duncan produced the two items. "You'll see everything's on the up-and-up."

Alan pulled a rectangular pad from his back pocket. As he wrote, the kid's cocky attitude fell away like peeling paint under a sandblaster.

"Hey, man. I wasn't speeding, and there's not a stop sign there. You can't give me a ticket."

"I'd say taking a ninety-degree turn on two wheels at thirty miles an hour is reckless driving. What do you think?"

Alan leaned down to look into the car where Johnny Davidson sat in the passenger seat, face frozen in fear. At fourteen years old, he had no business hanging with the likes of Duncan. After resting an elbow in the window opening, Alan continued. "And then there's the whole contributing-to-the-delinquency-of-a-minor thing. That one comes with jail time." Of course, Duncan was a minor himself, so the threat was baseless. But Duncan didn't know that.

The kid's eyes widened. "No way. Look, I'll get him back to school right away."

"No, I'd better take him up to Davidson Paint Supply. Then it'll be up to Mr. Davidson to decide whether he'll want to press charges."

Alan stifled a grin. If there was a contest for who looked more scared, he would have been hard-pressed to choose a winner. Johnny shook his head vigorously. "Officer Alan, please don't. My dad will kill me."

"If I let you go, how do I know you won't be right back out here tomorrow?"

"I promise I won't. I'll never skip school again."

"That would be good. Otherwise, I'd have to arrest Duncan here. And we don't want that to happen, do we?"

The "no" came in chorus.

"All right then. Get back to school." He brought his focus back to his pad.

"You're not still gonna give me a ticket, are you?"

Alan answered without looking up. "Yep."

"Aw, man."

The kid needed to learn a lesson. Granted, he had it bad at home. But he had choices. Hopefully, with consequences, he would start making the right ones.

After tearing the sheet from the pad, he handed it to Duncan along with his driver's license and registration. Then he watched the Impala turn around and drive away. It would be headed back to Harmony Grove Junior High, no doubt, to return Johnny to his studies. After the car rounded the corner and disappeared, Alan got back into his own car, dropping the ticket pad into the seat next to him.

The ticket pad.

His jaw went slack. Kayla. A traffic stop. An unmarked car. He'd almost forgotten.

Three or four weeks before Kayla had been killed, she'd told him about getting stopped shortly after dark. The car had been unmarked, but the officer had been in uniform. He'd claimed he'd stopped her because she hadn't signaled. She'd insisted she had. He'd run her license, given it back to her and let her go.

Or had he only pretended to run her license?

Had she instead been stopped by a killer in a policeman's uniform driving a car with a generic flashing light on the dash? Maybe he'd taken her license for the sole purpose of finding out where she lived. Was that what he did with all the victims?

He struggled to call up the conversation. Finally, he sighed. If Kayla had given him any details about the car or a description of the person who had stopped her, those facts were buried somewhere deep in his subconscious.

He cranked the car and headed toward the station. He had some phone calls to make. If Kayla's license had really been run, there would be a record of it. If not, maybe he had just recalled some valuable information about the killer.

Information they could use to set a trap.

SIX

———————

LEXI LAY STRETCHED out on the couch, a half-read paperback in her hands and Suki wedged between her legs. Itsy lay curled up on the floor next to her. Midnight was probably somewhere in the house looking for trouble. The youngest of the three, he had far too much energy and a mischievous streak a mile wide.

A pleasant odor wafted from the kitchen, and her stomach rumbled. She looked up from the book to check the clock. 6:15. She'd already fed the cats, but her own dinner still had another fifteen minutes to bake. She hadn't talked to Alan today, but he was probably home, getting ready to eat and wind down for the evening.

Or not. Spending so much time with her was probably putting a major crimp in his social life. Now that he had a free evening, even though the start of the weekend was twenty-four hours away, he wasn't likely to let it go to waste. He was probably out with one of the hopeful single ladies of Harmony Grove. That thought didn't bother her. Really, it didn't.

She once again picked up the book. Whatever Alan was doing, he probably wasn't stretched out, surrounded by cats. Of course, she didn't know that. He might have a menagerie by now. She hadn't been to his place since that night long ago, when Lauren had met her at the door with her shiny new engagement ring.

At this point, she didn't even know where "his place" was. Each time he'd worked with her over the past week, she'd picked him up from Harmony Grove P.D., or he'd met her at her house.

Seven years ago, his place had been an apartment he'd recently rented in Winter Haven, not far from Polk State College. Now all she knew was that he had a house somewhere in Harmony Grove.

A faint buzz sounded behind her, her phone still on vibrate from a meeting she'd attended earlier in the day. She twisted to retrieve it from the end table. When she glanced at the screen, her heart beat a little faster. Apparently, Alan *wasn't* with one of the Harmony Grove ladies.

"Hey, what's up?" She was smiling, and it came through in her tone.

"I saw Sheriff Judd on the six o'clock news."

"Yeah, the segment has aired a couple of times." She'd seen it, too. Now that they'd learned the killer was impersonating a cop, everyone had decided it was time for another press conference.

"He definitely got the point across. If I was a young woman, I'd think twice about opening *my* door." Alan paused. "I actually have another reason for calling. I did a traffic stop this morning."

"Yeah?" Not earth-shattering news, unless he'd happened to stop the killer. "Who?"

"One of the local teens, kind of a trouble maker.

Making the stop reminded me of something I'd forgotten. About two weeks before Kayla was killed, she told me that she got pulled over by a cop in an unmarked vehicle. I didn't think anything of it at the time. She said that he insisted she'd made a turn and hadn't signaled, but she was positive she had. He supposedly ran her license, then told her he was going to let her go with a verbal warning."

Lexi's pulse accelerated. "Do you think he's our guy?"

"Knowing our killer is impersonating a cop, it's possible, maybe even likely."

"It would be easy enough to check." Officers never made traffic stops without announcing their intentions to dispatch, giving the location and the vehicle's tag number.

"I already did, this afternoon. Kayla had said she was on State Road 540 between Lakeland and Winter Haven when she got stopped. No one called it in, not Polk County, Lakeland, Winter Haven, or even FHP."

Lexi's heart was pounding in earnest now. "Maybe the killer sees women who fit the description of what he's looking for, then stops them and pretends to run their license…"

He finished her thought. "And what he's really doing is taking note of their addresses. He stakes out the houses to make sure the women are alone, then abducts and murders them."

Joy and excitement swelled inside, with a lot of pride mixed in. "Good work, Officer White." She swung her feet onto the floor, and Suki released a meow of protest. "Kayla didn't happen to give any details, did she, like what he looked like or what kind of car he drove?"

"I've racked my brain trying to remember. If she mentioned anything, it's somewhere inside this thick skull of mine, buried deep. I'll check with her friends and see if she said anything to them. Maybe one of them has a little more information than I do."

"She might have said something to Evie and Miranda. I'll talk to them."

"We also need to find out if any of the other victims reported traffic stops by a cop in an unmarked vehicle."

She nodded, even though he wasn't there to see it. "If this is what the killer is doing, we can use it to set a trap."

"I hope you're not including yourself in that *we*."

"Why not? I'm single. I'm right in the middle of that age group. But there are some important differences between the victims and me. First, I'm onto him. If I see red or blue lights behind me, I won't stop without checking with dispatch first. Second, I'm armed. He puts his victims out with chloroform before kidnapping them. If he tried that with me, he'd end up with a hole in his chest."

"You're thinking of being bait." A heavy sigh came through the phone. When he spoke again, it was with uncharacteristic somberness. "I'm worried about you, Lexi. You need to be extra careful."

The concern in his voice warmed her from the inside out. After marriage to Lauren, a subsequent divorce and seven years of living separate lives, whatever tenderness he had at one time felt for her should be gone. But it wasn't. If she looked too deeply into his eyes, she saw it—traces of everything he'd once professed to feel.

Like last night, in the hospital parking lot. He'd looked at her with such warmth and tenderness, it had threatened to topple every wall she'd ever erected. If he had tried to kiss her then, she might have let him.

"Thanks, but I'll be fine, really."

A distinct beep overrode Alan's reply. She pulled the phone away from her ear and frowned at the display. "Tomlinson's calling. I'll call you back."

She touched the screen to switch calls. At her greeting, Tomlinson's bass voice came through the phone.

"Is this a good time for you to talk?"

"I'm home alone with my cats. What's up?"

"Apparently someone doesn't appreciate the time and effort you're putting into this."

The ominous tone sent a chill trickling over her. She shook it off. "Of course not. He's scared. He left a live witness."

"He also left a message. For you."

"Me?" Her palms grew suddenly clammy. "What kind of message?"

"Sweet and to the point. A single sheet of paper, folded in thirds, and taped to a light pole in the sheriff's department parking lot. It had 'Detective Simmons' typed across it in about a forty-eight-point font."

She gripped the phone more tightly. The chill headed straight for her stomach, condensing into a solid, icy lump. "What did it say?"

"'Back off. Or you'll be next.'"

Lexi closed her eyes, her heart pounding. The killer

had her name. She sucked in a calming breath. Of course he did. She was lead detective on three of the five cases. She'd spoken with dozens of possible witnesses. Her business cards were out there. "He's grasping at straws. He knows he messed up, abducting Denise without thoroughly planning things out in his usual OCD way. Now there's someone out there who can identify him. And that's got him scared."

"Which is why we've been keeping such a close watch on her."

"She wants to go stay with her aunt and uncle in Ocala. They have a horse farm up there." Lexi had talked to her that afternoon. Denise wasn't adjusting well. She refused to leave the house and, according to her father, jumped at the slightest sound. A change of scenery would do her good.

"It might be the safest place for her. We'll keep it quiet but alert the authorities up there anyway, just in case. And we'll have the detectives continue watching the Andrews house even after she leaves."

"Good." Denise's purse had never been recovered. The killer had probably disposed of it in a Dumpster somewhere, after he'd looked up her address. His best shot at undoing his mistake would be to finish what he'd started. If he tried, they would be ready.

Tomlinson sighed. "Just be careful."

She smiled at the words that so closely echoed Alan's of a few minutes ago. "I will. Also, Alan remembered an interesting conversation he'd had with Kayla Douglas a couple of months ago." She related what he'd told her.

"Interesting. That fits with the fake cop persona and gives him a great way to find out where his victims live in a less conspicuous way than trying to follow them home."

"I want to find out if any of the other victims relayed anything similar to their friends or family members."

After ending the call, she redialed Alan.

"What was Tomlinson calling about?"

She pulled her lower lip between her teeth and tried not to grimace. Alan wasn't going to be happy. Maybe she could give a non-answer and change the subject.

"I filled him in on what you said about the conversation with Kayla. He was impressed. We're definitely going to pursue the lead."

"That's what *you* told *him*. That doesn't tell me what he called about."

She winced again. There was no getting around telling him. Tomlinson had only had one reason for calling.

"Someone left me a note."

A heavy silence stretched through the phone. "Who? What kind of note?"

"Short. 'Back off. Or you'll be next.'"

"The killer."

"Or a prankster impersonating the killer."

"Lexi, this isn't good." His tone was thick with worry. "You're a target."

"All he has is my name. It wouldn't be that hard to get. Polk County isn't L.A. or New York City. We have a grand total of ten homicide detectives. Besides, my name's out there. I think you and I have talked to half the population of the county."

An insistent buzz sounded from the kitchen. Fifteen

minutes was up. She encouraged Suki out of her lap with a gentle push and received a scolding meow. Lexi ignored the protest.

"Maybe I have become a target. I can't say that would be a bad thing." After shutting off the timer and the oven, she pulled a plate from the cupboard. "If he comes after me, I'll be ready for him. I'm more than willing to act as bait if it will get me closer to catching Kayla's killer."

"You might be willing, but I'm not."

Something in his tone rubbed her the wrong way. It wasn't his decision. It was hers. "Then it's a good thing for the case that it's not up to you."

"You're making this too personal, Lexi. I'm sure Sergeant Tomlinson would agree. This might be a good time to step down."

Fire shot through her. She recognized his not-so-subtle attempt at control. She'd had plenty of experience. Her mom was the queen of manipulation.

"Don't you threaten me with Tomlinson. This is my case, and I'm going to work it how I see fit."

He blew out an exasperated breath. "When did you get so stubborn?"

"When did you turn into such a control freak?"

"I'm not trying to control you." His tone was low, but the words were thick with tension. "I'm trying to keep you alive."

"That's not your responsibility." Maybe at one time. But he'd given that up when he'd jumped into bed with Lauren instead of waiting for her. "Look, I'm determined to catch this guy. And I won't be deterred by idle threats—yours or the killer's."

She ended the call without waiting for a response,

then put the phone on the end table with a little more force than necessary.

Alan didn't understand. He would never understand.

She put her all into every case. She had no choice. It was at her very core, a driving need to bring to justice those who held no regard for human life. If her best chance of catching the killer would be to let the department use her as bait, then so be it.

For Kayla, she would do it.

She'd do it for Denise, too.

And for every one of the other four victims.

Alan stepped from his Mustang and approached the shop nestled between Harvey's New and Used Books and Hometown Cafe. The stenciling on the door spelled out *BethAnn's Fabrics and Crafts*, with *Artistic Design and Decor* below.

BethAnn's had occupied the space for the past eight years. The special events decorating company was a newer addition, begun after Jessica Dalton returned to Harmony Grove and decided to stay. His partner, Shane, had had a lot to do with that decision.

Alan swung open the door and stepped inside. He wasn't interested in fabrics and crafts, and he didn't have any special events coming up. He was there because both women had been friends of Kayla's.

Jessica emerged from the end of an aisle lined with colorful bolts of fabric and greeted him with a broad smile. "What brings you in today?"

He returned her smile. She'd been his friend longer than she'd been his partner's wife. "It's about Kayla. I was hoping you ladies might have some information

I'm looking for."

"BethAnn's finishing up a macrame class right now, but I'll be glad to help in any way I can."

He moved to the nearby counter and leaned against it. "A couple of months before Kayla was killed, she told me she'd been stopped for making an improper turn."

"Yeah, I remember."

His pulse picked up. "She told you about it?" Maybe her memory was better than his.

"She told both of us. She and BethAnn and I had dinner plans, and getting stopped made her run late. She wasn't happy about it, especially since she knew she hadn't done anything wrong. The cop said she hadn't signaled, but she knew she had. After he let her go, she even pulled over to make sure the bulb hadn't burned out or something. It was working, so she didn't understand why he'd stopped her."

"But he didn't give her a ticket."

"No, just checked her driver's license, ran her tag and let her go. BethAnn and I were teasing her that maybe he was looking for a date." Her eyes widened. "You don't think that had anything to do with her murder, do you?"

"Possibly. The guy who stopped her wasn't really a cop. Nothing about the stop was reported to dispatch."

Jessica leaned against the counter next to him. "Oh, my."

"Did she describe the guy at all?"

"She said he was too old for her."

"How old was *too old*?"

"She said middle thirties."

"Any other description?"

"She said he reminded her an awful lot of the last guy she dated—same build, same short haircut, just a little older." She grinned. "Being reminded of one's ex is never a good thing."

"Which ex?"

"Matthew Badcock."

The name wasn't familiar. The relationship obviously hadn't progressed far, or Kayla would have mentioned him. "Do you know where I can find this Matthew Badcock?" It wouldn't be as good as having Kayla around to do a composite, but depending on how much the supposed cop resembled him, having a picture of Mr. Badcock could give them a starting point.

"He's a substitute teacher, taught at her school a few times. That's how she knew him."

Voices reached them from the back of the store, proof that the door to the room where BethAnn held her classes had been opened. Soon a half dozen ladies made their way toward the front door. One deviated, making a beeline for him. An oversized cloth bag hung over one shoulder, likely containing her project. She was sporting her usual beehive hairdo, posture eager. Carolyn Platt was always in fact-gathering mode.

She nodded a silent greeting at Jessica, then stopped to stand in front of him. "Since that's your Mustang sitting out there, I take it you're not here on official police business."

Actually, he was, but he didn't need to explain his reasons for being there to Carolyn. "I just stopped in to talk to BethAnn and Jessica."

"I've seen you and Lexi together a lot around town

lately. Looks like some old sparks might be getting reignited." She waggled her eyebrows.

Alan resisted an eyeroll. Carolyn prided herself on knowing everything about everyone, before anyone else, and wasn't about to let an insignificant thing like manners hinder her in her pursuit of knowledge.

"No sparks." At least on Lexi's end. For him, those sparks Carolyn referenced stirred to life any time she got within twenty feet of him. By now they should have flickered and gone out, or at least been reduced to dying embers. "It's strictly business. We're working on a case together."

That eagerness faded to disappointment. Her shoulders even sagged a little. Carolyn lived for gathering and disseminating "news," even if she had to embellish it, and he hadn't given her anything to work with.

She told him goodbye, then walked out the front door the same time BethAnn appeared from the back. "Another class finished."

Alan asked her the same questions he'd asked Jessica, but she didn't have anything additional to add. When he returned to his car, instead of starting the engine, he dialed Lexi's number and waited through the first ring. He hadn't spoken with her since she'd hung up on him last night. He probably wasn't her favorite person at the moment.

Another ring.

He understood where she was coming from. He wanted Kayla's killer caught, too. But Lexi was too stubborn for her own good.

A third ring.

Maybe she was debating whether to take his call.

She was going to have to talk to him sooner or later. But she could always let him stew awhile. If she would pick up the phone, she would agree he had a good reason for calling.

She answered midway through the fourth ring, a curt "hello."

He tried for a friendlier tone. "Hey. I was afraid you were going to avoid me."

"I thought about it, but I figured you'd just keep calling."

Her tone was flat. Either she seriously didn't want to talk to him or she was joking. He couldn't tell which. He used to know her inside out. But things had changed.

He sighed. "I'm sorry about last night." An apology never hurt.

"Yeah, me, too."

"I didn't mean to upset you."

"It's all right. I might have gotten a little defensive."

A tension he didn't even realize he had seemed to drain from him. Now that they'd fallen into a sort of cautious friendship, he didn't like being at odds with her. "Where are you?"

"Leaving Harmony Grove. I checked in on Mom."

"How about meeting me at Pappy's for an early supper. I've got some information on Kayla."

"Can't you just tell me over the phone? I need to get home and feed the cats."

"It's early. If they eat at seven instead of five-thirty, I don't think it'll hurt them. From what I've seen, none of them look to be on the brink of starvation."

"I'm tired."

She was weakening. He could tell. "Then you

could use a relaxing dinner out. I'm guessing you really don't feel like cooking."

A heavy sigh came through the phone. "All right. But I don't want to stay too long."

"We'll be in and out before the late crowd gets there. I promise."

When he pulled into Pappy's parking lot ten minutes later, Lexi's Mazda was already there. She'd apparently left her department-assigned SUV sitting in her carport when she'd gone to check on her mother. He stepped from the car and walked through a parking lot that was already half full. Over the next hour, it would get even more crowded. Pappy's was always busy, but on Friday nights, the wait times at the popular pizza joint often exceeded ninety minutes.

When he stepped inside, a slender arm raised, drawing his attention to a booth in the back. Without waiting for someone to seat him, he made his way past tables adorned with red and white checkered tablecloths. In the center of each, a candle burned inside a pint-sized mason jar.

He slid onto the padded bench opposite Lexi. "You got here fast."

"I was driving past when you called."

Two glasses sat on the table, condensation on their outsides. Lexi had already ordered their iced tea. He picked up the one nearest him and took a long sip. It was perfect. Half sweet, half unsweet. Lexi knew how he liked it.

"What is this earth-shattering news you have for me?"

Before she could respond, Autumn Jenson approached wearing one of Pappy's green and white server uniforms. Alan smiled up at her. "You're missing Tori's cookout."

She lifted her eyebrows, then drew them together. "What cookout?"

Just what he thought. The cookout was a spur-of-the-moment idea that wouldn't materialize unless he agreed to attend. "When I saw her yesterday, she invited me, but I told her I would probably be working…which is what I'm doing, by the way." Even though it didn't look like it. "I guess she changed her mind."

"Yeah, I'm sure she did." An eyeroll accompanied the words.

Autumn was probably the most settled of the four girls. She had one more year of college. Then she'd probably ditch both the part-time server job and the roommates and move on to greener pastures.

As soon as she had walked away with their order, Lexi stared at him, eagerness radiating from her. "Okay, we're here and pizza is on the way. Tell me what you learned."

"I just came from BethAnn's, talked to her and Jessica. They have more information than I did on the guy who stopped Kayla."

"What kind of information?"

"A better description of his appearance. He reminded her of the last guy she dated."

"The substitute teacher."

"Yeah. You met him?"

Lexi shook her head. "She told me about him, but she only went out with him a few times. He ended up getting back with his old girlfriend and dumped Kayla. Then he moved somewhere out of state. I don't even remember his name."

"Matthew Badcock."

"Yeah, that's it."

Alan frowned. He hadn't counted on the guy having left the state. "The Polk County School system should have his phone number. People usually keep the same cell even when they move. If he'll cooperate and send us some pictures, it might give us a rough idea of who we're looking for."

"It's a great place to start, anyway." She gave him a broad smile. "Good job."

Warmth spread through his chest. This was the second time she'd praised him in less than twenty-four hours. He could get used to that.

"We'll work on tracking him down tomorrow." She paused. "I have a little information of my own. There's an orange grove next to the woods where Denise was found, with some tire tracks going in. Looks like whoever made them left in a hurry, spun up quite a bit of dirt. Almost got stuck. Near the tire tracks, one of the detectives saw something glinting in the sunlight. It was a half-buried ring."

"What kind of ring?"

"A class ring. Lake Region High School, class of 2002."

"Any distinguishing symbols or anything?"

"Yeah, ROTC."

"That narrows it down a bit."

"Another thing, the stone is a garnet. Lake Region's colors are black, silver and blue. My guess is the garnet is a birthstone."

"For?"

"January."

He nodded. "That narrows it down a lot."

"We're hoping the company that made the ring will be able to provide us with a name, if they keep records back that far."

"If not, just taking those in the 2002 graduating class who have January birthdays and were in ROTC should give us a workable number."

"I hope so." She heaved a sigh. "I can't tell you how ready I am for this to be over."

The weariness in her tone went straight to his heart. For five months, she'd been trying to catch this guy. Now, at the end of another long day, her face reflected her fatigue.

He reached across the table and covered her hand with his own. "We're getting closer. I don't know where the Matthew Badcock contact will lead, but we at least have a live witness now."

Autumn approached and Lexi pulled her hand free. After topping off their tea glasses, she left them alone. When she appeared again, she was balancing a tray holding a large mushroom, onion and pepperoni pizza.

Alan thanked her, then pulled two steaming slices onto each of the plates. "How's your mom?" He couldn't bring the case to a quick close, but maybe he could take her mind off of it while she ate.

She released her breath in another sigh. "Mom's just Mom. She sprained her ankle a couple of weeks ago. I've been dropping by to help her with laundry and cleaning and stuff. But I get the distinct impression she's milking it."

Alan laughed. "That doesn't surprise me."

"She's getting to see me almost every day, so it's

given her some sense of control. If she had her way, she'd be orchestrating every detail of my life, right down to how many animals I have and what time I go to bed at night. I've always been her project, but it's worse since Dad died."

"At least you're not living under the same roof. Once the laundry or cleaning or whatever is finished, you get to walk away."

"Except she saw the press conference and ever since, she's been insisting that I come and stay with her."

"It's not too often that I agree with your mother, but in this case, she's got a good point."

"I'd rather take my chances with a killer."

She stabbed a bite-size piece with a little more force than necessary. Maybe her mom wasn't a good topic of conversation.

For as long as he'd known Lexi, there'd been a tug-of-war between her and her mother. Even during those times when there hadn't been an actual battle raging, there had still been an underlying tension— Lexi's annoyance when Patty laid out yet another path for her, and Patty's frustration when Lexi didn't follow it to a tee.

For the rest of the meal, Alan managed to steer the conversation away from both the case and Lexi's mother. After the bill and the leftover pizza had been split between the two of them, she stood and gathered her purse from where it lay on the bench beside her. "I'll meet with you tomorrow morning. I made a lot of phone calls today. Of those I talked to, no one heard the victims mention being stopped, but I have a lot more people to call."

"I'll have my dialing finger warmed up and ready."

She hooked her purse over her shoulder and moved toward the door. "If we find out this is a link between the cases, we need to somehow get the word out to women in the twenty-to-twenty-five age group."

"And keep the killer from knowing what we're doing."

"That's the hard part. If we go to the press, there's too good of a chance we'll tip him off."

He held the door for her, flashing her a scheming smile. "Where can we find a lot of people in that age group all together?"

She returned his smile. "College."

"We've got several in the county."

She nodded. "Polk State, Warner, Florida Southern, Southeastern…"

He continued laying out the plan. "We'll pass out flyers asking women to call if they get stopped by an officer but not ticketed. And we'll ask them to pass along the info to all of their friends."

"And if we get a lead, we'll stake out the girl's house and wait for the killer to strike."

He nodded, trying to ignore the vise that suddenly clamped around his stomach. Somehow the thought of Lexi participating in a stake-out for a killer didn't sit well with him. But it was her job. She was trained for it, just as he was.

She pressed her key fob and the locks on her Mazda clicked open, accompanied by a beep. She turned to face him at the door. "First we've got to find out whether the other victims had been stopped."

"And we'll start that tomorrow."

He smiled down at her. She seemed to stand a little

straighter and anticipation had replaced a little of the fatigue in her eyes. He fought back the urge to pull her into his arms. He would do anything to take some of the load off of her.

Because no matter what happened, he would always have a soft spot in his heart for Lexi.

SEVEN

PALMS ROSE SKYWARD, fronds swaying in the gentle breeze. Beneath them, wide walks stretched past beds filled with lush greenery and overflowing with color. Spring in Florida was always beautiful, but Southeastern University went all out.

Lexi fell in behind a group of students moving around the campus, talking and texting. She could be one of them, except for the pistol at her side.

For the past several days she and Alan had contacted friends and family members of the other victims. Three out of four of the women killed had mentioned getting pulled over and having their licenses run. And there was no record of any of the stops. Today she and Alan were hitting the colleges.

She had also made contact with Matthew Badcock. Hearing about Kayla's murder had obviously upset him. He'd sworn he'd never meant to hurt her, that he'd dated her on the rebound, and when he and his girlfriend had worked out their differences, he'd felt terrible dumping Kayla. Now he felt even worse.

When Lexi had asked him to send pictures, he'd complied. She'd printed and tucked them into Kayla's file, a half dozen of them, along with statistics like height and weight. The pictures would never be made public. That wasn't their purpose. It was to give those investigating a general idea what the killer might look like, since Kayla had said the cop who stopped her reminded her of Matthew.

The problem was, "reminded" was a pretty loose term. Did they really look a lot alike, or was it less tangible things that had brought Matthew to mind? Things like mannerisms, the timbre of his voice, even posture.

Lexi removed her phone from her purse and pulled up a familiar number.

Alan answered on the third ring. "How's it going?"

"I'm finished. Just leaving Southeastern." She had taken Winter Haven and Lakeland and given Alan the rest of the county. "How about you?"

"I'm headed to Lake Wales to hit Webber. That's my last stop."

"Good."

"Everyone's been really cooperative. The office staff has promised to get the flyers into the hands of the professors to distribute to all the students. I've even had a couple offer to do all the copying."

"Same here. They're willing to do anything they can to help protect their students."

She looked down at the stack of pages she held. HELP US CATCH A KILLER stretched across the top of the page. Below that, the first paragraph revealed the same details the sheriff had given at the press conference. The second mentioned the traffic stops, with a request that anyone stopped and not ticketed by a cop in an unmarked vehicle call the number printed at the bottom. It was Lexi's cell phone number, something she'd had to fight Alan for. He'd insisted that publicizing her number put her in unnecessary danger. She'd insisted that it was her case, and if a young lady got stopped, she wanted to know any hour of the day or night. She'd won the argument.

"Let me know when you finish at Webber." She slid into the driver's seat of her Explorer and closed the door. "After that, we wait and hope for our big break."

A beep sounded in her ear and she glanced at the display. "I've got a call coming through—352 area code."

"That's north of here."

Ocala. Her pulse picked up speed. Maybe Denise had remembered something else. She switched the call over.

"Hey, Lexi? It's Denise."

It was only four words, but the strength behind them surprised her. Denise no longer sounded like a petrified adolescent. The time spent in horse country was apparently doing her good.

"I remembered something else. I don't know if it's important, but I wanted to let you know, just in case."

"That's great. Anything you can tell us might get us that much closer to catching this guy."

"That's what I thought. When he went to the trunk, I saw a piece of paper sitting in the console. It had a list of girls' names. Some of them were crossed out."

Lexi pulled a pen and pocket memo pad from her purse, her heart pounding. "Do you remember any of the names?"

"Lysandra."

"What?"

"Lysandra. L-Y-S-A-N-D-R-A. I remember it because it's so unusual."

Lexi jotted down the name. "Tell me everything you can about this list, starting at the top."

"The first four or five names were crossed out."

"Do you remember any of them?"

A long stretch of silence passed before Denise finally answered. "Tiffany. Tiffany was one of the crossed-out names. And Amber. I don't remember the others."

"You're doing great. How about the rest of the names, the ones that weren't crossed out?"

"Lysandra was the first one. Then Jeanie. There were two or three others. It was a list of probably nine or ten names, including the crossed-out ones, but those four are the only ones I remember."

"Anything else you can recall?"

"No. I'm sorry."

"You did great. That helps us a lot." If she had given them a list of Janes and Anns and Marys, they wouldn't have had any useful information. But Denise was right. Lysandra was an unusual name, which greatly increased their chances of finding the killer's Lysandra.

Tonight, Lexi would call Alan. Denise had told her at the hospital that the killer kept calling her Jeanie and saying that it wasn't her time yet. It wasn't her time yet, because Lysandra was supposed to be next. Or someone who represented Lysandra.

Tomorrow she would start a nationwide search of the name. Since the killer was choosing women in their twenties and the offense happened ten years earlier, the man they were looking for was probably in his thirties. That assumption fit with what both Kayla and Denise had said about the supposed cop who had stopped them.

Lexi dropped her phone into her purse and cranked up the SUV. As the soothing melody of an Evanescence song filled the confined space, her spirits lifted and she sang along. It was the first real hope she'd had since learning that their Martin Jeffries lead was dead.

She pulled onto Longfellow belting out the notes, unable to tamp down the excitement. If they could find this Lysandra, she could probably lead them to the killer.

The excitement stayed with her all the way to Auburndale. She turned into the driveway and brought the Explorer to a stop in the carport, next to her Mazda. Alan would probably be calling shortly, once he finished his last stop. In the meantime, she'd feed the cats, then work on feeding herself.

As she picked up and cleaned the porcelain dishes, three sets of eyes stayed fixed on her, and Suki let out a yowl.

She looked over her shoulder. "You're not going to starve before I get your food dished up. I promise."

The vocal Siamese responded with another indignant meow, while Midnight paced back and forth across the kitchen. Itsy lay in the corner, patiently waiting. Except her non-demanding pose was probably due more to laziness than patience.

After putting the dishes on the floor, she laid out ingredients for tuna casserole. It was something quick and easy that made great leftovers. Twenty minutes later, she had the pasta, tuna and canned soup layered in a casserole dish, a generous coating of cracker crumbs spread across the top, dotted with butter. She slid the casserole into the oven, then cleaned up the kitchen. Soon the pleasant aroma of dinner filled the room.

The timer had seven minutes to go when the doorbell rang, sending tension spiking through her. She didn't get a lot of visitors. At least unexpected ones.

She tried to shake off the uneasiness. Granted, she'd been threatened. The note Tomlinson had told her about had put her on edge. But it was probably just an idle threat, someone trying to scare her off the case. Or a prank. Besides, the killer didn't know where she lived. She hadn't had any traffic stops.

She moved through the living room and checked the peephole. Prank or not, she wasn't unlocking the door without knowing who stood on her porch.

It was Alan. She swung open the door.

"What are you doing here?"

He flashed her a teasing smile. "You told me to let you know when I was finished at Webber."

"What I had in mind was a phone call."

"This was right on my way home. Sort of."

She backed away from the door to let him in.

"Mmm, something smells good."

"Tuna casserole."

He held up both hands. "Don't worry, I'm not going to invite myself for dinner."

"No, you're just going to drop hints and hope I will."

She walked into the kitchen and pulled two plates and glasses out of the cabinet. The company would be nice. Eating alone meal after meal sometimes got old. Besides, they had strategies to discuss.

Alan slid into one of the kitchen chairs. "What did you learn from Denise? At least, I assume that was who called."

"It was. It seems our killer is working off a list."

"What kind of list?"

"Girls' names. Denise saw it in the console the night he abducted her. She said the first four or five names were crossed off."

Alan pressed his lips together. "I'm guessing it was five."

"Yeah, me too, one for each of the girls killed. Then there were another four or five names that weren't crossed off yet."

"His remaining victims."

"Yep." She dropped a pot holder in the center of the table and sat opposite him. "The next name on the list is Lysandra, then Jeanie."

Alan nodded slowly. "We can probably assume Lysandra is next, or someone who represents Lysandra. Unless he deviates."

"My guess is he won't deviate again, especially after this last time. He almost got caught. Besides, he's too methodical."

The oven timer buzzed, and she rose from the table. "That would be the dinner bell. You've probably figured out you're invited."

"Yeah, the second place setting sort of gave it away."

She took the casserole from the oven, and put a serving spoon into it. After she placed the dish on the wooden hot pad that she'd set in the center of the table earlier, Alan piled a spoonful onto each plate.

"I'm glad you didn't throw me out after letting me smell this for the past five or ten minutes. That would have been cruel."

"I wouldn't want to be accused of being cruel." She scooped a steaming mouthful onto her fork and blew on it. When she looked across the table at Alan, he was sitting with his head bowed. She raised her brows. He hadn't done that at Pappy's. Or maybe he had and she just hadn't noticed.

She waited until he opened his eyes and picked up his fork. "When did that start? The prayer thing."

"About five and a half years ago. I'd hit bottom, pretty well messed up my life. My personal life, anyway. I figured I could use some help straightening things out."

"Did it work?"

"It did. I'm not perfect. I still make mistakes, but the consequences aren't as far-reaching. There's a lot to be said for divine guidance."

Maybe so. But it didn't take divine guidance to know that getting Lauren pregnant had been a bad idea. She could have told him that up front and saved him some heartache.

She scooped another bite onto her fork. "I'm glad it's working for you."

"It's for anyone who wants to accept it, you know."

Yeah, she knew that. Her parents hadn't taken her to church; her mom had been more into attending social events. But Lexi had occasionally gone with friends. And she'd actually listened. She had liked the songs and the stories and the kindness of the people. She'd even prayed some. That was when she and God were still on speaking terms, before Abby and Dad and Kayla.

"What did you pray for?"

"Thanked God for the food, asked for help finding Kayla's killer." His eyes locked with hers and held. "Prayed for a chance to undo some past mistakes."

"There were mistakes on both sides. But it's all in the past." She offered him a weak smile. "Let's just leave it there. We have a case to solve."

Alan nodded, but there was reluctance in the gesture. "We now have names. What next?"

"We do a nationwide search for women named Lysandra, then eliminate anyone over the age of forty and under the age of twenty-five."

"And we pay some Lysandras a visit."

"Or at least make some phone calls."

After they'd dished up and finished seconds, Alan stood to clear their empty plates. "Thanks for feeding me, even though I sort of invited myself. That wasn't my intent when I dropped by. The aroma sort of roped me in."

"No problem. It gave us a chance to bring each other up to speed on everything."

He stepped onto the porch. "Lock the door behind me."

"Believe me, I will."

As she watched him walk to his car, an unexpected longing rose up from within. The past that she had successfully avoided all through dinner surged forward with a vengeance.

At one time, he was her life. She'd loved him with all her heart and had known without a doubt that they would someday commit to spending the rest of their lives together. Unfortunately, *someday* had arrived sooner for him than it had for her.

Now, seven years later, *someday* seemed set off in some distant universe. Because regardless of what she felt for Alan, and no matter how desperately she longed for something more, nothing had changed.

Nothing had changed, yet everything had changed. Instead of heading off to her second year of college, reveling in her new-found independence, she'd become solidly set in her way of life—solitude, freedom, no one to consider except her cats.

It was really kind of nice. Was she ready to give that up?

Would she ever be?

———

Alan laid aside the spy novel he'd been reading and picked up the remote. He'd checked out the movie lineup earlier and had actually found something that spurred his interest.

It was another Friday night at home. What had once been a rare event was becoming a regular occurrence. But ever since Lexi had come back into his life, at least on a professional level, casual dating didn't hold the appeal it once had. Besides, he didn't have the time. He was sort of working two jobs— official Harmony Grove police officer and unofficial Polk County Sheriff's Office assistant detective.

He wasn't complaining, though. He was enjoying his dual role. Searching for clues. Uncovering the mystery one layer at a time. Working side by side with Lexi. The last was the most appealing of all.

The hours they were spending together had gone a long way toward rebuilding burnt bridges. The long-term tension between them had all but vanished, and during unguarded moments, slivers of emotion slipped past her defenses. He could see it in her eyes—signs of what had once been there long ago.

When this was over, maybe they could continue a friendship. He wasn't willing to set his sights on anything more. Maybe her priorities had shifted. Maybe she'd come to realize that money and prestige didn't always equal happiness and satisfaction. But he'd already had his dreams shot down once and wasn't ready to go for round two.

He clicked the TV remote and opening credits filled the screen. Soon other music mixed with the orchestral score streaming through the surround sound—his phone's ringtone. It lay on the coffee table, screen lit. Lexi was calling. He muted the volume on the TV.

After his "hello," the thud of a door closing came through the phone, followed by the sound of an engine turning over. "Hey, I'm leaving Mom's. She's still on crutches with her ankle sprain, so I cooked for us and ate with her. Are you home?"

"Yeah."

"Alone?" The last word came out with a little hesitation.

"Yeah, I'm alone. What's up?"

"After I finished cleaning up the kitchen, Mom started getting a little overbearing."

So what else is new? He kept the thought to himself.

"I told her I needed to go, that you and I had some work to do on Kayla's case."

Alan smiled. Any time Lexi's mother was involved, having an escape route was never a bad idea. "I'll be glad to help supply your getaway excuse. You want to stop by?"

"Yeah." She paused. "I don't know where you live."

He gave her the address. "I'm right around the corner from BethAnn's house."

"I'll be there in less than five minutes."

"What about the cats?"

"I took care of them before I went over to Mom's."

When he opened the front door a few minutes later he sputtered a greeting. He was used to seeing her in her business attire, tailored suit, hair secured in a clip or a tight braid, weapon strapped to her hip. Professional all the way.

That wasn't who stood on his porch, though. This was the old Lexi, relaxed and casual in a pair of snugly fitting jeans and a scoop-necked tee. Her hair fell past her shoulders in wavy blond cascades, pressed in by previous hours in a braid.

His chest tightened, and his thoughts flew back to other times she'd arrived at his door, happy and in love. First it had been his parents' house right there in Harmony Grove. Then he'd rented an apartment near Polk State's Winter Haven campus.

That had been where Lauren had deftly inserted herself into his life. And where he'd blown his last chance at any possible future with Lexi. The memories left him with a keen ache and a hollow emptiness.

He swallowed hard and forced an easy smile. "Come in, and let's get started on that case work. We want to be able to tell your mother how we slaved away."

She returned his smile. Hers didn't seem to reflect any of the emotions that churned inside him.

He led her into the living room and, after offering

her a seat on the couch, sat down next to her. "Okay, tell me what you've got."

"We found the owner of the high school ring. Definitely a dead end. He works for Wilkins Irrigation. They do work there. A month or so ago, he got to the job on a Monday morning, realized he still had his ring on and took it off and put it in his pocket. When he got home, it was gone. He figured it was lost for good. He was really happy to get it back."

"Did anyone check out his story?"

"Yep, Jim Wilkins himself says that the guy has worked for him for five years."

"How about Lysandra? Anything there?"

She opened the manila file folder she had carried in. "According to my search, there are five Lysandras in the U.S. that are between the ages of twenty-five and forty. I've eliminated three of them. One married right out of high school and is raising her five children with her farmer husband. I called her, and she said she had a friend in grade school named Amber, but she's lost contact with her. She has an acquaintance named Jeanie, but doesn't know any Tiffanys. And she can't think of any circumstances where someone might be hurt or angry enough to want to take this kind of vengeance."

"What about the other two?"

"One's a marketing executive and one's a nurse. Neither of them had prior connections with the other names on the list. And, like the first Lysandra, neither could think of anyone from their pasts who would have reason to do something like this."

"We're striking out so far."

She flipped to another page in the folder. "There

are still two left. Lysandra Yearwood is no longer at the job that shows up for her. We've got a cell number but she doesn't have her voice mail set up. We can try her again tonight."

She turned to the last page in the folder. "The fifth is a Lysandra Tucker. She went to Florida State for one year, stayed in one of the sorority houses. Then she got busted for drugs and dropped out of school. Never went back. She's thirty now, works as a bartender at a club over in Tampa, Ybor City. I get the distinct impression she's avoiding me."

"How so?"

"I've called three times over the past couple of days. Each time, the person who answered has told me to hang on, then comes back and says she's not available. I even called back when she was supposed to be on break."

"You think she's hiding something?"

"It sure looks that way." She pulled out her cell phone and pressed in the number, then put it on speaker phone.

"Club Dynamo, your place for a good time." The words were shouted over the music blasting in the background.

Lexi glanced at him and smiled. "May I please speak with Lysandra Tucker?"

"Who's calling, please?"

"Detective Alexis Simmons with the Polk County Sheriff's Office."

For several moments, the only sound that came through the phone was the high-energy techno beat. The club employee's span of silence was just enough time to flash someone an unspoken question and receive a silent answer.

"I'm sorry, she's not here tonight."

"How about if I call back tomorrow evening? Will she be working then?"

"Might be. I don't know for sure."

Lexi ended the call and gave him a conspiratorial wink. "How about a trip to Ybor tomorrow?"

"I'm game."

"This Lysandra isn't going to be able to avoid us if we're standing right in front of her."

"True. How about Lysandra number four—Yearwood?"

Lexi referred back to the page in the folder, punched in a number and pressed the phone to her ear. Several seconds later, she stiffened, posture alert.

Alan waited through the one-sided conversation. She was obviously getting further with this Lysandra than the last. Finally, she ended the call.

"Well?"

"We've just eliminated our fourth Lysandra. Same basic story as the other three. But I'm putting all my hope on this last one. There's a reason she's avoiding us, and my guess is it has something to do with this case." She closed the folder and slid forward on the couch, preparing to stand.

He wasn't ready for her to leave. "You want to watch a movie with me?" Of course, the one he'd intended to watch was already thirty minutes in. But he'd gladly change his plans if she'd stay.

"I probably should go. It's been a long day."

He steeled himself against the disappointment filling his chest and walked her to the door. "You know you can drop by anytime. It doesn't have to be about the case." He grinned down at her. "Or escaping your mother."

"Thanks. But I don't want to bother you."

He rested his hand on the doorknob but didn't open the door. "You used to never worry about bothering me."

"Things were different then."

Yes, they were. Did she feel the loss as acutely as he did? He couldn't tell. Her eyes were shielded, her emotions hidden behind the walls she'd erected to keep everyone—at least him—at a distance. Though her clothes no longer screamed *professional*, her entire demeanor did.

He lifted a hand, determined to reach through those walls to the sweet, softhearted woman he'd fallen in love with. "Why did you say no?" He slid a finger down her cheek. "Why wouldn't you marry me?"

"I was nineteen and had just gotten out from under my mother's thumb. I was enjoying my freedom and didn't think I was ready for commitment. The last thing I expected was to come back a month later and find you engaged to Lauren." She turned away. "It didn't take you long to replace me."

There was no bitterness in her tone, but the hurt that underlined her words sliced right through him. "I had already gotten your message."

"What message?"

"The one you had your mom deliver to me."

She looked at him again, mouth parted and eyebrows drawn together. "What?"

His chest grew tight with the suspicion that he'd made a huge, life-altering mistake.

He wrestled in a deep breath. "You had already said

we should date other people." She'd told him that before she'd left for school that year. He'd fought it, insisting he didn't mind waiting for her to finish her criminal justice degree and come home. He'd already waited through one year. What was another three?

But it hadn't been *his* lack of freedom she'd been concerned about. It had been her own. He'd finally given in and done some casual dating but still called her every chance he'd gotten. Meanwhile, she hadn't even seemed to want to talk to him.

"Every time I called you, you were heading to class or studying for an exam or had some other reason why you couldn't talk. I was beginning to feel as if you were avoiding me. Then came the visit from your mom."

She stiffened and an icy hardness entered her gaze. Anger flowed beneath the surface, carefully held in check. "What did my mom say?"

"That you had met someone. That the two of you were serious, were even discussing marriage. She made it a point to tell me that he was studying to be a doctor and would be able to give you all the things you deserve."

Her anger erupted, springing forth like a geyser. "And you believed her?" Her voice was raised, her question ending on a particularly shrill note. She sliced one hand through the air. "You never once thought you should verify what she said with me?"

"I never considered that she might have been lying to me. She convinced me you didn't want to talk to me and that's why you sent her. And frankly, your actions hadn't exactly convinced me otherwise."

"I was busy. I was carrying a full load while working

part-time." Her tone was defensive, but some of the fire had gone out of her. "I came back at Christmas to tell you that I was ready, that if you were willing to wait until I finished school, I wanted to marry you."

A lead weight slid down his throat and settled in his gut. He'd thought she had finally worked up the courage to dump him herself. The last thing he'd wanted was to hear the words from her own mouth. He'd shut her down by telling her he'd moved on and was marrying Lauren.

"Lexi, I'm so sorry." He rested both hands on her shoulders, pleading with her to understand. "I cared for Lauren, but I didn't love her. When she found out you had left me, she was right there, eager to step in, pushing for marriage. I knew you were the only one I would ever love. But since I thought I would never have you, raising a child with Lauren didn't seem like such a bad second choice."

She looked up at him while he spoke, eyes once again veiled. Then she twisted from his grasp and bolted toward the front door. She swung it wide, leaped off the porch and flew down the short drive.

"Lexi!" He ran after her, but she didn't turn back. As she slipped into the driver's seat of the Mazda, tears glistened in the glow of his porch light. The sight tore his heart in two.

He watched her back from the drive. When he'd returned to the house, he closed the door and sagged against the wooden jamb.

Dear Lord, what have I done?

EIGHT

———

LEXI WIPED AT the tears streaming down her face. Alan wasn't the only one who had betrayed her. Her mother had, too.

She was used to her mother's manipulation. She'd dealt with it all her life. But going behind her back to talk to Alan, trying to eliminate any chance of reconciliation? That was over the top, even for the queen of control.

How would she ever trust her again? Forget trust. How would she ever forgive her?

She turned onto Main Street to head out of town. Her mom had been conniving and deceitful, but Alan had let her manipulate him. All it would have taken was a simple phone call. Instead, he'd not even bothered to question what he'd been told, had just believed the worst.

As she sped down Highway 17 toward Winter Haven, she swiped at the tears once more. She would deal with her mother later. And Alan…well, nothing had changed. He still had no excuse for sleeping with Lauren.

Up ahead, a brightly lit service station beckoned her. She wanted nothing more than to go straight home, curl up with her cats and have a good cry. But the "low gas" light on her dash killed those plans, or at least delayed them.

She stepped on the brake and pulled up to one of the pumps. While the gas poured into her tank, she leaned against the car, letting her gaze drift down the street that ran alongside the station. A car sat some twenty yards away with only its parking lights on.

A shiver passed through her. Had the driver followed her off the highway when she'd pulled into the station? She'd been so upset, she hadn't paid attention. Dumb mistake. Distractions like that could get her killed.

She finished pumping her gas and as she pulled back onto Highway 17, she cast frequent glances in her rearview mirror. Moments later, the same car eased to a stop at the intersection, then turned onto the highway, headed in her direction.

Now she had no doubt. She was being followed. But she couldn't even identify the vehicle. It was too far back, nothing but a couple of headlights piercing the blackness of the cloudy night.

She slowed, allowing the car to catch up. But it slowed, too, maintaining the same distance. Another vehicle slipped between them.

She touched a button on her headset. "Call Tomlinson."

She waited through two rings.

"Please answer." No way was she going to go home with someone following her. And no way was she going to pull over. If she couldn't reach Tomlinson, she'd call 911.

Relief washed over her at her supervisor's warm

greeting. She dispensed with the pleasantries.

"I'm being followed. The car is light, a four-door." That was as detailed as she could get. Whoever it was had been careful to park well out of the glow of the streetlights. All she had to go on was what she'd seen in her rearview mirror as he'd made his turn onto the highway. "I'm not sure, but it could be our guy."

"Give me your location."

"On 17, turning onto Winter Lake Road." She cast several glances in her rearview mirror. The suspicious car turned, too. Now it was directly behind her but still hanging back, too far away to identify.

"Hold on. I'll get a couple of units dispatched."

He didn't disconnect the call. Soon she heard him on the other line, issuing directions.

Tomlinson came back on the phone. "You doing okay?"

"So far. I've made a right on Spirit Lake and he's still behind me. I think it might be a Toyota Camry, but I'm not sure." The light ahead turned red and she pressed the brake. "I hope our people get here fast."

"They're being dispatched now."

By the time she braked to a stop, the light had turned green again. She accelerated through the intersection. But the car didn't follow. Instead, it veered into a squealing right turn, as if having had a sudden change of plans.

"He just turned right on Coleman." She braked for a hard right onto Seventh Street, then made the one-block jaunt to continue down Coleman. But the light-colored Camry, or whatever it was, was gone.

Why had he suddenly given up the pursuit? It was almost as if he'd been listening to a police scanner.

She couldn't rule it out. If he had a strobe light, he could certainly have a police scanner.

She heaved a sigh. "I lost him. I think he cut through one of the subdivisions off of Hatfield. He knew we were on to him."

She disconnected the call and during the final miles home, her heart rate gradually returned to normal. That was close. She had to remain more alert. No matter what happened, she needed to be constantly aware of her surroundings. She had let down her guard, just for a few minutes. If she hadn't stopped for gas, she might have led the killer right to her home.

Before pulling into her driveway, she scanned the street in front and behind her. She was alone—no strange cars, no distant headlights. She pulled the Mazda into the double carport next to her county vehicle, and for the first time ever, wished she had a garage instead. Auburndale was small. If someone really wanted to find her, it wouldn't be that difficult.

When she opened the front door, Suki met her in the foyer, loudly berating her for leaving. When she headed toward the kitchen for a drink of water, the cat almost plowed her over getting there.

"I already fed you." She bent to pick up the talkative Siamese and the meows immediately turned to purrs. "Just because someone comes to the kitchen doesn't mean it's time to eat again."

After putting the cat back on the floor, she drank the glass of water, then walked into the living room. It was too early to go to bed, and she didn't feel like watching something on TV. She didn't want to read, either.

Tomorrow she would be spending the afternoon

with Alan. There was no way around it. She had already invited him on her investigative trip to Ybor City. There would be plenty more shared excursions before this was all over. She needed to just buck up and forget about what they'd shared in the past.

She heaved a sigh and let her gaze circle the room. The old spinet piano in the corner called to her. Two months after moving in, she'd found it at a yard sale for fifty bucks. The seller had even moved it for her.

She sank onto the bench and ran her hand over the keys. She had her mother to thank for her skill on the piano. But it wasn't until recently that she'd considered that skill a gift. As a child, she'd sat through endless piano lessons and spent countless hours practicing and participating in contests and recitals. She'd hated every minute of it. Playing the piano had always been her mother's passion, not her own.

Now she took comfort in the activity. There was no one to tell her she had to practice, no impossible standard to live up to, no pressure to perform.

She put her hands on the keyboard and started to play Beethoven's *Für Elise*. Her fingers glided over the keys and she closed her eyes, letting the emotion of the piece swell inside her. The tinkling melody filled the room and circled around her, soothing her frayed nerves. She would never tour the world as a concert pianist. She had no desire to. Playing for her own enjoyment was more than enough.

All the glitz and glamour had been her mother's dream. She might have achieved it, if she hadn't met and married Lexi's father. She had given up a lot for love. And regretted it ever since.

Lexi's eyes snapped open and she sat frozen, hands

suspended over the keys, Beethoven silenced. All her life, she'd thought her mother was trying to make her into what she'd wanted her to be. She'd been wrong. Her mother was trying to make her into what she wished she herself had become. Always trying to live her dreams through her only child.

Patty Simmons regretted not pursuing the career path she'd chosen at a young age—living in the spotlight, praised for her talent, loved by thousands. So she'd forced that dream onto her daughter.

She had regretted not marrying someone with the financial means and social status to allow her to continue living in the upper echelons of society. When she'd seen Lexi about to make the same "mistake," committing her future to a lowly police officer, she'd stepped in and taken action. Her actions had ruined two lives. Three, counting Lauren's.

As long as Lexi could remember, her mother had fought to get her way, cajoling and manipulating people and circumstances in an attempt to force her world into what she'd wanted it to be. When that hadn't worked, she'd turned to deceit and lies.

Lexi and Alan had both played right into her hands.

Lexi hadn't wanted to give up her independence, her right to make her own decisions without having to consider someone else's wishes, so she'd severed her relationship with Alan. The fact that she'd changed her mind a month later didn't matter, because Alan had believed her mother's lies and had already turned to Lauren. Her mother had gotten her way.

She was still getting her way. Although working on Kayla's case had thrown them together on a professional level, the events her mother had orchestrated seven years ago were still keeping Alan and her from finding happiness together.

Lexi dropped her hands to her lap. As long as she held onto her pain and resentment, she was continuing to award her mother control over her life. She'd been doing exactly what her mother wanted—pushing Alan away, keeping herself shut off from him.

Her mother's demand for control had created the prison walls around her, but it was her own anger and determination to protect herself that had given them their power. Was it possible that freedom was just a decision away? Was happiness within her and Alan's reach after all?

She shook her head and released a heavy sigh. It was all far too complicated, and tonight she was too tired to try to sort it out.

She lifted her hands to the keyboard and began to play.

———◆———

Ybor's Club Dynamo stood hemmed in between a tattoo parlor and a nail salon, little more than a hole in the wall. Music pulsed through the closed door and neon script in the windows enticed patrons with a promise of the booze they would find inside. Across the mansard roof, more neon lights flashed the name of the establishment. At least, that was the intent. Instead, "Club Dyna" was what beamed into the darkness, since the last quarter of the sign wasn't lit.

Alan swung open the wooden door and paused, steeling himself against the onslaught to his senses. Lights strobed, reflecting off the smoke curling through the air, and the music, now unobstructed, reverberated through his rib cage.

Lexi walked in ahead of him. He had one word to describe her—hot. Black stretch jeans disappeared into knee-high boots with four-inch heels. Her blouse, with its red and black swirly pattern, flowed over her curves. Its uneven hemline ended between upper and mid-thigh. Her hair was loose, its blond waves framing her face and brushing her shoulders.

A teardrop-shaped ruby bordered by tiny diamonds hung over the curved neckline of her blouse. The necklace had been the last thing he'd bought for her, other than the engagement ring. He'd given it to her for her birthday, a month before she'd left for school.

The fact that she'd kept it all these years instead of selling it had to be a good sign. It meant the piece held sentimental value and she hadn't been able to part with it.

Or maybe it was a bad sign. Maybe there'd been no sentimental value, and she'd been able to wear it without a thought of the love that had gone into its purchase.

Or maybe she'd kept it put away for the past seven years, unable to part with it or wear it. In that case, taking it out tonight could be a good sign.

He gave himself a mental scolding. He needed to stop trying to assign meaning to what were probably insignificant decisions and focus on the case. That was obviously what Lexi was doing. Since she'd avoided any mention of their discussion last night, he hadn't brought it up, either. There would be time for meaningful conversations later.

She turned her head and leaned into him. "We

should have come armed with earplugs."

"Not a bad idea." His voice was several decibels louder than normal. How people conversed in settings like this, he'd never understand.

He followed her as she wound her way toward the bar, past a dance floor filled to capacity with writhing bodies. A thin leather purse hung at her side, large enough to accommodate the manila folder she had slid into it before she left the house.

When she climbed onto a bar stool, he took the one next to her. Two female bartenders moved back and forth, filling drink orders and chatting with patrons. One was blond, petite and pretty. And much too young to be their Lysandra. Maybe a USF student, taking on the weekend shift to work her way through school.

The other was older and tougher-looking, lacking the youthful innocence of the blonde. Her jet-black hair was cut short in a jagged, chopped style and highlighted with streaks of purple. Some kind of hair gel stiffened the uneven clumps, accentuating the unconventional cut.

Lexi nodded toward the older bartender and put her mouth close to Alan's ear. "You think that's our Lysandra?"

"I'm almost positive."

The blonde looked over at them and held up a finger. After setting two drinks in front of a couple of ladies at the other end of the bar, she hurried in their direction.

"What can I get you folks?"

He smiled up at her. "Not that I don't like you, but I was hoping to be served by Lysandra."

"Not a problem." She turned and shouted to her coworker halfway down the bar. "San, this one's yours."

Lysandra's gaze drifted over the other patrons and came to rest on Alan. The friendly smile she had for her customers widened and she closed the distance between them. Even in the poor lighting, at close range, the heavy makeup did nothing to hide the creases that surrounded her mouth and marked the edges of her eyes. If she was thirty, those were some hard thirty years.

She stopped in front of him and leaned on the bar, mouth curved upward in invitation. "Hey, big boy, what can I get you?"

Lexi tensed next to him, almost imperceptibly. It might even have been his imagination. But he wasn't imagining the prickly vibes she was sending out now. Maybe she felt something for him, after all.

But this wasn't the time to explore possibilities. They had finally found the elusive Lysandra. Now to get her to talk.

He returned her smile. "A Coke, and the same for the lady."

One side of her mouth rose a little higher. "The hard stuff. Be back in a sec."

She returned to set a glass in front of each of them.

Alan smiled up at her again. "You're a hard lady to get a hold of."

"If I'd have known you were trying, I'd have made it a little easier." She ran a painted nail along the back of one of his hands. She wouldn't have been nearly as friendly if he'd been dressed in his usual working attire. She would probably have slipped out the back door and not come back until someone had told her the coast was clear.

He resisted the urge to pull his hand away. Shallow flirtiness had never appealed to him. Lexi's genuine air was much more refreshing. "My friend here has tried for the past three days to reach you, with no success. If I didn't know better, I'd think you were trying to avoid us."

She pulled away from the counter, back ramrod-straight and green eyes guarded. Distrust flashed in their depths, pushing aside all hint of the invitation that was there only moments earlier. "Jake's trying to pin everything on me, isn't he?" She crossed her arms in front of her. "It's not going to work, because I wasn't there. I figured out he was trouble and was going to pull me down with him, so I dumped him."

Alan nodded. "That was a wise choice. But Jake isn't the reason we're here."

Lexi went on to explain. "We have a serial killer stalking young women in Polk County. We're pretty sure what he's doing is retribution for something that happened ten years ago." She pulled the folder from her bag and laid it on the counter, still closed. "We have some names of the women who were involved. One, of course, is Lysandra. There was also Amber, Tiffany and Jeanie."

Recognition flitted across her features, but she shook her head.

"I'm sorry. I can't help you."

Lexi rested her hand next to the folder. "We just need to ask you a few questions, see what you can remember."

Lysandra shook her head again. "I'm sorry, I don't

know any women by those names."

Alan studied her. She was lying. He opened Lexi's folder enough to pull out the stack of photos. After fishing through them, he pulled out one the killer had taken of the first victim. It wasn't one of the earlier ones, with nothing more than some minor bruising. It was the last one, head cocked unnaturally to the side, bulging, lifeless eyes, discolored face and ugly brownish-red ring around the neck. This time he *was* going for shock value.

He slammed the photo face up on the counter. "Look, lady, young women are dying, and you might be able to stop it."

She cast a glance at the picture, then jerked away, lips turned out in revulsion. For several moments, she stood motionless, indecision set in her features.

Finally, she cast a glance at her coworker. "Cover for me."

After she came out from around the counter, she led them to a table in the corner, farthest from the massive speakers pumping their racket onto the dance floor. Not that it helped. There was probably no peace and quiet to be had within a three-block radius.

Lysandra slid into a chair, her expression somber. "Amber, Tiffany and Jeanie—we were all in the same sorority at Florida State."

Lexi nodded. "Anyone you can think of who might have had a bone to pick with you ladies?"

Lysandra gave a dry laugh. "Yeah, a whole bunch of guys. Where do you want to start?"

"How about the why? Then we'll get to the who."

"It was all part of joining."

"What was?" Alan asked.

"Using our feminine wiles to lure a guy into a really embarrassing situation."

He nodded. Hazing was illegal, but that didn't stop it from happening. "Do you remember the names of any of these guys?"

Lysandra thought for a moment. "Frank. I remember him, because he's the one I set up."

"What was Frank's last name?"

"Thompson or Thomas, maybe Tomlin. I'm not good with names."

Lexi made some notes on a blank sheet of paper in her folder. "Any others you can remember?"

"No, that's it."

Lexi continued. "So one of the requirements of getting into the sorority was to lure some unsuspecting guy into a compromising position. Then what?"

"Then we took pictures, posted them to social media and plastered them all over campus. The guys got a lot of ribbing."

Alan's pulse sped up and he cast Lexi a meaningful glance. The killer's photos weren't trophies. They'd already known that. But they weren't for the purpose of publicity, either. They were for revenge. His tormenters photographed him at his worst, so he photographed his victims at theirs.

He brought his attention back to Lysandra. "Any of those guys seem especially upset over your pranks?"

Lysandra shrugged. "Most of them took it in stride."

"Most, but not all?"

She stared down at her hands clasped on the table. When her gaze again met his, it was intense, as if she had suddenly realized the import of what she'd participated in.

She nodded slowly. "There was one. He didn't laugh it off like the others."

"How so?" Lexi asked.

"He was really angry, not like an explosive, blow-up-and-get-violent anger. More like a seething, beneath-the-surface anger that would simmer and stew." She frowned. "That's the most dangerous kind. When I passed him on campus the next day, he glared at me with a cold hatred. He scared me." An involuntary shudder shook her shoulders. "That was the last time I had any part in the hazing pranks."

Lexi took a swig of her Coke. "Do you remember his name?"

Lysandra looked toward the back wall, her brows pulled together in concentration. "Gary maybe? I don't remember for sure, but I think it was Gary." She shook her head. "I can't believe he might be killing people over this."

She lowered her head to stare at her hands. "A few months after this, I was gang raped. I figured it was retribution for all the bad stuff I'd done over my life. You know, karma." When her eyes again met Lexi's, they glistened with moisture. "I thought I'd paid my dues, but apparently not."

Lexi put her hand over Lysandra's, resting on the table. "Don't blame yourself. These deaths are the responsibility of the killer and no one else. But we're asking you to help us catch him, before he kills again."

"Tell me what I can do."

"Give us the names of all your sisters who had any involvement in Gary's prank."

"There were about ten of us. I can give you the

names, but I've lost touch with all of them. I only went to Florida State for a year."

Yeah, they knew that. And they knew why. But there was no sense bringing it up now.

Lexi continued. "Do you have any photos?"

"Not of Gary, but I know I have some of my friends. Photography was one of Tiffany's hobbies. She had a thirty-five-millimeter camera. She'd upload the photos to Shutterfly and get enough copies printed for all of us. I took pictures, too, with my phone, but I've lost my really old ones. I don't think my cloud storage goes back that far."

"Can we look at them?"

Lysandra nodded. "I live only two blocks from here. Let me get Josie to cover a few more minutes. Then I've got to get back to work."

Alan followed Lysandra and Lexi out the door. This had been their most productive day yet. Not only did they have a motive, but they also had a first name.

And maybe somewhere in all that college memorabilia, there would be a photo that Lysandra had forgotten about.

A photo of Gary.

NINE

———◆———

LEXI FOLLOWED LYSANDRA down the sidewalk, thankful for Alan's presence next to her. The neighborhood seemed a little on the rough side, with trash on the edges of the street and burglar bars on most of the windows.

But Lysandra didn't seem to mind. She walked along at a good clip, chatting as she went. "I stuck everything from my college days in a box and have lugged it with me everywhere I've gone. I'm sure I've got some pictures in there, too."

Lexi smiled. That box had probably been through a lot of lugging. Hopefully its contents would prove valuable.

With each of the people they had talked to, Alan had let her lead. It was, after all, her investigation. He'd surprised her tonight when he'd come down hard on Lysandra. He was always so even-keeled. The tough stance had worked, though. Their witness had gone from being unwilling to get involved to wanting to do anything she could to help them catch the killer.

Lysandra cast a glance over her shoulder. "That box is tucked on the top shelf of my closet. I haven't been through it in forever. I'm not even sure why I keep all that old stuff."

She veered off the sidewalk and headed toward a narrow wrought-iron stairway that hugged the side of a chipped stucco building. At the top, she put the key into the lock and swung the door wide.

"Well, this is home. It's not great, but it's all I could afford when I left Jake. I've come to the conclusion that sometimes it's better to be alone."

She led them into the apartment and closed the door behind them. Fresh paint covered sections of missing plaster that had never been repaired, but the place was neat and tidy.

Lysandra headed down the hall. "Are you guys together?"

Lexi followed but stopped in the doorway. "Yes and no. We work for separate departments, but we're working together on this case."

"No, I meant, are you a couple?" She turned to face them in the bedroom. "You look like you belong together. There's good energy between you."

Lexi opened her mouth to respond, but before she could compose her thoughts, Lysandra had already crossed the room to open a laptop that was sitting on the dresser.

"While this boots up, I'll check the box."

Alan followed her to the closet and lifted it down from the shelf. After he had set it on the bed, she folded back the flaps. Lexi circled the bed to stand next to her. A Seminoles pennant lay across the top of the items in the box. Beneath it were a mug, a blanket and some other FSU memorabilia. A shoe box was at the bottom.

She pulled out the shoe box and removed the lid.

"These are the pictures Tiffany took." After picking up a handful of photos, she thumbed through them. "Here you go." She handed one to Lexi. "This is Amber."

Lexi showed it to Alan. "Stephanie."

Lysandra looked up from the pictures she held. "Who?"

"Stephanie Wilson, the third victim. Amber resembles her. Or I should say, Stephanie resembled Amber."

Lexi held on to the photo, and Lysandra flipped through a few more pictures.

"Here's one of Amber and Tiffany together."

"Do you have a close-up of Tiffany?"

"Probably." She sat on the bed to finish what she held, then pulled out another one-inch stack. "Here's a shot of Tiffany, closer up."

Lexi handed the picture to Alan.

He lifted a brow. "Donna Jackson?"

"I'd say so." Tiffany's face was a little more rounded than Donna's, but the resemblance was definitely there. Similar build, same wavy, shoulder-length hair, deep brunette.

Lysandra released a heavy sigh. "So he's finding girls that look like us, killing them and taking their pictures."

Over the next several minutes, they were able to link five of Lysandra's friends to the five victims. A sixth, Jeanie, could have passed for Denise's sister. Lexi held four other pictures, girls who Lysandra claimed were involved in the prank but whose names were apparently farther down on Gary's list.

"I think that's all of us." She removed the last

handful of photos. Suddenly she stopped. "Oh, my goodness! I didn't know I still had this one. Most of the pictures we took went up around campus."

"Gary?" Lexi's pulse jumped to double time and she stepped closer to see what Lysandra held. Her jaw dropped. "How in the world...?"

"Bridgett did it."

Bridgett, represented by Meagan Bowers, victim number one. She must have been incredibly persuasive, because she had somehow convinced Gary to dress in nothing but a T-shirt and a pink tutu.

The problem was, he was running away from the camera. All they had to go on was some longish brown hair, a white T-shirt thinly concealing a bony back, and a tulle-covered rear end.

Lysandra sighed. "It was quite a feat. The hard part was sneaking him past our house mom. The rest was easy. Bridgett promised him a great party, lots of booze and wild, beautiful women. But she told him that to be initiated in as one of our fun party guys, he had to let go of all his inhibitions. And putting on that pink tutu was what he had to do to prove it. When he came out of the bathroom and Bridgett led him into the rec room, we were waiting for him... with phones, Polaroid cameras and lots of laughter."

But Lysandra wasn't laughing now. In fact, she looked as though she was going to be sick. Lexi couldn't blame her. Their silly pranks had likely created a killer. He had started with Bridgett, the orchestrator of his humiliation, and was methodically working his way through each of her friends.

Except the women paying the price were innocent, their only crime being unfortunate enough to resemble his tormenters.

Lysandra shook her head. "I had no idea."

Lexi placed a comforting hand on her shoulder. "I know you didn't. None of you had any way of knowing something like this would happen."

"I wish I could take it back. I'd do anything to go back and relive that year."

Lexi let her hand fall from Lysandra's shoulder. "Is it all right if we put names on the backs of these and take them with us? We'll make copies and send them back, if you give us a mailing address."

"Sure." She laid the last of the pictures on the bed with the others, then picked up a pen from her nightstand to label the ten photos with first and last names. When she'd finished, she handed them back to Lexi and walked to the dresser. "I'll check my cloud storage now."

It didn't take her long to determine that the oldest photos she had were from three years after her time at Florida State. She returned to the bed to repack the unneeded photos.

Alan held up a hand. "Before you put all those back, do you have any pictures of yourself?"

"I do." She fished through the piles on the bed, talking while she searched. "I looked a lot different then. This isn't my natural hair color." She gave a short laugh. "Obviously the purple isn't natural. But the black isn't, either. My true hair color is a mousy brown, sort of like that dresser over there." She tilted her head toward the other side of the room. "In college, though, I was blonde. Ah, here's one."

She handed the photo to Alan, and his complexion seemed to grow several shades paler. He lifted his gaze to Lexi's, and the fear she saw there sent slivers of apprehension through her. She didn't want to know, but she moved closer anyway.

When she looked down at what he held, the floor seemed to tilt sideways. She could almost have been looking at a picture of herself.

Lysandra's voice cut into her thoughts. "I hadn't noticed before, but you and I could almost be sisters." Realization flashed across her face, and she grasped Lexi's arm. "He might come after you. He would see you as a good substitute." She sank onto the bed with a groan. "I wish it could be me."

"I'll be all right. I'm a cop, remember? We're going to catch this guy. The information you gave us is going to help us do that." She stepped back. "Now we need to get you back to work."

Lysandra nodded. "You're right. If I don't get back soon, Josie is going to string me up."

She rose and led them from the apartment. When they got back to Club Dynamo, Lexi stopped at the door. There was no reason to endure the assault to her eardrums or her lungs.

"Thanks for talking to us." She gave Lysandra an encouraging smile. "You were a big help."

"No problem. If there's anything else I can do, anything at all, let me know. I'm afraid I won't live long enough to atone for my part in this."

"You don't have to." It was Alan who spoke. "God's forgiveness is there for the asking, but you'll also have to learn to forgive yourself."

Lysandra gave a brief dip of her head and disappeared inside. As Lexi walked with Alan to his car, an unexpected warmth filled her chest. Alan's compassion and tenderness were two of the reasons she had fallen in love with him. That, along with his integrity and sense of justice. Those boyish good looks hadn't hurt him any, either.

Now at twenty-six, his looks were no longer boyish. Some intense gym time had helped him fill out his clothes in a way he never had as a teenager, and his dark hair, which had previously been a little on the long side, was cut in a close, layered style that tamed the natural curl.

But the good looks were definitely still there. Enough to turn female heads, Lysandra's included.

They made their way down the sidewalk, past the tattoo parlor to the lot that was designated as parking for all three establishments. A nearby streetlight cast them in its soft glow.

Lexi looked up at Alan. "Lysandra ended up being a lot more helpful than I anticipated."

"Yeah. I was pleasantly surprised."

"I wasn't sure how things were going to go at first. While we were sitting at the bar, she acted like she could hardly keep her hands off you. I was beginning to think you'd acquired a new girlfriend."

He grinned over at her. "You jealous?"

Lexi rolled her eyes. "Not hardly."

He opened the passenger door of the Mustang and she slid into the seat. She waited until he'd settled himself behind the wheel before continuing. "Our conversation last night got me thinking, though."

"Oh?"

She laid her head back against the seat and stared through the windshield. "We let her win. She doesn't deserve that."

Alan didn't respond. He would know who she was talking about. She didn't have to explain.

"For seven years, she's had her way. She prevented me from marrying you, but she's still not happy. She'll never be happy until I'm married to a disgustingly wealthy corporate executive or touring the world, wowing millions with my musical brilliance. As long as I'm single, she's going to keep doing everything she can to make that happen."

Alan cranked the car but made no move to back from the parking space. "What do you have in mind?"

"I don't know." She certainly wasn't ready to accept that ring she'd rejected so many years ago.

"Do you still care for me?" His voice was soft.

"It's not that simple."

He leaned back against the seat with a sigh. "Because of Lauren."

"Lauren is just part of the problem."

"Lauren was the biggest mistake of my life. She came to me in trouble, pregnant and alone. And I let my kindhearted nature get in the way of good sense. At the time, I didn't feel I had anything to lose." He reached across the console to cover her hand resting in her lap. "I thought I had already lost what was dearest to me—your love."

His palm was warm against the back of her hand, his touch comforting. But inside, her mind was whirling. Had she heard him right?

She turned to look at him. "Lauren was pregnant when she came to you?"

"Yes. Otherwise, we would have waited and that ill-fated wedding would never have taken place."

"So the baby wasn't yours."

He pulled his hand back suddenly. "Of course not. She was almost two months along when we started seeing each other. I took her out several times, more as a friend offering encouragement and support. But when I told her about your mom's visit, that was when she really ramped up her pursuit. Next thing I knew, we were shopping for a ring. She instigated it, but I went along with it. And I've regretted it ever since. Even more so since working with you."

"What happened?"

"A month after marrying, she had a miscarriage. She didn't need me anymore and took off. As much as I hate to admit it, I was almost relieved when she left. We never loved each other. She was using me, and I still loved you."

Lexi shook her head, trying to wrap her mind around what she had just learned. Lauren had already been pregnant.

Alan was still watching her. "Where do we go from here?"

She took a deep breath and turned to look at him. "How about we start over and take it slow?" She cared for him. Maybe even still loved him. But she had a lot more thinking to do before she was ready to cast aside her independence.

A warm smile spread across his face, and her stomach did a little flip.

"All right. I won't push. We'll take it slow." He leaned across the console and pressed his lips to her forehead.

She closed her eyes, relishing the sensation of his warm breath against her face.

Slow was going to be difficult. Because right now

she wanted nothing more than for him to wrap her in his arms and kiss her fully and deeply.

The way he used to.

———◆———

Alan strolled along the winding walks of Harmony Grove Park, Lexi's hand in his. Curved flower beds hugged the edges of the wide concrete path that circled the fountain up ahead. Sometime in the distant past, the ladies of the Harmony Grove Garden Club had taken over responsibility of those beds. Now it seemed their goal each spring was to outdo what they'd accomplished the prior year. Lush greenery formed a dramatic backdrop for blooms in every color of the palette, not leaving a single square inch of any bed bare.

He led Lexi around the fountain and toward the lake at the back of the park. They had just finished a picnic lunch. He couldn't get her to accompany him to church that morning, but she had agreed to an afternoon in the park. The other would come. The fact that he was even here with her, strolling the park, her hand in his, was a miracle in itself. If God wanted them together, He would work in the area of her faith, too.

Slow. That was what he had to keep reminding himself. Lexi was willing to explore the possibilities of a relationship, as long as he was willing to take it slow. God would touch her heart, too, but it would be in His time.

Alan inhaled the floral-scented air. The weather couldn't have been better if he'd custom ordered it: A balmy seventy-eight degrees under a sunny blue sky with a spattering of fluffy white clouds. Now, with a belly full of chicken and potato salad and a heart overflowing with contentment, life seemed exceptionally sweet.

After walking only a third of the one-mile perimeter of the lake, Lexi stopped in front of a bench shaded by a huge oak. She smiled up at him, lips touched with some pinkish-colored gloss, reapplied after lunch. Lexi never was one for heavy makeup. She didn't need it. With her soft features, she possessed a clean, natural beauty.

"Do you know where we are right now?"

He gave her a crooked smile. "We're at the park."

She sat on the bench, pulling him down with her. "I know, but do you know what's significant about this exact spot?"

He looked out toward the lake, where a pair of mallard ducks was gliding on the surface a short distance away. It wasn't where he'd asked her to marry him. That had happened on the front porch of her house, with the two of them sitting on the swing, pleasantly full from Thanksgiving dinner.

She hadn't taken the ring. Instead, she'd jumped to her feet, rambling about how she was busy with school, and that it wasn't fair for her to tie him down and expect him to wait for her, and that they'd agreed to date other people, and that actually, it would probably be better if they severed ties completely.

He'd hoped for a "yes," knowing a "maybe" was more likely. The last thing he'd expected was for her to panic and break everything off. He'd left that evening with a lump in his throat and a hole in his heart.

But he wasn't going to think about all that. Now he was with her, and God was possibly giving them a second chance.

"I give up. What's significant about this spot?"

"This is where you kissed me for the first time."

He grinned over at her. "Are you sure about that?"

"Positive. It was after the Memorial Day cookout. We'd just finished watching fireworks and were walking around the lake. You stopped right here and kissed me."

"Then you're right. It *is* a special place." He released her hand to wrap his arm around her and pull her to his side. The memory she brought up stirred something in him, carrying him back to those early days, when love was new and the future was bright with promise. Would it be even sweeter the second time around?

He had promised her he would take it slow. But how slow was slow? He could really use some clarification, because he was so ready for a replay of that first kiss.

He cleared his throat and reined in his thoughts. His safest bet was to let her set the pace. When she was ready, he would know. Maybe. She was much harder to read than she used to be.

She sighed and stretched out her legs in front of her, crossing them at the ankles. "After Dad died, I used to come down here a lot. Mom thought I had gone to hang out with friends, but I was right here, sitting, staring out at the lake, trying to find answers."

"Did you ever find any?"

"Nope, never did. All these years later, I still haven't. Now there are even more questions, but still no answers."

"If the question is why, sometimes there isn't a really good answer. We have to accept that bad things happen in a fallen world and recognize the good as a gift."

"So in the bad times, God basically just turns His back on us."

"No, just the opposite. When we walk through the valley, He is with us. He comforts us. The Bible says we're going to have heartaches. Those valleys are dark places, and the shadows are deep. But the valley isn't our destination. We're just passing through. And God has promised to be right beside us."

She shook her head. "I have a hard time serving a God who allows so much evil in the world."

He smiled over at her, his tone gentle. "You don't want anyone to try to control you, but you're expecting God to do just that."

"What do you mean?"

"He created us with free will. Evil is never part of His plan, but he allows us to make our own choices, even if those choices hurt ourselves and others. God didn't create us to be a bunch of puppets."

She heaved a sigh and seemed to sag against him. "I'm just tired of people dying."

The sadness in her tone stabbed through him, and he pulled her closer. It wasn't just her father and Abby and Kayla. There were countless others she'd encountered whose lives had been snuffed out before their time. Being a homicide detective had to wear a person down, especially someone as compassionate as Lexi.

She hiked up her shoulders, then let them fall,

shaking off the melancholy that had descended on her. Lexi was compassionate, but she was also strong, and she wouldn't let herself wallow in sadness for long.

She pushed herself to her feet to continue her course around the lake. When they got back to his car, he turned to face her. "How about taking in a movie with me?"

She gave him an apologetic smile. "I think I'm going to pass. As much as I've enjoyed our outing, I should probably be getting home."

"Already?"

"I wanted to run the names Lysandra gave us last night through the database. Tomorrow, I'll get any additional information I can from Florida State. If we can locate Lysandra's friends, maybe one of them will remember Gary's full name."

He wasn't ready for their time together to end. "Can't you just goof off this afternoon? Even God took a day off. He spent six days creating the world, then rested on the seventh."

"I can't take a day off as long as women are dying."

Yeah, she would look at things that way. He opened the passenger door for her to slide into the seat. "Anything I can help with?"

"Not tonight. When I get some addresses and phone numbers, I'll have you help me contact them."

A few minutes later he braked to a stop in his driveway, right next to the gold Mazda. He had wanted to pick her up, but she'd insisted on meeting him, saying she needed to check on her mother anyway.

Now she was getting ready to drive home. Alone.

"How about if I follow you?"

She leaned back against her car and looked up at him. "That's not necessary. I'll be fine."

He stepped closer. There was more he wanted to say, but he'd been putting it off. It was going to be a point of contention between them. They could discuss it all day long and probably never agree. But he had to try to talk some sense into her.

"Lexi, you're the spitting image of the young Lysandra."

She tensed. "I saw the photo the same time you did."

He ignored the annoyance in her tone. "What if the killer has realized that fact, too?"

"I'm being careful."

"I know you are. But I'm worried about you. Ever since I saw that picture, I haven't been able to get it out of my mind. Let me stay with you."

His idea got the raised eyebrows he expected. "That's not necessary."

"Come on, Lexi. That's the one thing all the victims had in common—they lived alone. If you won't let me stay with you, ask someone else. Or go stay with a friend. BethAnn."

"I have three cats."

"Bring them. BethAnn wouldn't mind, under the circumstances."

"Considering she's allergic, yeah, she probably would." Her eyes softened, and she draped both arms over his shoulders. "My job has its risks. If we're going to make this work, you'll have to accept that and trust me to make the right decisions."

He stared down at her, heart twisting. How was he

supposed to stand idly by while she did things that put her in direct danger? Granted, it was in the line of duty. She wasn't being reckless, taking unnecessary chances. But still…

He gave a small nod. What choice did he have? He couldn't expect her to stop activities that were part of her job, and he couldn't be there to protect her twenty-four/seven. She wouldn't want that, anyway.

She dropped her arms from his shoulders. He should probably step back and give her some space. But he couldn't get his feet to obey. She didn't seem to be in any more of a hurry to leave than he was to let her go. She stood staring up at him, gaze warm and lips slightly parted. A fresh, clean fragrance drifted toward him, some kind of lavender-scented hand lotion or body wash, the same scent that had teased him off and on at intervals throughout the past three hours.

What would she do if he kissed her? He had refrained all afternoon. Was that slow enough? Maybe so, because the next moment she stood on her tiptoes and brushed a soft kiss across his lips. "I'll call when I get home. I promise."

He stood frozen, fighting for control, afraid that if he moved, he would crush her to him and kiss her back. And it wouldn't be the sweet, casual peck she'd just given him.

He stepped away and forced a smile. "All right. If I don't hear from you within thirty minutes, I'm sending out the search parties."

As he watched her back out of the drive and start up the road, his heart clenched. Somewhere out there was a killer. And Lexi was vulnerable. After seven long years, he was so close to winning her back. He couldn't lose her again.

Lord, please protect her.

Her taillights disappeared from view and he turned to walk into the house. His recliner beckoned, but he didn't bother to settle into it. There was no way he could sit still. Instead, he paced the living room. If only she would go stay with her mom or take in a roommate.

But he knew Lexi. She would do none of those things. She was far too independent. There was nothing he could do.

Or maybe there was. He stopped pacing and pulled out his phone. Maybe she wouldn't let anyone stay with her. But she couldn't stop people from checking on her.

He pulled up the non-emergency number for the Polk County Sheriff's Office and, after identifying himself, asked for a return call from Sergeant Tomlinson. "You can tell him it's regarding the Kayla Douglas case."

Maybe he was overstepping his bounds. Lexi would think so. But he'd leave that opinion up to Tomlinson. Something told him the sergeant would be on his side on this one.

His phone rang ten minutes later. The number displayed wasn't familiar. He swiped the screen and pressed the phone to his ear. "Alan White."

"Brent Tomlinson. Is Lexi all right?"

"She's fine right now. But I was wondering if you could have some units drive by her place on a regular basis and check on her. I'm worried about her."

"Is something going on that I need to know about?" His tone was heavy with suspicion.

"We talked to Lysandra last night. I'll let Lexi fill you in on the details. Knowing Lysandra is the next name on the killer's list, we're pretty sure that his next victim is going to be someone who looks like Lysandra did ten years ago."

"What's that got to do with Lexi?"

"Ask her to show you Lysandra's picture. She and Lexi could be sisters."

"Oh, that's not good." Tomlinson was concerned. Alan didn't need to see the man's face. It all came through the phone.

"I'm not asking that she be taken off the case. I was just hoping everyone could keep an eye on her, because I know Lexi, and she's not going to back down. Though I don't agree with her, I understand. She's determined to find her cousin's killer and doesn't want to leave it in someone else's hands."

"Kayla Douglas was Lexi's cousin?"

Uh-oh, he'd said too much. "Please don't tell her I told you. I just wanted to let you know the possible danger she's in so everyone can be watching out for her."

"We'll do that. Thanks for letting me know, son."

Alan ended the call and laid his phone on the end table. Conflicting emotions churned in his gut—relief that deputies would be checking on her, and fear that she would find out he'd talked to Tomlinson.

And regret, because she *would* learn of the conversation. And when she did, she'd be furious.

Whatever walls had come down over the past two days would go right back up.

And she'd be lost to him all over again.

TEN

———◆———

LEXI STOOD AT the water cooler, watching the ice-cold water slowly fill her thirty-two-ounce 7-Eleven mug. Ever since that morning's briefing, she'd been holed up in her cubicle, searching databases, poring over names, trying to gather contact information. She'd gotten what she could from Florida State. Some of what she'd obtained had been helpful. Some had been enough out-of-date to require a lot more digging.

She was getting closer. She'd already made contact with two of Lysandra's friends. She'd obtained the contact information of three others, but hadn't succeeded yet in getting a hold of them. The last four were still at large.

She released the lever to stop the flow of water and took a long swig. When she turned, a line had formed behind her. A line of one, anyway.

She smiled up at Greg, one of the department's patrol deputies. "Sorry. I didn't mean to hog the water cooler." She stepped aside. "Help yourself."

"No problem. I'm not in a hurry." He extended his right hand and flashed her a friendly smile, revealing straight, white teeth. "I don't think we've been properly introduced. Greg Lanning."

She returned his smile and took his extended hand. "Lexi Simmons."

He was a good-looking guy, with closely-shaved dark hair and eyes a vivid shade of blue. Judging from the broad chest and muscular arms, he was a regular visitor at the gym.

His smile broadened. "I'm pleased to meet you, Lexi. I've heard a lot of good things about you. You're well-respected."

"Thanks."

He filled his own mug, talking to her over one shoulder. "I hope to someday join you. I applied to homicide several months ago, but there haven't been any openings. You guys get in and stay."

"I know." She'd just joined the division nine months ago herself, after one of the older detectives had retired.

She raised a hand in farewell. "Good luck on that promotion."

She headed back to her cubicle and had just settled in at her desk when a large figure filled the opening. Tomlinson might be old enough to be her father, but he hadn't lost any of his bulk.

She smiled up at him. "How's it going?"

"Can I see you in my office?"

It was phrased as a question, but she wasn't under any delusions. It was a command, not a request. His stern manner underscored the fact that this wasn't going to be a relaxed, friendly chat.

She sprang to her feet and followed him past a stretch of cubicles to one of the offices at the edge of the bay, uneasiness settling in her stomach.

He closed the door behind her, then motioned toward one of the two chairs that faced his desk. "Have a seat."

Once he had settled into his padded office chair, he leaned back, fingers intertwined over his abdomen. "How did your trip to Ybor go?"

She raised a questioning brow. She'd already done a report, and he'd shared the details with everyone in that morning's briefing. He'd even seen all the pictures, since she'd included those with her report. What was he getting at?

"It was productive. Even though we only have the suspect's first name at this point, I'm hopeful one of the women is going to remember more about him, like a last name, maybe even where he's from. I'm working on making contact with each of them, but all we know about him at this point is that he has brown hair and is thin, or was at the time." She forced a smile. "And he doesn't look good in pink tulle."

Her attempt to inject some levity into the situation fell flat. Tomlinson's expression remained stony.

She cleared her throat. "Anyway, as I said in my report, five of her friends bear a strong resemblance to the five victims, and a sixth looks a lot like Denise."

"What about Lysandra herself?"

Lexi's uneasiness intensified.

"Dark hair, heavy makeup. Pretty tough."

"Dark hair, huh?"

"With purple streaks."

"How about ten years ago?"

Okay, she was busted. She'd hoped Tomlinson wouldn't notice the resemblance between her and the ten-year-old photo of Lysandra. She should have known better. Tomlinson was too observant to overlook important details.

She frowned. "Blond."

"Like you."

"Like me." She gave him a tense smile.

He didn't return it. "Why didn't you tell me you were related to one of the victims?"

Sparks shot through her. Her sergeant might have noticed the resemblance between her and Lysandra on his own, but he didn't learn of her relationship with Kayla through reading her report. Alan had ratted her out.

She sighed. "I was afraid you would take me off the case."

"You lied to me, Lexi."

"No, I didn't lie. I told you I knew Kayla."

"You withheld important information."

Her eyes drifted to her lap and she took a stabilizing breath, trying to gather her wits. If she didn't do some fast talking, he was going to assign someone else to lead the investigation.

She brought her gaze back to his and kept it there, unwavering. "Sir, I'm sorry I wasn't completely honest with you. I was afraid you would make me step down. This case is important to me. It was before Kayla was killed, and it's even more so now. We're making headway. Please let me continue. Please don't take this away from me."

Tomlinson stared at her, his expression unreadable. If the sternness had lessened, it wasn't by much.

Finally, he sighed. "Lexi, you're one of my best detectives. But you're too close to this. It's way too personal for you."

"That isn't affecting my performance, not in the slightest. Look how far I've gotten."

"Your relationship to Kayla could make you take bold risks. Unnecessary risks that you wouldn't take if it was just another murder investigation."

"I won't. I'm careful. I know I can't do Kayla or the other victims any good if I'm dead."

"You look like Lysandra, the next one on the killer's list, which makes you a shoo-in to be his next victim."

Tomlinson was coming up with one argument after another. No problem. She could think fast on her feet, too. She would refute each one as soon as it left his mouth.

"I can be bait. Better me than some naive young girl. I'm trained. This might be our best chance of catching this guy."

"It's not safe. I'm not putting you in known danger. He's already threatened you."

"We don't know that for sure. It could have been a prank. Anybody could have typed up that note."

"Sorry, Lexi. I'm assigning Detective Kaminski to take over the case. It's for your own good and for the good of the case."

She heaved a sigh and her shoulders sagged. Greg had told her he'd heard a lot of good things about her. She had a great reputation around the department. She was well-respected, he'd said. A lot of good it was doing her now. "Sarge, please."

He held up a hand, signaling the end of the discussion, and rose from the chair. "I want you to go over everything with Kaminski and bring him up to speed on these latest developments."

She walked from his office, the weight of disappointment bearing down on her. There was no changing his mind. Thanks to Alan, she was off the case. He had betrayed her.

She returned to her cubicle, gathered up her papers and threw her purse over her shoulder. It was lunchtime. Usually, she would grab something from the Publix deli right up the road. Now she wanted to be alone.

What had she been thinking? How could she have even considered a future with Alan? She was better off alone.

She slid into the Explorer and tossed her purse and file into the passenger's seat. When she pulled into her driveway fifteen minutes later, her mood wasn't any better than it had been when she'd left the station. It wasn't likely to improve, either, until she'd had the opportunity to unload on Alan.

She wasn't going to let him off the hook. Allowing him to get close to her had made him think he had the right to interfere in her life. He'd tried to convince her to step down from the case. She wouldn't, so he'd gone behind her back to make it happen, not leaving her a choice in the matter. He was treating her just as her mother always had.

She wasn't going to put up with it. After eighteen years of living under her mother's controlling, manipulative thumb, she'd finally won her independence. For the past eight years, she'd enjoyed that independence. She wasn't about to trade it for the male version of what she'd endured for most of her life.

She unlocked and pushed open the front door.

As always, Suki met her in the foyer. If she took a sandwich into the living room and plopped down in front of the TV, she'd probably have all three cats nestled in around her. The idea had appeal. After an hour of watching Court TV, listening to someone else's problems instead of thinking about her own, she'd be ready to face the rest of her day.

This afternoon she would brief Detective Kaminski. It wouldn't take much. He had helped investigate all five of the murders, so he was already well acquainted with each of the cases. All of the detectives were. As soon as they'd discovered the second victim and realized they had a possible serial killer on their hands, all ten detectives had been pulled in, and the information had been disseminated agency-wide.

Lexi topped off the cats' dry food, then slathered mayonnaise on two slices of bread. After piling on a liberal amount of cheese and turkey breast and adding a handful of chips to the paper plate, she took her place on the living room couch. Soon she had company. Times three. As she clicked the remote and began a channel search, Midnight and Suki jumped up to press themselves against each of her sides. Itsy situated herself on the floor, front paws and chin resting over Lexi's feet.

This evening she would check on her mother. She was still angry with her, probably would be for a long time. Lexi had already confronted her about her lies. Her mother had offered profuse apologies. But Lexi wasn't fooled. She was never sorry for her actions, only sorry she'd been caught.

Once she checked on her mom, there would be one more Harmony Grove stop to make. Alan would probably be expecting her. He couldn't really believe she would accept his betrayal and go on as if nothing had happened. He had to know her better than that.

At least she'd realized her mistake before she'd gotten in too deep. There was no ring, no seriously hurt feelings on either end. They could both easily jump back to where they were a month ago—two professionals temporarily working together.

Alan had done her a favor. She was used to being alone. She'd been on her own for so long, just her and her cats. There was no reason to upset her routine. She was happy with her life. Content and satisfied.

But that didn't make Alan's actions hurt any less.

———————

Alan drove slowly down Main Street, window down and arm resting in the opening. The sun sat low on the horizon, staining the western sky vibrant shades of orange, pink and lavender. Another sunny spring day coming to a close, another uneventful shift ended.

As he rolled past Pappy's Pizzeria on his way to the station, enticing aromas drifted to him on the early evening breeze. His stomach rumbled an impatient response. It was tempting. But Pappy's was better shared. Tonight, it would be iced tea and a frozen dinner for one in the company of evening sitcoms.

He cast a glance to his left where a huge oak occupied the vacant space between Dani's Bakery and Westbrook Insurance Agency. Two sets of legs dangled from one of the lower branches.

He frowned. Dani's had closed an hour ago, Westbrook two. No one had any legitimate reason to be hanging around either business. Probably a couple of kids up to no good.

He eased to a stop in one of the parallel parking spaces. As he stepped from the car, the legs disappeared. Yep, definitely up to no good.

And he was reasonably sure he could identify one of the culprits. Whenever there were any kind of shenanigans going on, Duncan Alcott was usually at the center of the mess.

As Alan stepped onto the sidewalk, sounds came from the tree—a whisper, followed by a harsh "Shh." Whoever they were, they weren't being very stealthy.

He crossed the sparse lawn and stopped at the base of the tree. Two sets of eyes looked down at him. He zeroed in on the instigator, who had apparently tried unsuccessfully to hide a crinkled paper bag in a crook of the branch above him.

"Whatcha got there, Duncan?"

"Nothing."

"Doesn't look like nothing to me. You wanna toss it down here? Otherwise, I'll have to climb up there and get it, and that won't make me very happy. You don't wanna see me unhappy, do you?"

Duncan shook his head and reached for the bag. Alan waited. A moment later, it dropped into his hands with a thunk and a muffled slosh. He didn't have to look inside to know that he wasn't holding Kool-Aid or Pepsi.

"Where'd you get this?"

"It's my dad's."

"Correction. It *was* your dad's." He unscrewed the lid and poured out the pungent substance.

"Aw, man. My dad's going to be ticked that you

dumped out his booze."

"Your dad needs to keep his booze out of the hands of minors."

He focused on the other occupant of the tree, this one female.

"You don't look twenty-one, either."

"No, sir, I'm sixteen."

"So you're too young for this stuff, too."

She shook her head. "Oh, no, sir, I don't drink."

Right. No one ever admitted guilt, even when caught red-handed. Except for some reason, Alan was inclined to believe her. Maybe it was that clean, wholesome girl-next-door look. Maybe it was the sincerity and innocence in her eyes. That wasn't likely to last long, hanging with Duncan Alcott.

Which was a shame. She seemed like a nice girl. With blond hair and wispy features, she sort of reminded him of Lexi at that age. He'd seen her before. She and her family had moved to Harmony Grove about a month ago. The past two Sundays they'd occupied seats not far from the front at Hope Community Church.

"What's your name?"

"Juliette Nolan."

"Do your parents know where you are?"

"Yes, sir. Well, no, not exactly. But they know that I went for a walk with Duncan. They just said I had to be back before dark."

Alan cast a glance upward, where the sky was rapidly darkening to deep blue. "Then you'd better get moving."

"Yes, sir. That's what I told Duncan right before you drove up." She scrambled down out of the tree,

Duncan right behind her.

He watched them hurry toward the sidewalk. "Young lady?"

She turned, brows raised. "Yes, sir?"

"Be careful how you choose your friends."

"Yes, sir."

Something in her smile told him she knew exactly what she was doing. Maybe she was going to have a good influence on Duncan rather than the other way around. He hoped so. The kid needed some positive examples in his life.

He climbed into the cruiser and drove the short distance to the police station to swap vehicles. He'd just settled into the driver's seat of his Mustang when his ringtone sounded. The caller was Tomlinson. Alan had saved him in his contacts last night, just in case. He touched the screen and pressed the phone to his ear.

Tomlinson's deep voice came through the line, crisp and professional. "I'm calling to update you on some changes."

Here we go. "What kind of changes?"

"I've pulled Lexi off the case."

Alan released a long breath. It hadn't taken long. He'd talked to the man less than twenty-four hours ago. Lexi was going to be furious. "I was afraid you might."

"I didn't tell her I had talked to you."

"Thank you."

Of course, he wouldn't have had to. Lexi would have made the connection to him immediately.

Or maybe she hadn't. She would have prepared a report and submitted the photos to the Sheriff's

Department. Tomlinson would have seen Lysandra's ten-year-old picture and would have instantly recognized the resemblance to Lexi. That in itself was a good reason to remove her from the cases, even without the fact that the latest victim was a family member.

Tomlinson continued. "I'm putting Detective Sam Kaminski in charge. I want to still keep you in the loop because of your connection to Harmony Grove and the latest victim. Can you write this down?"

"Hold on." He pulled a pen and notepad from the console. "Okay, shoot."

Tomlinson repeated the name and rattled off a number. After finishing the call, Alan backed from the parking space. He would program the information into his phone when he got home.

As soon as he turned onto his street, worry tightened his chest. The Mazda sat in his driveway, Lexi at the wheel. Was she there to vent about being sidelined or to attack him for causing it to happen? He pulled in next to her and killed the engine. She had traded the County vehicle for her own but hadn't taken the time to change clothes. She was still in her working attire.

She exited the vehicle the same time he did and slammed the door a little harder than necessary. The stiffness of her shoulders and the set of her jaw underscored her displeasure. Hopefully, it was aimed at the situation rather than at him.

"You ratted on me."

"What are you talking about?" Maybe he could get away with playing dumb.

"You talked to Tomlinson."

He tried not to flinch under the accusatory glare. "Let's go inside."

She snapped her mouth shut and followed him to the house, boots clicking hard against the concrete drive. After unlocking the door, he motioned her inside. She stepped over the threshold and spun on him before he even had the door closed. "I trusted you, and you squealed on me."

He closed the door with a soft thud. "Tell me what happened."

"Tomlinson took me off the case."

He sighed. "I'm sorry, but once you made your report and turned in those photos, did you really expect any different? Tomlinson would have to be blind to not see how much you resemble the young Lysandra."

She planted both hands on her hips. "Nothing in my report *or* the photos revealed that Kayla was my cousin. That had to have come from you."

Now he did wince. What she'd said was true. "I'm sorry. I didn't mean for Tomlinson to pull you off the case."

"Oh, yeah? Then what *did* you mean? You called him and volunteered the information that Kayla happened to be my cousin. And I'm sure you were happy to point out the resemblance between Lysandra and me. What did you think Tomlinson was going to do with all that? Just ignore it and leave everything be?" Her voice held a steely edge, but it wasn't raised. Lexi had never been a blow-up-and-throw-things kind of girl.

"I called to ask him to have some units patrol past your house. That's all. I'm worried about you." He stepped toward her and put a hand on her shoulder.

"Don't touch me." She jerked away from him and stalked to the other side of the living room. "It wasn't your place to interfere, period. You knew how important this is to me. Now Tomlinson is afraid I won't be able to be impartial, that I'll take unnecessary chances to catch this guy because of my relationship with Kayla."

"I'd say that's a legitimate concern."

"You're saying I can't be professional."

"I'm saying you're human. No one should be expected to do what you're trying to do. Let someone else handle this."

She crossed her arms in front of her, further shutting him out. "You've left me with no choice."

He strode across the room, but this time had the good sense to stop two feet in front of her. "I wasn't trying to get you taken off the case. I was asking for the backup, explaining to him why I was so worried about you. I told him you were determined to find your cousin's killer, and that I really didn't blame you." He sighed. "It slipped. I wasn't intentionally telling him something you didn't want him to know."

She stared up at him, arms still crossed. "You put me in a really bad position. Tomlinson feels I lied to him."

"I'm sorry. That wasn't my intent."

"But you still interfered. If everybody would just stay out of my business and let me live as I see fit, I'd be a whole lot happier."

She crossed the room with angry strides, brushing past him on her way to the front door. After swinging it wide, she spun toward him. "I'm sick and tired of people trying to control my life." A second later, the door slammed shut.

He moved to the window and separated the slats in the mini-blinds in time to see her slide into the driver's seat of the Mazda. As she backed from the driveway and sped off down the road, intense emptiness stabbed through him, so keen it was painful. The sensation was familiar. It was that void left by thoughts of a future without Lexi.

Seven years later, he was falling for her all over again.

He almost snorted. Who was he kidding? *You can't fall when you never got up to begin with.* All these years later, he'd never fully recovered from her rejection. He'd told himself he'd moved on, but he'd never stopped holding out that small sliver of hope that she would one day come back to him. Even while he'd dated his way around town, she had always occupied some almost-forgotten corner of his heart. The casual friendships he'd had with the single women of Harmony Grove had only been cheap substitutes for what he'd longed for with Lexi.

Just this weekend, he'd begun to penetrate those barriers. Doors were beginning to crack open, just a little. Now she wanted nothing to do with him. She wouldn't even let him touch her.

He would give her time, let her cool down and think about it. Maybe she would realize his good intentions and forgive him for interfering in her life. Maybe she'd give him the chance to prove that he didn't want to control her, that he only wanted what was best for her.

But wasn't that exactly what her mother would

claim? Everything she'd ever done was what she'd felt was for Lexi's good. Even running him off.

Why would Lexi forgive him when he'd done exactly what her mother had always done, and for all the same reasons? She wouldn't. He'd blown it with her.

If he could turn the clock back one day and not make that fated phone call, would he change what he'd done? Probably not, because it all came down to one unquestionable fact.

He cared for Lexi more than life itself.

And he'd rather she be mad than dead.

ELEVEN

———◆———

L EXI PUT THE last of the clean dishes into the cupboard and closed the cabinet doors. Music drifted in from her mom's living room, a Mendelssohn piano concerto, backed by a full orchestra. The house was always filled with music. If her mother wasn't producing it herself, a well-planned lineup of her favorite pieces cycled through a top-of-the-line stereo system.

Lexi drew in a deep breath and rolled her shoulders. Between cooking, eating and cleaning up, she had spent most of the past two hours in the kitchen. When she stepped into the living room, her mom sat in a recliner, an open book in her lap. Although the leg rest was raised as far as it would go, her injured ankle was propped on a thick pillow, elevating it even further.

Her mom looked up from her reading as soon as Lexi entered the room. "Thank you, dear, for the wonderful dinner and for cleaning everything up."

"No problem. But I need to be heading home. Anything else I can get you before I leave?"

"I can't think of anything." She heaved a forlorn sigh. "I guess if something else comes to mind, I'll just have to figure out how to get it myself."

Lexi lifted her chin. It was time for the semi-weekly guilt trip, but she wasn't falling for it.

"I think you'll do great. You ought to be an old pro by now getting around with those crutches." She'd had plenty of practice. Not many people could nurse a mild ankle sprain for three and a half weeks.

Her mom chose to ignore the enthusiastic pep talk. She could be as optimistic as the next person, but only when it suited her.

"Sweetheart, I wish you'd consider moving back home, just temporarily. You know, until I can get back on my feet. It's hard to take care of myself. I'm having to hobble here and there on crutches, and I could really use some help."

Lexi gathered her purse and bent to place a kiss on her mother's forehead. From the time Lexi finished college, her mom had dropped hints about her coming back home. But the suggestions had gradually grown more and more insistent. With Lexi's dad gone and Lexi living on her own, her mom had no one left to control. It was driving her crazy.

"I'll keep coming by and helping you with your laundry and cleaning as long as you need me." She moved toward the door before her mother could say anything else. "'Night, Mom."

As she slid into her car, she shook her head. Her mother needed something to occupy her time. A pet or a job or something.

No, not a job. Her mother had never worked a day in her life. She'd been pampered by her parents growing up, then pampered by Lexi's dad. The latter had been to a lesser degree, but it wasn't for lack of trying on his part. In the end he'd made the ultimate sacrifice. He'd succumbed to a heart attack and left her well-fixed with a couple of really good insurance policies. For the past nine years, she'd been able to continue her standard of living without having to get a job.

Money wasn't a problem, but she still needed something to do. No, what she needed was a pet, some little foo foo dog that would obey her every whim and stare at her with undying devotion.

Lexi put the car in reverse and backed from the drive. Four blocks down, a familiar road branched off to the right, drawing her attention. Night had fallen, and a handful of streetlights dotted its edge. Alan's house was almost at the end. He was probably inside, stretched out with a book or chilling in front of the TV. Or maybe he was out on one of his dates. That was fine with her. If he was with someone else, at least he wouldn't be meddling in *her* life.

She turned onto Highway 17 and pressed the pedal to the floor, watching the RPMs spike before backing off to press the clutch and shift to the next gear. There were times when she was thankful that she had moved away from Harmony Grove. This was one of them. Being able to put distance between herself and Alan was a good thing. Now that she'd been taken off the case, it would be even easier.

His good looks and sweet ways had almost sucked her in. Spending so much time together, working toward a common goal, connected by their love for Kayla—the whole experience had wreaked havoc with her defenses. Sunday's picnic in the park and romantic walk around the lake had almost finished her off.

But that hadn't lasted long. It had taken all of two days for her to remember why she valued her independence. Being pulled from the case was the pits, but Alan had done her a favor.

She eased off the gas at a Reduced Speed Ahead sign and frowned. She had accused Alan of being like her mother. There was one big difference that she hadn't acknowledged, though. Her mother's attempts to control her stemmed from her selfish desires to mold Lexi into what she wanted her to be. Everything Alan had done was out of concern for her safety. He didn't have a selfish bone in his body.

But control was control, regardless of the motivation behind it.

A ring tone cut into her thoughts, and she tapped her Bluetooth. Driving, she couldn't check who was calling. Hopefully it wasn't Alan. She wasn't ready to talk to him. Actually, she didn't feel much like talking to Tomlinson, either. Same with her mom. She'd take a sales call over any of the three.

After her "hello," a vaguely familiar female voice came through the phone. "Is this Lexi?

"Yes."

"This is Jennifer Rushdan."

No wonder the voice was familiar. Jen had grown up two doors down from the Simmons house. "Jen, hi."

"It *is* you."

"What's me?"

"Alexis Simmons, the name at the bottom of this flyer."

Lexi sat straighter and squeezed the steering wheel

more tightly. "Yeah, that's me."

To all her peers, she had always been simply Lexi. Jen wasn't exactly her peer, but she was the kid sister of one of her peers. And she'd somehow gotten a hold of one of Lexi's notices.

"You have a flyer?"

"I got it from a guy I work with. His younger sister goes to Polk State."

"I see. Have you heard about anyone being stopped?"

"Yeah, I got stopped late today on my way home from work."

Lexi's heart jumped to double time and her palms grew damp against the wheel. "By someone in an unmarked car?"

"Yep. It was dark where I was, not well-lit, so I waited until I got into a more populated area. I still couldn't see the car that well, since it was directly behind me with its headlights on, but I think it might have been a light-colored Toyota Camry. The flashing lights looked like they were coming from the dash. As soon as he stopped me, he turned them off."

That would make sense. He wouldn't want to attract any more attention to himself than necessary. Otherwise, a real officer might stop to offer assistance and would instantly recognize him for a fraud.

"Tell me what happened."

"He asked for my license and registration and insurance information. When he looked at my license, he asked if that was the correct address. I told him it was. He took my stuff back to his car, sat in there for a couple of minutes, then brought everything back to me."

"Did he say why he stopped you?"

"Yeah, he said I was speeding. I was, too. But he didn't give me a ticket. Just told me to slow down."

"What did he look like?"

"He was in a dark green uniform."

"You're sure?"

"Positive. But you know how they normally have patches on the sleeves and a name plate over the shirt pocket? Well, his didn't have any. It was just a plain dark green uniform. But there was a silver star over the pocket. It said 'Sheriff,' but that's all."

Definitely not a real sheriff's deputy. But close enough to fool someone not paying attention. Or someone who wasn't previously warned.

"What else can you tell me about him?"

"He had like a buzz cut. His hair was a brownish color."

"How about height and weight?"

"Since I never got out of the car, I don't know about his height. But he was average weight. Pretty muscular."

"Age?"

"Maybe thirty, maybe a little older."

"Any tattoos, distinguishing characteristics, jewelry?"

"No, none of that. I was looking, too, because Darrel just gave me the flyer yesterday."

The light ahead turned yellow, and she eased off the gas. "You did good, Jen."

"So what now?"

"We'll get some officers to stake out your house. They'll be there every night until the threat is over."

There was a long pause, as if Jen had just now

considered the possibility that he might come back looking for her. "Could you stay with me?" Her voice had grown thin and weak.

Lexi stopped at the light, now red. When a pickup truck pulled up in the lane next to her, she glanced into the cab. The kid at the wheel couldn't have been more than seventeen. The girl with him was sitting close enough, she could help him drive. No threat there.

She looked back up at the light. "How about staying with your parents tonight? From tomorrow night on, the detectives will be there. They'll be right outside, so you'll be safe."

"I can stay with them tonight. But what about after that? I don't want to be alone in the house. I'm scared. Please?"

"All right. I'll stay with you." Tomlinson probably wouldn't be happy. But Jen was bait. If she wanted company, she would have it.

The light changed, and she eased off the brake. As soon as she disconnected the call with Jen, she phoned Tomlinson. He answered on the second ring.

"You know those flyers that Alan and I passed out? If you remember, it's my number that's at the bottom. We just got a bite."

"Tell me about it."

"She's twenty-five, finished school three years ago. But a coworker of hers got a flyer from his younger sister who's a student at Polk State. It's been a few years since I've seen her, but she used to be a blond, similar build to Lysandra." *Similar build to me.* She kept that thought to herself.

"She said the uniform was dark green, like ours,

but she didn't see the sheriff's department patch on the sleeve. I'm going to check to see if anything was actually run."

"*You're* not doing anything." Tomlinson's voice was low but held a forbidding edge. "Give the girl's info to Kaminski."

Lexi sighed. "Come on, Sarge. I'll be stuck behind a computer." She tried to keep the resentment out of her tone, but wasn't quite successful.

"I'm not backing down on this, Lexi. This isn't your case anymore. It's Kaminski's. Get the girl's info to him, and we'll stake out her place. I assume she lives alone?"

Lexi let her head fall back against the seat, her shoulders slumping. "Yeah. I've known her all her life. She grew up a couple doors down from me. But she's been on her own for the past three years."

"Another Harmony Grove resident. I'll tell Kaminski to include Alan on this."

Oh, yeah, rub it in. Alan would be hiding out, ready to spring, while she sat tucked away in Jen's house. If Tomlinson even allowed it. "She asked me to stay with her."

"No."

"She begged me. I promised her I would."

"I don't want you anywhere near there. I don't trust you to not jump in and get involved."

"Come on, Sarge. She's scared to death. Let me stay with her."

Silence stretched through the line while he thought. Finally, he sighed. "Okay, Simmons. I'll allow it this time. But you stay inside with the girl. I don't want to hear of you taking any unnecessary chances."

"Yes, sir."

She would do as Tomlinson said. She would stay inside.

But if it came down to Jen being drugged with chloroform, ready to be dragged away and murdered, no way was she going to stand idly by, hoping that backup was just outside.

She would take the creep down.

———◆———

Alan tried to wipe the rain from his eyes with cold, wet fingers. It didn't help. Heavy droplets dripped from the hood of his raincoat. Below the slicker's hem, the bottom half of his jeans were soaked, and his tennis shoes sloshed with every step he took. Although the rain had slowed to a light drizzle, he was wet and sticky and miserable.

For the past two hours he'd huddled under the overhang of Jen's cottage while wind gusts drove cold droplets into his face. Detectives Kaminski and Ford were also there, Ford on the opposite side of the house and Kaminski behind the hedge that ran the length of the front, broken by the porch.

Lexi was inside. Dry and comfortable. The same place she'd been for the past two nights. She was probably still mad at him. At least he assumed so. He hadn't actually talked to her. She'd ignored his texts and let every call go to voice mail.

He pushed himself away from the wall and walked out into the yard. The worst of the rain had passed, but heavy clouds obscured the night sky. A brilliant three-quarter moon was up there somewhere. He'd seen it the past two nights.

On those nights, Lexi had been inside, probably seething. His presence there would have been like salt in a wound after she'd been removed from the case. Tonight, she was likely gloating, figuring a little bit of discomfort served him right.

He pulled the rain gear away from his chest to allow in some fresh air. Though his shirt wasn't soaked, it held a sticky dampness. A hundred percent humidity had a way of finding its way underneath the best rain slicker. What he wouldn't give for a long, hot shower. Some dry clothes wouldn't be bad, either. It was going to be a long night.

A long, *unproductive* night, if it was anything like the previous two.

The suspect showing up tonight was a long shot. If he didn't come out when the skies were clear and the air a balmy seventy degrees, he wasn't likely to show up on a miserable night like this. That meant they'd be right back out here tomorrow night. And the night after that and the night after that. At least, someone would. Eventually, their break would come. They knew the "where." The "who" was Jen. But the "when" was anybody's guess. Alan only hoped it would be on his watch.

With a sigh, he headed toward an oak tree that dominated the front yard. That had been his hiding place before the downpour had chased him up against the house. The tree trunk was large enough to hide behind but offered him a clear view of Jen's front yard and the front and one side of the Carson place. The two houses shared a drive. It ended in a "Y," the right branch leading to the Carsons' garage, the left to Jen's cottage.

Alan crossed his arms and leaned back against the trunk of the tree. The boredom was getting to him as much as the heavy slicker trapping moisture against his body. One hour blended into the next, no different from the last, each one passing with excruciating slowness.

He shifted his gaze toward the end of the street. A car turned onto Oakwood Lane. A dead-end road, it hadn't seen much activity since dark. None in the past hour.

The vehicle moved closer, passing under a streetlight. It was definitely a Toyota Camry. Tension drew his spine straight as he waited. Was it the same Camry that had stopped Jen?

Suddenly the headlights went out. His pulse went into overdrive. There was only one reason to cruise down the street with lights off. To avoid being seen. Even if the Camry driver wasn't their killer, he was up to no good.

He pulled out his phone and keyed in a quick text to Kaminski—*We might have something.*

The car continued to move at a crawl, barely visible in the distant glow of the streetlight. It passed in front of the Carson house, then disappeared from view. Alan held his breath and waited. Soon it reappeared and came to a slow stop at the end of the driveway. After several tense moments, the wheels turned hard to the right, and it moved slowly up the drive, tires crunching against gravel.

Yes! The suspect was falling for their trap. He keyed in a second text—*Target coming up drive.* If all went as planned, once Jen opened the door and the suspect pulled out his chloroform-soaked cloth, they would storm the house and capture him. In a few minutes it would all be over. Six months of hard work would be brought to a satisfying close.

Instead of continuing up the drive, the Camry stopped. The wheels turned again, this time to the left, and the car backed toward the Carsons' garage. What was he doing?

Then realization extinguished his excitement. *No, not there!* Number 410 was the left side of the fork. *Come on, it's marked.* Right at the beginning of the drive.

Alan watched from fifty feet away, praying the killer would figure it out. Finally, the driver's door swung open. But the dome light didn't come on. He'd turned it off. The guy was careful. He stood next to the car, door open. He seemed to be scanning the area, looking for danger.

Alan strained into the darkness. If he could just get a little closer, maybe even try to get a tag number. But he didn't dare. The guy was on edge, super alert. It was obvious in the way he stood, the tension that emanated from him. Nothing would escape his notice. A rustle of clothing, the snap of a twig, and he would take off.

Finally, he moved away from the car and walked toward the house. The *wrong* house. The Carsons were home, and though it was almost eleven, they hadn't gone to bed. Several lights were on inside, and a television filled one room with a soft, bluish glow.

The suspect stepped from view, presumably headed to the front door. Alan cast a glance at Kaminski, who was watching from around the corner of Jen's house. After a nod and gesture from the older detective,

Alan sprang from his hiding place to sprint toward the Carson house. Plans had just changed.

He stayed in the shadows as much as possible, moving from tree to tree and finally ducking behind one of the shrubs that sparsely lined Jen's drive. He'd just straightened to dive behind the next one when the driver reappeared, hurrying toward his car.

Alan crouched behind the shrub and waited. Maybe the suspect realized he had the wrong house and would just continue up the drive. When he did, they would all be waiting for him.

Instead of driving into the trap set for him, he took off in a spray of gravel, rear end fishtailing. Alan made a diagonal path across Jen's yard, moving at a full run. As he reached the road, the car sped past, lights still off. By the time he'd radioed the description to dispatch, both Kaminski and Ford stood next to him.

Kaminski, the older one, was breathing harder than Ford. "Did you get a good look at him?"

Alan shook his head. "It was too dark, and I couldn't get close enough."

"Tag number?"

"I couldn't get that, either. He kept his lights off all the way to the end of the street. By the time he passed under the streetlight, he was too far away."

"Which way did he turn?"

"Right." Away from Harmony Grove, which wasn't any surprise.

"Something obviously spooked him." Kaminski headed toward the drive, Ford beside him.

Alan followed. "I'm going to talk to Willie Carson, see if he saw or heard anything."

Just as he passed the corner of the garage, the front

door of the house swung open and Willie Carson stepped onto the porch. He was barefoot, dressed in plaid cotton pajamas that were a little too short for his tall, lanky frame. Alan had given the Carsons sketchy information earlier in the week, letting them know they would be there. But this was the first night Willie had ventured outside.

Alan met him at the edge of the porch. "Did you see something?"

Willie nodded. "Sure did. The missus and me was gettin' ready for bed, and I was turnin' off lights. When I walked into the livin' room, someone was at the window. He saw me and took off."

"Can you describe him for me?"

"'Fraid not. Couldn't see him that good through the screen, lights being on inside and all."

"Anything else you can tell us?"

"That's it."

"If you think of anything that might help us, give me a call."

"Sure will." Willie's head bobbed. "Anything I can do to help. If he comes back, I'll get my twenty-two."

Alan held up a hand. "Let's not get carried away. Just call me. No shooting anybody."

Willie nodded again, his enthusiasm a little more restrained. He'd worked in one of the phosphate mines all his life and recently retired. This was probably the most excitement he'd had in a while.

When Alan rejoined the others, they'd all gathered in the cottage. Jen and Lexi sat at the kitchen table nursing what looked like two glasses of iced tea. Ford stood behind a third chair, and Kaminski leaned against the doorjamb, pose casual.

Kaminski raised a brow at Alan. "Well?"

"I know why the suspect ran. Willie Carson went to turn off the living room light and came face to face with him."

"Description?"

"Nothing. It was too dark."

"What do you think the chances are that he'll be back?"

Alan thought for a moment. "Probably not good. If he thinks Jen lives in the Carson house, he believes she's not alone. And he only targets women who are alone."

He looked at Lexi, his gaze intentional, and she lifted her chin. She didn't need the reminder, but he would give it anyway. Every chance he got.

He continued. "Even if he realized his mistake and figures out Jen lives in the cottage on the left, he still probably won't be back. He knows we're watching her place. My running to the road guaranteed that. But it was our best chance at getting a tag number and identifying the guy. At this point, I'm sure he'll look for another slender blond who he feels would make an easier target."

Lexi narrowed her eyes, but he ignored the daggers she was sending his way. The other two men seemed not to notice.

Kaminski pushed himself away from the doorjamb. "I think we're through here tonight. What do you say we all go home and get into some dry clothes?"

Alan smiled. "You won't get any argument from me."

Ford and Kaminski moved toward the front door, but Alan hung back. Creases of concern had settled into Jen's face as she watched the two detectives leave. His reasoning about the killer not returning apparently hadn't done much to allay her fears.

He looked at Lexi. "You staying?"

"I will for tonight."

Tension seemed to drain from Jen, and her breath escaped in a relieved sigh. "Thanks. I think I'll go stay with Mom and Dad for a while until this is all over." She directed a weak smile Alan's way. "Just in case."

"That's a good idea." He returned her smile, then moved toward the door. "I guess I'll leave you ladies alone."

Once outside, he headed up the gravel drive and to the house on the opposite side of the Carson property. He'd left his Mustang there. Kaminski and Ford had ridden together in Kaminski's Forerunner, which they had parked across the street. Now it was gone, of course. Lexi's Explorer was in the Carsons' garage. At least that was what he'd been told. He hadn't personally seen it. She always managed to get there a little ahead of him.

He'd hoped for a chance to talk to her. It hadn't come. Three straight nights and he hadn't had a single opportunity to be alone with her. Maybe he should just show up at her house. With flowers. And a sincere apology.

He slid into the driver's seat of his Mustang and shut the door.

Yep, a bouquet of flowers was a good idea.

TWELVE

————◆————

"SIMMONS, MEET ME in my office."

Tomlinson caught her before she even made it to her cubicle. He walked at a good clip, holding a file folder, Greg Lanning a pace or two behind. Lexi changed direction and followed. At least this time she wouldn't get a dressing down, not with Greg present to witness it. Tomlinson didn't work like that.

When he reached his office, instead of rounding the desk to sit behind it, he leaned against the front, propping a hip on top. "We had a call from a waitress at a local wings place. Seems one of her frequent customers wasn't getting enough of her with his wings and beer. He started stalking her outside of work. He never tried to talk to her, just kept showing up where she was. Even joined the same gym so he could watch her work out."

"Perv." Though Lexi muttered the word under her breath, Tomlinson heard it, if the quirk of his lips was any indication.

"He was so bold about it that she got a restraining order. That was two weeks ago. This morning we found him sitting in his vehicle across the street from her apartment complex, a pair of binoculars in front of his face and a camera with a monster zoom lens next to him."

"He's been taken into custody?"

Tomlinson nodded.

"Good." The creep would probably say she brought it on herself with the short-shorts and eye-popping cleavage. But that didn't excuse what he did.

"Anyway, we've put in for a search warrant and should have it anytime now. I want you two to go through his place and see what you can find."

Lexi nodded. She was a homicide detective. Chasing stalkers was a far cry from solving murders. But since she was no longer investigating Kayla's and the other four girls' murders, her case load was fairly light, and nothing new had come in during the past couple of days. Besides, the behavior of the suspect they were investigating was exactly how a lot of killers started—obsessed and perverted. Maybe she could take this one off the street before some innocent girl lost her life.

Lexi looked at Tomlinson. "What can you tell us about the suspect?"

"The guy's name is Wendell Moorehead. White male, forty-three, five foot eleven, a hundred eighty pounds. He works part-time for one of the aluminum contractors, keeping the shop cleaned up. Lives in a two-bedroom house on the edge of Lakeland. Apparently has a roommate."

She glanced over at Greg. He hadn't spoken but was busy taking notes. When she looked back at Tomlinson, he was eyeing her.

"Go on over there. I'll call you as soon as we have the warrant."

She followed Greg into the hall, but Tomlinson stopped her from proceeding farther. "Simmons, hold on." He motioned her back into his office with a tilt of his head. Greg continued down the hall. *Great.* Maybe she was a little premature in her confidence that she wouldn't get a dressing down. Although she hadn't done anything deserving of any kind of reprimand. The entire time she'd been at Jen's, she had explicitly followed Tomlinson's orders to stay inside.

Tomlinson closed the door but didn't offer her a seat. That meant the exchange would likely be short.

"Lanning has been wanting to get into homicide when a position comes open."

Ah, so this wasn't about her. "He mentioned it when I ran into him at the water cooler last week."

"Detective Quinn is looking to retire sometime during the next six months. Lanning is in the running for the position. He's been with us for three years and was with Orlando P.D. for four years before that. His record is exemplary. I believe he'll be a good addition to homicide when a position opens up."

She nodded. There was a reason Tomlinson was telling her all this. She just wasn't sure what it was.

"Chances are good, this guy you're checking out is just a simple stalker, but you never know what might turn up once you get inside his place. Sometimes there are surprises. I'd like for Lanning to see how you work, your investigative methods. If it does happen to turn into a homicide, it'll be your case from start to finish."

"All right." Tomlinson was hoping she could give Greg a little "pretraining." Wonderful. Nothing against Greg. He seemed nice enough. But she wasn't a trainer. She got too wrapped up in her own investigating to take the time to explain what she was doing to someone else.

When Tomlinson opened the door and dismissed her, Greg was standing at the other end of the hall, well out of hearing range. She headed in his direction, then walked through the station with him and out to the parking lot.

"I'll drive." Her tone didn't leave him any room to argue.

He buckled himself into the passenger seat of her Explorer and waited until she had left the parking lot to strike up conversation. "How long have you been with the department?"

"Four years, the last nine months in homicide."

"Like it?"

"Oh, yeah. It's challenging." She glanced over at him. "How about you?"

"I've been here three years, was with Orlando P.D. before that. I was still finishing my criminal justice degree at UCF when I got on with them. I like patrol, but like I told you before, I'm really hoping to get into homicide. Finding killers and bringing them to justice, that's where my heart is."

"Yeah, mine, too." She pressed the radio dial, and soft rock music filled the confines of the vehicle.

"Are you single?"

She cast him a sideways glance. Maybe he was just making friendly conversation. She hoped so. Regardless of what happened with Alan, she wasn't in the market for romance, especially with a coworker. That scenario had *disaster* written all over it.

"Single and not looking to change that status anytime soon." She cringed at the snarky tone that came through in her voice. It wasn't Greg's fault that Alan had gotten her pulled off Kayla's case. "How about you?"

"Yeah, I'm single. My wife dumped me and ran off with my best friend."

That was more than she needed to know, but she couldn't help feeling sorry for him. A bad experience could sour one on love for some time. How well she knew. She hoped he'd get over it and find someone who appreciated him. "Sorry to hear that."

"Don't be. I say 'good riddance.' For the past nine months, it's just been me and my dog."

"What kind of dog do you have?"

"A German shepherd. I rescued him from the pound. Now he thinks the sun rises and sets on me. I think *he's* pretty cool, too. Much less demanding than a woman." He smiled over at her. "No offense."

"None taken."

"Do you have a dog?"

"No, three cats."

By the time she stopped in front of the Lakeland address Tomlinson had given her, he had called with news of the warrant, and she had heard half of Greg's life story. At least his adult life.

She stepped onto the porch and pounded on the front door. "Police! Open the door!" After waiting for a half minute or so, she pounded and called out again. "Search warrant! Open the door!"

All was silent. The roommate was probably at work. There were no vehicles in the drive. But kicking in doors was a last resort.

A quick survey of the property, however, left them no choice. The front and side doors were locked, with no keys hidden outside, and the dog that guarded the back yard appeared none too happy about two strangers roaming his territory.

She left the dog barking and growling inside the back fence and walked to the side door. Before she could kick it in, Greg stopped her.

"Here, let me."

Whatever. She didn't have anything to prove. She stepped away and, after a quick thrust of Greg's booted foot, the door swung open, exposing a splintered jamb.

A hallway led them past a small laundry area and into the kitchen. She scanned the room. Definitely the residence of a couple of stereotypical bachelors. Dirty dishes filled the sinks and sat on the countertop in haphazard stacks. The dishwasher was open, its racks almost empty. From the looks of things, they were one meal away from dirtying their last clean dish.

After they entered the living room, Greg headed toward a closed door on one side, and she walked down a short hall to a bedroom at its end. An open pizza box sat on a computer desk, one piece of dried-up pizza still inside. Clothes overflowed a hamper in the corner, and the bed was unmade, the sheets wrapped around the comforter in a jumbled mess. As she stepped further into the room, Greg called to her from the other side of the house.

"Lexi, you better come and look at this."

She hurried back to the living room. The closed door she'd seen earlier was now open. The space was a second bedroom. Greg stood inside, looking at a corkboard mounted over a desk. There were two others just like it, all covered in photos. A couple of expensive-looking lenses sat on the desk. Deputies would have taken the camera and at least one lens into evidence when they arrested the suspect.

She approached one of the boards. The photos all seemed to be of the same woman. Young, attractive and well-endowed, with shoulder-length dark hair. Judging from the attire in some of the pictures, she was the wings waitress.

Lexi moved to the next board. This subject was blond, equally attractive. In some of the pictures she wore a medical uniform.

Greg wrinkled his nose. "Was the guy stalking the nurse at his doctor's office?"

Lexi frowned. "That's what it looks like."

The last board held photos of yet another subject. This one appeared to be Asian. None of the pictures revealed what she did for a living. They were all candid shots—shopping, standing on a sidewalk, getting into her car, hanging with friends. Lexi leaned forward. With those exotic features and jet-black hair, she was gorgeous.

Greg let out a low whistle. "How much you wanna bet none of these women had any idea they were being photographed?"

"No doubt. He was probably fifty feet away, shooting them with a zoom lens."

She looked around the room until a bookcase in the corner snagged her gaze. The entire top shelf was packed full of what appeared to be photo albums. She pulled one from the center.

"People don't usually have this many photo albums. Proud parents, maybe. A single guy living with his roommate? Not likely."

She flipped through the pages. Just as she expected. More pictures like those on the boards—candid shots of beautiful women, probably all taken with a zoom lens.

She slid the album back into its slot on the shelf and pulled out another one. It held the same. So did the next, and the one after that. Album after album, all filled with photos of women.

"How long do you think he's been doing this mess?" Greg had stepped up beside her and stood watching her flip the pages.

"Apparently a long time."

After sliding the last book onto the shelf, she moved toward the closet. The door stood open. It was a walk-in, with racks of clothes on two sides and shoe cubicles built into the back. When she flipped the light switch, nothing happened. Probably a dead bulb.

She stepped inside and scanned the high shelf that ran along all three sides. It held lots of miscellaneous stuff—several shoe boxes, a camera bag, a stack of magazines, some games, a bowl of loose change and...

She stiffened as coldness swept through her and settled in her core. Sitting on the shelf in plain view was a policeman's hat.

She pushed hangers down the rod with sharp flicks of her wrist, her pulse picking up speed. Near the end of the rack, she found it—a policeman's uniform. There was a patch on the left sleeve, three V-shaped stripes. A silver star was pinned over the right pocket, and a pair of handcuffs hung down the front, looped over the hook of the hanger.

Her heart was pounding in earnest now. Had Tomlinson taken her off Kayla's case, then unknowingly put her in the killer's house?

"Check this out, Greg." She clicked on her flashlight and shone it on the uniform as he stepped up beside her.

"A police uniform." His voice was hushed. "We might have found your killer."

"The problem is, it's navy." Even by flashlight in a darkened closet, she could tell the uniform wasn't dark green.

"Maybe the girl who was abducted was confused. I mean, she was probably too shaken up to be very reliable with the details."

"But Jen wasn't shaken up."

"Who's Jen?"

Oh, yeah. Although all the divisions had been informed about the case, Greg wouldn't necessarily have the latest details. "The girl he stopped last week and pretended to run her license. Jen paid attention. It was dark, but she got a pretty good description of the guy. He was average build, but fairly muscular. And he had a buzz cut."

Greg ran a hand over his closely shaved head and grinned. "That describes a lot of us nowadays."

She returned his smile. "True. But she said the uniform was dark green, and there weren't any patches."

Greg studied the uniform hanging in the closet, lower lip trapped between his teeth. "This patch is on the left sleeve. My guess is if we pulled it out of the closet, there wouldn't be anything on the right, and that's the sleeve she would have seen."

Lexi nodded slowly. They wouldn't test his theory, not until after everything was processed. But he had a point. And in the dark, navy blue could possibly be mistaken for dark green.

But there was another inconsistency. "Both witnesses put him around thirty. This guy is forty-three."

"Maybe he looks young for his age. Or maybe the two girls aren't good at guessing how old people are. You know how it is when you're young."

"Maybe." But even in her teens, someone would have to be a young forty for her to mistake him for thirty. "There's also the name. How would someone get Gary out of Wendell?"

"According to the information Tomlinson disseminated, the witness thought the name was Gary but wasn't sure."

True again. Greg followed her into the living room, where she pulled her phone from the pouch on her belt and dialed Tomlinson. As soon as he answered, she jumped in. "We'd better get Crime Scene out here. We found pictures. Hundreds of them. And a police uniform."

She filled him in on the rest of the details. When she finished, an unexpected chuckle came through the phone. "I removed you from the case, and it looks like you might be close to solving it anyway. Good job, Lexi."

"Thanks. What kind of car was Moorehead in when they picked him up this morning?"

"A truck. A Ford F-150."

She frowned. "Not a Camry?"

"No, but maybe he has a second vehicle."

"Maybe." She stepped back into the room and lowered her voice. "By the way, I'm impressed with Greg. He has a good head on his shoulders. Analytical, thinks things through, looks at the situation from all sides."

"Great. That's what I'd hoped to hear."

The front door creaked open and a hesitant male voice called out, "Hello?"

She spun in that direction. "Someone's here. I'll talk to you later."

As she exited the room, a man stepped from the entry area into the living room. He was a throwback from the sixties' era, with blond hair graying at the edges, pulled back into a thin ponytail that almost touched his waist.

"What's going on? I come home for lunch, and there are cops in my house." His eyes shifted from Greg to her. "One cop anyway."

Lexi didn't address his question. "What's your name?"

"Jeff Underwood."

"Wendell's your roommate?"

"Yeah."

"How about showing us which room is yours."

His gaze shifted to Greg again, and he shrugged. He was the epitome of the laidback Southern country boy. "Sure. Right back here."

Lexi followed him down the short hall to the bedroom she'd entered on first arriving.

"This is mine."

"And where is Wendell's?"

"Off the other end of the living room."

She leaned against the door jamb. "Do you ever go into his room?"

"No, he keeps the door closed."

"Locked?"

"I don't know. I haven't tried it. He rents the room from me. I don't have any reason to go in there."

"Have you ever seen any of his pictures?"

"A while back, I knocked to let him know someone had stopped to see him. When he opened the door, I saw he had like a bulletin board with a bunch of pictures attached to it."

"Did you find that odd?"

"No. He's a hobby photographer. He's always carrying his camera around."

"These pictures, what were they of?"

"Girls, I think. At least some of them. I just caught a quick glimpse when he opened the door."

She pushed herself away from the jamb and pulled a pen and mini-notepad from her jacket pocket. "Let me get your phone number. We might need to talk to you again later."

After he'd given her the requested information, she nodded toward the front door. "We're in the middle of an investigation, so you'll have to go now."

"Is Wendell in some kind of trouble?"

"We can't say just yet."

"What about after work? Can I sleep here tonight?"

"You'd better make other arrangements. We'll let you take some clothes and personal items, but we'll probably be here for the next two days."

Not that she had high hopes of finding anything. It wasn't likely, since none of the victims had been brought there. If the killer was smart and careful enough to strip a whole crime scene of any smidgen of evidence, he wasn't likely to bring anything home with him.

Except pictures. Hundreds of them. The problem was, there wasn't a single photo of any of the five victims.

While Jeff gathered clothes and toiletries and stuffed them into a duffel bag, she and Greg watched. Considering the man was being denied access to his home for the next forty-eight hours, through no apparent fault of his own, he was surprisingly compliant. He packed the items without comment, then headed to the front door.

After stepping onto the porch, he turned to face them, brows drawn together. "What did Wendell do?"

"We can't share that yet."

Greg cleared his throat. "Who does the dog in back belong to?"

"He's Wendell's."

"Is someone going to take care of him while Wendell's gone?"

Lexi smiled. They were in the middle of a possible murder investigation, and he was worried about the dog. Nothing wrong with being an animal lover. She'd been lovingly called the crazy cat lady on more than one occasion.

"I take care of him any time Wendell goes away." Jeff stepped down from the porch. "You got a card or something so I can call and find out when I can come back?"

She pulled a business card from the slim, metal case in her back pocket. When she handed it to him, she looked past him, and her heart leaped into her throat.

A Toyota Camry sat in the drive.

It wasn't all the way white. It was two-tone, with that common beige-gold color at the bottom. But the majority of the car was white.

Lexi nodded toward the driveway "Is that yours?"

"The Camry? Yeah. Why?"

"Do you ever loan it to Wendell?"

"Once or twice a long time ago, when his truck was in the shop. Not in the past year. Why?"

"I'm afraid we're going to have to impound it."

"What?" The word exploded from his mouth. He wasn't so relaxed anymore. "I need it to get back to work."

"Detective Lanning here can take you." She cast a glance at Greg. "Pick him up some lunch, too."

"Come on, man. I'm okay with you taking over my house if Wendell's in some kind of trouble. But what's that got to do with me and my car?"

"If Wendell's gotten into trouble, he's done it in your car."

Jeff shook his head. "No way. If he took my car, I would have known it."

She didn't respond, just fished her keys from her pocket and handed them to Greg. They would get the warrant extended to include Jeff's car. If there was evidence to be found, that was where they would find it.

She watched Greg leave, Jeff in the back. The Crime Scene Unit would arrive anytime. Meanwhile, she would see what else she could find.

By the time Greg returned, more than an hour had passed. The drive-through lines must have been long. Crime Scene had already arrived and was processing the bedroom. As Greg made his way to the kitchen, an enticing aroma followed him. She smiled wryly. Her palate must have degraded to basement levels when she classified fast food as enticing. But she was hungry.

After wiping a wet paper towel across the kitchen table, she washed her hands over a mountain of dirty dishes. Greg made the smart decision and retreated to wash up in the bathroom.

When he returned, he pulled out two wrapped sandwiches from the bag and handed her a third. "I got you a grilled chicken. You don't look like a greasy cheeseburger kind of girl."

Frankly, she was a whatever-was-fast kind of girl. She sank into the chair and unwrapped her sandwich. With the dirty dishes piled up three feet away, it wasn't like eating in her kitchen at home. But she'd eaten in worse settings. At least there wasn't a body nearby.

Greg took the chair across from her. "Sorry it took me so long to get back here. The drive-throughs were packed, and I had to hit two of them. Jeff wanted Chinese. Since I wasn't sure if you did Chinese, I went for the All-American."

She held up her sandwich, now a third of the way eaten. "As you can see, you made a good choice."

"Anything exciting happen while I was gone?"

"Not really. Last I checked, Crime Scene was processing the uniform. Of course, they'll bag it up and take it with them."

He looked around the kitchen. "Looks like nobody's tackled this room yet."

"No. They'll do the whole house before it's all over

with, but they're starting in Wendell's room."

Greg nodded. "What's next? After we're finished here, I mean."

"If they find any evidence linking Wendell to the victims, it'll be turned over to homicide."

"Evidence other than the uniform."

"Yeah. That in itself isn't strong enough. Pictures of the victims hidden somewhere in the room would help, or even better, DNA evidence in that Camry we're impounding. Meanwhile, we'll go ahead and get some crime scene tape up. Then I'll get you back to the station." There was no reason for Greg to hang out there the rest of the afternoon while the investigators did their tedious work.

When they'd finished eating, Greg crumbled up his sandwich wrappers. "If you want to go get the tape, I'll clean up our mess from lunch. Although if what we've got here is classified as *mess*, I don't know what you'd call the rest of this."

She smiled and rose from the table. Tomorrow she would talk to the suspect. If he was, in fact, their guy, hopefully during the course of the next few days, they'd find the evidence they needed to put him away for good.

She walked to her vehicle, her heart feeling lighter than it had in months. Tonight, she would go see Alan. She was still upset at him for talking to Tomlinson. He'd had no business interfering in her life.

But she was possibly just hours away from solving the case.

And for some reason, he was the first one she wanted to tell.

THIRTEEN

———◆———

A LAN PULLED INTO the driveway of the small brick house and slumped in the seat. The gray Explorer was sitting in the drive, but the Mazda was gone. It was eight o'clock. He'd hoped she'd be home by now.

He glanced over at the frosted-glass vase held somewhat secure by the passenger seat belt. Two dozen red roses could atone for a lot of wrongs. At least that was what Sandy at Flanagan Florist had said.

He turned off the engine and brought up Lexi's number. She answered on the third ring. At least she was taking his call. And her "Hello" didn't sound the least bit annoyed. Judging from the background noise, she was driving.

"Where are you?"

"I'm headed to Harmony Grove."

"Going to see your mom?"

"No, you."

He grinned. "In that case, turn around. I'm sitting in your driveway."

"What are you doing there?"

"I'm here to see you."

"Dumb question, huh?" There was a smile in her

tone. "I'll be there in about ten minutes."

He ended the call, all his doubts falling away. Whatever had happened over the past several days, her anger with him seemed to have evaporated.

True to her word, ten minutes later she rolled to a stop next to him. By the time she killed the engine and removed her seat belt, he was at her door, roses in hand.

"I come bearing gifts. And words of apology. I'm sorry for going behind your back and talking to Tomlinson. It'll never happen again." He held up a hand. "Scout's honor. Forgive me?"

She climbed from the car and took the roses from him. "The jury's still out on that. But this definitely helps." She flashed him a smile, that same beautiful, sweet smile he had fallen in love with.

She turned to face him at the front door, the porch light bathing her in a soft glow. Her smile had faded and her features held seriousness. "Sorry I've ignored your calls and texts the last few days. I needed time to think. I accused you of trying to control me, just like my mother has always done. There's a big difference, though, something I recognized right away but didn't want to admit."

She unlocked the door and led him into the house. "With my mom, everything is all about what *she* wants. That's never the case with you."

Warmth swelled inside his chest. She was right. Everything he did was centered around what was best for Lexi, because Lexi was the center of his world.

She closed and relocked the door. "I'm not excusing it. You shouldn't have called Tomlinson behind my back. But I understand. Even though I have a problem with what you did, I do appreciate the thought behind it."

She dropped her purse on the coffee table and continued to the kitchen. "There's another reason I wanted to see you tonight. I have good news." Excitement shone from her eyes, and her smile returned. "We might have caught our killer."

His chest tightened. If they'd caught him, that meant he'd struck again. Another young girl traumatized... or dead. No, if that was the case, sadness would temper Lexi's excitement. "How?"

She set the vase in the sink and topped off the water before continuing. "We picked up the suspect on a completely unrelated case, stalking. When we checked out his place, we found hundreds of photos."

"What kinds of photos?"

"Women."

"The victims?"

"Other women."

"If they're not pictures of Kayla and the other women, what makes you think he might be the killer?"

"After looking at the photos, I checked out his closet. I found a police uniform. It's generic, nothing identifying it as being associated with a particular department. It's navy instead of dark green, but since it was dark when both Denise and Jen had their encounters with him, they could be mistaken on the color."

"I don't know. Both women seemed pretty sure." Polk County was going to have to come up with a lot more than that to charge the guy with murder.

"That's what I thought. Then his roommate showed

up. In a white Camry." She lifted the vase from the sink and set it on the counter. "Thank you for the roses. I'm keeping them up here so Midnight doesn't eat them. You may have noticed I don't have a single houseplant. He's the reason why. But he's usually pretty good about not getting up on the kitchen counter."

He followed her gaze to the flower-eating bandit, who was currently weaving in and out of her legs. The vocal Siamese was, too. The big gray one hadn't appeared yet. Lexi looked down at them, shaking her head. "I fed you an hour ago. Nothing else till bedtime."

She headed into the living room, and both cats followed. As he settled onto the couch next to her, Suki made herself at home on her lap, voicing her contentment with loud purrs. Midnight stretched out on the back of the couch, behind her head. Itsy was probably still trying to work up the motivation to come out from wherever she was napping.

"Anything else tying him to the killings?"

"We don't have anything back yet from Crime Scene, but I did check out his book-in photo. Both Denise and Jen described the guy that stopped them as muscular with closely-shaved hair, and Kayla said he reminded her of Matthew Badcock. I compared his mug shot with the pictures Badcock sent us, and there's a little bit of resemblance. The suspect could possibly even pass for mid-thirties, so everything fits. We're going to do a lineup to see if Jen can identify him. We'll do the same for Denise."

She ran a hand down Suki's back and the cat purred even louder. "That poor girl will finally be able to come home. If she even wants to. The times I've talked to her, she seemed pretty content up there with her aunt and uncle and their horses. I'm afraid Polk County holds too many bad memories."

He frowned. "It's probably better that she stays put. In case they've got the wrong guy."

"What's the matter?" She cocked a brow at him. "You don't seem convinced."

"You say he's got all these photos of women, right?"

"Hundreds."

"But he apparently didn't kill any of them."

"We don't know that. We'll be running them through the databases over the next few weeks. Of course, we know one of the women. She filed the restraining order that got him picked up."

"But there isn't a single picture of any of your five victims."

"He's too smart to leave behind that kind of evidence."

He shook his head. "I don't know. You pick the guy up for stalking, and he just happens to be the killer. It seems too easy. Too coincidental."

She turned to face him more fully and grinned. "Haven't you been praying for divine help?"

"Yeah, but—"

"You don't think your God is big enough to drop the guy in our lap?"

"I have no doubt that God's big enough. I'm just saying that something about this feels off."

She studied him, the smile still there. Finally, she gave a short nod. "I've missed you."

"You have?"

"Yep. Our brainstorming sessions, bouncing ideas

off each other. We make a good team."

He returned her smile. "We do."

He had missed her, too. And it wasn't just working together on the case. It was everything. Eating together, laughing, talking, walking hand-in-hand at the park.

And it wasn't just this week. He'd missed her for the past seven years.

"How about letting me take you out to dinner Friday night?"

As soon as the words were out of his mouth, he wished he could retract them. He was rushing things again. "You know, to discuss the case. Not as a date or anything."

The teasing smile she gave him shattered his reservations.

"What if I *want* a date with Harmony Grove's most eligible bachelor?"

He matched her smile with one of his own. "Then I'd be happy to oblige."

"I'm looking forward to it."

Her smile faded and her eyes grew warm, emotion flickering in their depths, traces of what used to be there every time she looked at him. Was he really seeing what he thought he saw?

He reached up to cup her cheek. What he wanted to do was to kiss her. But that *would* be rushing things.

"I'm going to leave and let you get some rest." He pushed himself to his feet.

She moved Suki off her lap and let him help her up. "I'm going to question the suspect tomorrow morning. I'll let you know how it goes."

"You want some company?"

"Mmm, probably not. If he feels like we're ganging up on him, he'll be more likely to clam up."

He nodded and moved toward the door. "You might be right. Keep me posted."

"I will. And keep the prayers going, will you?"

"You're acknowledging that maybe God does listen?"

"I'm leaning a little in that direction." One side of her mouth lifted in a quirky smile. "Who knows? I might even show up at your church one day."

"I'll save you a spot."

A ring tone sounded from her purse on the end table and she hurried to retrieve her phone. She looked at the screen, then cast him a glance filled with anticipation. "It's Tomlinson."

She pressed the phone to her ear, and moments later, her brows lifted. "That's too much to be mere coincidence. I'm going to the jail tomorrow to interview him. I'll bring that up."

In the next span of silence, her face fell. "Come on, Sarge. I know it's Kaminski's case, but let me do this. If Moorehead's not our killer, this is just a stalking case, and you've already assigned it to me. If he *is* our killer, he's locked up. I'm safe either way."

After another brief pause, the corners of her mouth lifted. "Thanks. And no need to call Alan. He's here." Her cheeks flushed a little pink at the admission.

She ended the call and dropped her phone into her purse, features radiating excitement. "A bottle was retrieved from under the suspect's kitchen sink."

"What kind of bottle?"

"Brown, made of glass. It has some kind of liquid in it. According to one of the crime scene techs, it's sweet-smelling, made him kind of light-headed."

He raised his brows. "Chloroform?"

"If it's not, I'll eat my socks."

"How did Tomlinson respond to your argument for letting you interview the suspect?"

She grinned over at him. "He accused me of liking to push the boundaries. But he's letting me do it." She crossed her arms and leaned against the doorjamb. "I know none of the photos Moorehead has are of the dead girls. But what are the chances of him having a police costume, a roommate with a Camry and a bottle of chloroform under the kitchen sink?"

"Pretty slim."

"He *has* to be our guy."

"Unless the chloroform belongs to the roommate. The Camry does."

"But the roommate doesn't fit the description of the killer. Based on the book-in photo, Moorehead does."

Alan nodded and stepped into the balmy evening air.

For her sake, and for the sake of the single young women of Polk County, he hoped she was right.

———

Lexi sat at the polished oak table, a manila file folder in front of her. It was closed. She didn't need to review what was inside. She had it almost memorized.

She flipped open the cover anyway and scanned the sheet on top. She might as well because the room she waited in certainly didn't offer anything of interest. Except for the table, four chairs and a fake plant sitting in the corner, the space was bare. No pictures decorated the plain white walls, just a simple clock—a clock that had advanced fifteen minutes since she'd entered the room.

She dropped her gaze back to her folder until the rattle of the doorknob drew her attention. The door swung open and a corrections officer led in an inmate dressed in the jail's orange jumpsuit.

"This is Moorehead." The officer turned toward the door. "I'll be waiting right outside."

She watched him leave the room then nodded toward the chair opposite her. "Have a seat, Wendell. It's all right if I call you Wendell?"

"Sure. Whatever."

He settled into the chair and leaned back, weight shifted to one side in a devil-may-care pose that he didn't quite pull off.

"I'm Alexis Simmons. I have a few questions for you. I spent a good bit of yesterday at your house."

A flicker of concern flashed across his features, so brief she might have imagined it.

"You have a pretty impressive collection of photos."

"I'm a hobby photographer. There's nothing illegal about that."

"There is when you're doing it thirty feet from a woman who has a restraining order against you."

He shrugged and one side of his mouth cocked up in an irreverent half grin. "I've been through this before. They're not gonna keep me that long."

He was right about it not being his first rodeo. Over the past four years, he'd had three other restraining orders filed against him. He'd violated two of them.

She leaned back and crossed one ankle over the opposite knee. "You might be a guest of Polk County longer than you think. So tell me, what's the police uniform for?"

"What's that got to do with anything?"

"Just answer the question."

"It's a costume."

"What for?"

"My company's Halloween party. We do it every year, the last weekend in October. It's a costume party. I've gone as a cop the past three years."

"What company is this?"

"Davis Aluminum."

That would be easy enough to check out. They were a good-size aluminum contractor, right on one of the main drags through Lakeland.

"How long have you worked there?"

"About four years."

She nodded. That cocky air was as pronounced as ever, but at least he was answering her questions.

"Where did you go to school?"

"Lakeland High School. I've lived here all my life."

"College?"

"I never went to college."

He could be lying, but it would be easy enough to verify, at least with Florida State. "What's in the brown bottle under your kitchen sink?"

"What brown bottle? You're going to have to be more specific."

"A brown bottle about five inches tall, glass, unmarked."

"How am I supposed to know? I'm sure there are all kinds of bottles under there."

"They tell me it smells an awful lot like chloroform."

He gave an irreverent smirk. "I don't know what

you're talking about."

"Chloroform. Puts people out. Women are a lot more cooperative when they're unconscious. Not nearly as feisty."

He stiffened and sat straighter. That cockiness was falling away by the second, and concern was moving in. "What are you trying to pin on me?"

"I'm not trying to pin anything on you. I'm just trying to get at the truth."

"You've already got the truth. I went out and took some pictures. That's the extent of it." He settled back in his chair and lifted his chin. But the fear on his face canceled out the confidence he was likely trying to project.

"When is the last time you drove the Camry?"

"What Camry?"

"Jeff's Camry."

"I don't drive Jeff's car. I've got my own."

"How about after he goes to bed at night?"

"Why would I do that?"

"I don't know. Maybe you don't want to be seen driving your own car?"

"What, has some kind of a crime been committed using a white Camry?" He gave a snicker. "Someone going around stealing donuts? Got you cops in an uproar?"

"Maybe. But we're more concerned about the girls who are being murdered."

His eyes widened and he raised both hands. "Hey, lady, that's not me. Okay, I admit it. I like women. I like to look at them and admire them and photograph them. But I'd never raise a hand to hurt one of them. If you're looking for a killer, you got the wrong guy."

The last trace of cockiness had dissolved with the word *murdered*. Nervousness had replaced the arrogance. A telltale tightness stiffened his jaw, and one leg bounced a rapid rhythm. She couldn't see under the table, but she didn't need to. The movement radiated all the way into his torso.

"You don't have anything on me."

"We'll see. My buddies are working hard at your place. And you'd better believe we're going to be thoroughly checking out that uniform of yours. It's amazing the stories that the tiniest of particles can tell. A strand of hair, a clothing fiber. And of course, we've taken in the Camry."

His jaw dropped. "You impounded Jeff's car? He's gonna kill me."

"He'll get it back when we're done."

He lifted his chin and cast her a disdainful glance. "You guys are grasping at straws. Do you know how many white Camrys there are on the roads?"

"A lot. But most other Camry drivers don't happen to have a police uniform hanging in their closet and a bottle of chloroform under their sink. That makes you a pretty good suspect."

"I'm not a Camry driver, and I don't know anything about any chloroform. Looks like you're batting one out of three. Not very good odds, I'd say."

Lexi pulled a photo from the folder and laid it in front of him. It was an earlier picture of the first victim. She was gagged and restrained, but not too badly beaten yet. "Do you know this lady?"

He gave the photo the briefest glance before he turned his head and pushed it back across the table. "I'm not saying anything else without a lawyer."

"No problem." She stood and crossed the room. After she gave two raps on the door, it swung open. "We're finished here."

She walked from the room, leaving Wendell Moorehead in the hands of the officer. Moorehead was a jerk and a creep and a pervert. But was he a killer? All the evidence pointed in that direction, but something in her gut told her no. She needed to go back to the station and talk to Tomlinson. Tonight, she would run everything by Alan. Maybe she would talk to Alan sooner.

She slid into the seat and plucked her phone from her side. When he answered, an involuntary smile crept up her cheeks. "What are you doing?"

"Working."

"Are you available for an interview this afternoon?"

"For you I'm always available."

A pleasant tingle swept over her. "Can you meet me at one? Davis Aluminum, 98 North. Are you familiar with it?"

"I'll be there with bells on."

"That's a scary picture."

She ended the call and made the twenty-minute drive to the station. As she walked in, she met Greg heading out. She nodded a greeting and he turned to follow her.

"Sarge says you're going to interview the suspect."

"Just coming from there."

She kept walking and he fell in beside her.

"Learn anything interesting?"

"Yeah. He says he got the cop costume to wear to his company's Halloween party. Says he's worn it for the past three years."

"What did he have to say about the Camry and the chloroform?"

"He claims he doesn't know anything about the chloroform and never drives his roommate's car."

"Do you believe him?"

She looked over at him and shrugged. "I haven't decided yet."

"How likely do you think it is that someone can have chloroform under their kitchen sink and not know it's there?"

"It depends on how observant they are. This was behind some cleaning supplies."

"I don't know. I think if a strange brown bottle showed up under *my* sink, *I* would notice."

"We also don't know for sure that what's in the bottle is chloroform. That hasn't been confirmed yet."

"Since it smells sweet and made the crime scene tech light-headed, I can't imagine what else it could be. If they find out it *is* chloroform, between that, the uniform and the Camry, it's too much to be mere coincidence."

"It appears that way." But something didn't sit right with her. It was that seed of doubt that had sprouted while she and Alan discussed the case and had grown even more after she spoke with Wendell. Though she couldn't pinpoint exactly why, she wasn't fully convinced. "Sometimes a big part of solving crimes is going with your gut. My gut tells me we might have the wrong guy."

He shrugged. "I'm sure the truth will come to light. I'm hoping that'll happen by the middle of next week."

She looked up at him. "What's happening next

week?"

"Vacation. I'm leaving Wednesday for the Jeep Jamboree in Oak Ridge, Tennessee. I go every year."

She stopped outside Tomlinson's open door and faced Greg. "So you're a Jeep guy."

"Yep. Got my first one fresh out of high school and have driven one model or another ever since."

When they entered Tomlinson's office, he looked up with a smile. "Have a seat, both of you."

After they had settled into the two padded chairs, Tomlinson's gaze shifted to Lexi. "Tell me how it went."

"As planned, I met with Wendell Moorehead. He's cocky, irreverent and a perv. Definitely rubs me the wrong way. But I can't say with confidence that he's our killer."

Tomlinson nodded slowly, then focused on Greg. "What do you think, Lanning? You don't have the advantage of having talked with Moorehead, but you spent several hours at his house. What's your take on all this?"

Greg seemed to sit a little straighter. Tomlinson was good at building morale in those under his supervision, making them feel valued and competent.

"I'm thinking we might have him, sir. The police uniform and the fact that his roommate has a Camry, those two things raised my suspicions. But if that bottle they found under the sink holds chloroform, that'll clinch it for me."

Tomlinson nodded. "That's what it holds."

Lexi perked up. "We got the results back already?"

"As of a few minutes ago. They rushed it for us."

Greg gave a sharp nod. "Then I'm convinced.

Unless some evidence shows up to the contrary."

Tomlinson continued. "They weren't able to lift any prints from the bottle, though."

"No surprise there." Lexi sighed. Even with the contents of the bottle verified, something didn't feel right. "Stalking women to collect their photos doesn't fit with what we know of the killer. He's out for vengeance, every murder a payback for wrongs done ten years earlier."

"Why would one have to rule out the other?" Greg shrugged. "I mean, just because he likes to stalk women and take their pictures doesn't negate the possibility that he's also on a vendetta. In fact, those pictures are a link between the two cases. Granted, a loose one, but still a link. That's one thing we know about the killer—he's obsessed with taking pictures."

"The killer's motivation for taking pictures is humiliation. That's why he's sending them to the *Ledger*. There's no admiration going on. Another thing, Moorehead claims he never went to college."

"If you were in the killer's position, would you admit a connection to where it all originated?"

"Probably not."

Greg paused and lifted both hands. "I'm just playing Devil's Advocate. You're the expert here."

"And you're raising valid points." For the good of everyone involved, she hoped her gut was wrong on this one. She respected Greg and would have no problem with him being right. Playing a big part in putting away a serial killer would make him a shoo-in for that detective position when it opened.

She looked back at Tomlinson. "I'm going to check with Florida State and see if they have any record of a

Wendell Moorehead attending ten years ago."

When Tomlinson dismissed them, Greg stood and walked from the room. Before Lexi could follow, the sergeant addressed her.

"Keep working on it. I'm leaving you in charge of the Moorehead case. But remember, the murder investigation is Kaminski's."

"Yes, sir." As she said the words, a pang of guilt passed through her, the sense that she wasn't being totally honest. At the time Tomlinson had reassigned the case, she'd already begun the work of locating and contacting Lysandra's sorority sisters. With messages left and searches half completed, it didn't make sense to stop midstream. Kaminski knew, but Tomlinson didn't.

"Sir, when you pulled me from the case, I was in the process of locating Lysandra's sorority sisters. I had already made some contacts and left messages. I'd like permission to continue."

"We've been over this, Simmons." That now-familiar stern tone was back. "I don't want you involved."

"Sir, I know you're trying to keep me out of harm's way because of my resemblance to Lysandra and my relationship with Kayla. I appreciate that. But all I'm doing is searching databases and making and receiving a few phone calls."

"I know you. You're not going to stop there."

"I've already proven to you that I will. All those nights I was at Jen's, I never stepped outside, even the night the killer showed up."

Tomlinson leaned back in his chair and crossed his arms, his expression unreadable. But he didn't shut her down. Maybe he was reconsidering.

Lexi continued. "I've gotten four return phone calls so far, and I'm waiting for some others. If it comes down to paying any of them a visit, someone else can do that. But with all the work I've put into this thing in the past six months, please at least let me finish what I've started."

A tense silence descended as seconds ticked by. Finally, Tomlinson uncrossed his arms and rested them against his desk, shifting his weight forward. "Simmons, you're like a dog with a bone. Once you sink your teeth into something, you won't let it go." Some of the sternness left his face, and the hint of a smile touched his mouth. "That's what makes you such a good detective."

Warmth spread through her at his compliment. "So can I finish making these contacts?"

"All right. Make your phone calls. Talk to your ladies. Then give the information to Kaminski. That had better be the extent of your involvement. Do you understand?"

She couldn't stop the smile that spread across her face. "Yes, sir."

With the leads Lysandra had given them, they were close to solving this thing. She had nine names. Nine women, besides Lysandra, who'd had contact with the killer.

Whether the killer was Wendell Moorehead or someone else, one of those women was bound to have something that would seal the case up tight.

FOURTEEN

———◆———

D AVIS ALUMINUM WASN'T any rinky-dink operation, if the elaborateness of its showroom was any indication. A mini screen enclosure stretched along half of one wall, with a glass room completing the span. The opposite wall held samples of awnings, roofing panels and handrails. Several framed photos filled the space behind the counter, showing off completed pool cages, carports and other product offerings.

Alan stood leaning against the end of one of the shelving units that held bins of screws, washers and other parts and pieces. Lexi roamed the room while a difficult customer harassed the harried clerk behind the counter.

The young woman heaved a sigh. "Sir, the warranties on our carports are for one year. Yours was built over five years ago."

"But it's got dings in the roof."

"That's normal wear and tear. You probably had some hail." She cast a glance at Lexi before returning her gaze to the old man. "How about if I have Mr. Davis call you?"

"You do that."

Alan watched him write down his phone number and make his way to the door with indignant steps. The old guy would be able to plead his case with the boss. Not that it would do him any good. Mr. Davis likely didn't build a successful business by giving away carports.

Lexi approached the counter and Alan stepped up beside her. Technically, she was working the Moorehead stalking case. But there was still that possible link to the murders, something that Lexi would no doubt be pursuing, so he was tagging along.

The young lady flashed them a pleasant smile. "Sorry about that. That's how it goes. The other folks all run off to lunch and leave me here by myself. That's always when the difficult ones show up. What can I do for you?"

After Lexi had introduced them, she pulled a notepad and pen from her purse. "We need to ask you some questions about Wendell Moorehead. He works here, right?"

"Yeah, he's our shop guy. He keeps the floor swept, organizes the materials, helps stage jobs and do inventory, stuff like that. He didn't show up for work yesterday. I heard he's in jail. What did he do?"

"He violated a restraining order, for starters. What can you tell me about him?"

"Well, he's worked for us for four years. He's single. Pretty much keeps to himself."

"Have you ever known him to have a girlfriend?"

"No. It's hard to picture him with a girl."

"Why?"

She shrugged. "I don't know, he just seems socially inept in the picking-up-girls department. He doesn't act very comfortable around women, at least younger, attractive ones."

Alan leaned against the counter. "Has he ever bothered you in any way?"

"No, not at all."

He nodded. She was cute, with a small, upturned nose and faint freckles spattered across her cheeks. But based on what Lexi had told him, "cute" didn't cut it. The girls he stalked were drop-dead gorgeous.

Lexi picked up the line of questioning. "Has he ever asked you out?"

"No."

"Ever done anything that made you feel uncomfortable?"

"Like what?"

"I don't know. Anything. Any inappropriate comments? The way he looks at you?"

"No, not at all. He's more shy than anything."

"Have you ever seen him get angry?"

"No. Everyone says he's really even-keeled. Nothing much rattles him."

Lexi tapped her pen on the counter before continuing. "Davis Aluminum hosts a Halloween party every year, right?"

"Yeah, a costume party."

"Does Wendell go to these parties?"

"Always. He comes as a cop, even brings a toy pistol and handcuffs. He seems to really get into the part, especially after he's had a couple of drinks. It's as though the costume makes him feel like a ladies' man."

"How so?"

"Not in an obnoxious or creepy way. It's more like

it gives him confidence."

"Anything else you can tell us about him?"

"Not that I can think of."

After she had thanked the clerk, Alan pushed open the glass door and let her walk out ahead of him. Gray clouds were beginning to gather on the western horizon, but it would be some time before Lakeland would benefit from the cooling effect. The sun was high in the sky, reflecting off the black asphalt parking lot and making it feel more like summer than mid-spring. Of course, between the heat and humidity, Florida felt like summer most of the year.

He let the door swing shut and walked with Lexi to her vehicle. "What do you think?"

"The same as I did before. I don't believe he's our guy."

"I agree." The killer was methodical, organized and highly intelligent. Whatever job he might have, it probably wasn't sweeping floors.

"It was confirmed this morning that the bottle taken from under the sink does, in fact, contain chloroform, but there weren't any prints left on it. Also, before heading over here, I put in a call to Florida State. Wendell Moorehead claims he never went to college, but I've got them checking to see if he was ever a student there."

"Good thinking. Where are you headed now?"

"I'm going to pay a visit to Jeff Underwood, Moorehead's roommate. You want to tag along? He works here in Lakeland, so you can ride with me. I want to see what kind of light he can shed on Moorehead's activities. I also want to know what the two of them were doing with a bottle of chloroform."

"That's a good question."

She unlocked her Explorer and he slid into the passenger seat. "Where does this Jeff Underwood work?"

"Phil's Tire and Automotive, about ten minutes from here."

When they pulled into the business's parking lot, the four bay doors were open, with vehicles occupying three of the four slots. Lexi stopped and pointed at the end bay. "That's him there, mounting a tire."

She stepped from the vehicle and headed straight through the bay door, not bothering to use the customer entrance. Two of the mechanics stopped their work to watch them enter. Lexi approached Jeff, ignoring the mechanics as well as the no-customers-beyond-this-point sign. Technically, they weren't customers.

"Do you have a few minutes?" She had to shout over the hiss and bang of the tire changing machine and the high-pitched drone of impact wrenches.

"Sure." He laid down the crow bar and pulled two foam plugs from his ears, leaving them dangling from the nylon string that rested against the back of his neck. "Let's go outside."

He led them around the side of the building to a wooden picnic table that sat on a concrete slab. A light breeze rustled the limbs of the cherry laurel shading the area. In the distance, the storm clouds were rolling closer. If he and Lexi didn't hurry and finish their business, they would probably get wet before the afternoon was over.

Jeff sat on the bench that ran along the back side of the table, and Lexi took a seat opposite him.

Alan settled next to her. This was probably where employees sometimes ate their lunches. Or where customers who preferred nature escaped the noise of the television that usually ran from opening to closing in the lounges of these places.

Lexi folded her hands and rested them on the table. "How long have you and Wendell been roommates?"

"About six months. He's quiet, minds his own business. And he's always on time with the rent."

"Has he ever invited any women over?"

"No. I've never seen Wendell with anybody."

"Does he date at all?"

"Not that he's ever mentioned. He really doesn't have much of a life outside of work and his photography hobby."

"These photos you saw that time you knocked on his door, there were lots of women, right?"

"What I noticed, yeah."

"Did they look like candid shots to you, maybe even shots taken without the women being aware?"

Jeff shrugged. "Maybe. I wasn't paying that much attention. I was just there to let him know someone had stopped to see him."

"Didn't you find it odd that he takes pictures of all these women but never seems to go out with any of them?"

"I don't get into his business. He can take pictures of whatever he wants."

"Has Wendell ever expressed any kind of anger or resentment toward women?"

"No. As far as I know, he likes women. I think he's just shy."

"What about you?"

"Yeah, I like women."

"Are you dating anyone?"

"Not right now. My last girlfriend and I split up about a month ago."

"Do you mind me asking why?"

He shrugged. "She was getting too possessive. After she called here a couple of times to make sure I was working, I figured it was time to get out."

"The chloroform, is that yours or his?" She'd shifted gears without a hitch.

Jeff's eyebrows shot up. "Chloroform? Isn't that the stuff they put people out with?"

"Yeah."

"You found chloroform in his room?" Either he was genuinely surprised, or he was a good actor.

"Actually, it was under your kitchen sink. Is it yours?"

"No way, man. I don't even know where you can buy the stuff."

"You can't. At least not legally. When did you last clean out that cabinet?"

"Not since I moved into the house." He gave her a sheepish smile. "You probably gathered neither of us are great housekeepers."

She returned his smile. "Most guys aren't known for their housekeeping skills. How long have you lived there?"

"I bought the place two years ago."

"Did the prior owners leave anything behind? Were there any drawers or cabinets or closets that they hadn't cleared out?"

"Just a little bit of junk in the shed in back."

Lexi pushed herself to her feet. "I think that's it for

now."

Jeff stood and rounded the table, ready to head back into the garage. "When can I go home?"

"This evening. They're finishing up this afternoon."

"Good. My buddy's couch doesn't sleep that great."

Lexi flashed him a sympathetic smile. "Thanks for being understanding about the process."

As they walked back toward her SUV, a gust blew through, carrying the earthy scent of rain. It picked up some strands of hair that had escaped her braid and laid them across her face. Alan caught himself midway through reaching up to smooth them back. Instead, he stuffed both hands into his pockets.

"Do you think he's lying about the chloroform?"

Lexi shook her head. "I don't think so. The problem is, Wendell doesn't seem to be lying, either. That's why I asked about the possibility of it having been left behind by the prior owners. I offered him a good out. He could easily have said there was stuff under there that he'd never gone through, but since he didn't, if I had to bank on one of them lying, I'd say it's Wendell."

She settled into the driver's seat and he slid in beside her. The murder case was far from being wrapped up. It would probably be at least another day or two before investigators finished processing whatever they had collected from the Camry. If they found nothing linking the car to any of the five victims, Moorehead's charges would remain as they were—stalking and violating a restraining order. With no other evidence and no prints on the bottle of chloroform, they probably wouldn't have enough to try him for murder. If he was guilty, he'd covered his tracks well.

Lexi cranked the SUV and backed from the parking space. "Yesterday afternoon, I talked to two more of Lysandra's sorority sisters. I learned that another one, Tiffany, was killed in a car accident a couple of years ago. Unfortunately, she was the photographer of the group, the one who took most of the pictures and provided copies to the other girls. I'm going to try to locate her parents and see if they might have a box from their daughter's college days tucked away in their attic."

She braked to a stop at a red light. "Other than learning about Tiffany, I didn't get anything of value from the two women I talked to. They admitted to playing pranks on guys, pretty much the same things Lysandra told us, but they don't remember names or descriptions. They didn't keep any of the photographs, either."

She sighed and let her head fall back against the seat. "Now that I'm two-thirds of the way through the list, I'm so afraid that I'm not going to get any more from the last women than I did the others. Then we'll be back to square one."

She let her head roll to the side, and her gaze slid over to meet his. A weight had settled over her, its heaviness reflected in her features.

He lifted his right hand to cup her jaw, then caressed her lips with his thumb. "We're going to catch this guy. Eventually we'll get our break. Then we'll nail him."

"I hope you're right. I just feel like we're missing something."

"Yeah, me, too." He let his fingers linger before he

lowered his hand.

The light changed, and she stepped on the accelerator. He had the same gut feeling she did. They were missing something.

Something important.

———◆———

Lexi approached the door leading into the station. She had a little paperwork to do and wanted to touch base with Tomlinson. Then her shift would be over.

She released a sigh. It had been a long day and an even longer week. But Friday had finally arrived and the afternoon was drawing to a close. Tonight was her date with Alan, and she was looking forward to it more than she wanted to admit.

He'd tried to make it nothing more than a meeting to talk shop. Maybe she should have left it at that. That would have been the safer route. Something told her Alan would be ready to jump back into a relationship. It was up to her to put the brakes on things.

If that was even what she wanted to do. She wasn't sure anymore.

She enjoyed her independence, no one making demands on her time or trying to control her actions. If she felt like having nachos and dip for dinner instead of cooking, that was what she did. She watched what she wanted to watch on TV without having to discuss her choices with anyone else. She read to relax and played the piano because she wanted to, not because she was pushed to try to fulfill someone else's dream. Independence was great.

It was also lonely.

She swung open the door and navigated her way toward Tomlinson's office. He was there. So was Greg. She hesitated in the open doorway, but her sergeant motioned her inside.

"Come on in. This involves you, too. At least part of it does."

She stepped into the room and nodded a greeting at Greg. He wasn't involved in the murder case. But he was involved in the stalking investigation. And the two cases were intertwined. Or at least they had been.

"Greg was just asking how everything came back on Moorehead."

She sank into the chair next to him. "Stalking and violating a restraining order. That's it."

"What about murder?" The question came from Greg.

"No evidence. Nothing solid, anyway. The uniform really is a costume he wears to his company's Halloween party every year. I heard back from Florida State, and the only Wendell Moorehead they have started attending six years ago, his junior and senior year. Besides the time frame being wrong, he's seventeen years younger than our Moorehead. The chloroform is suspicious, but there's nothing connecting it to him. We struck out with the Camry, too. Our biggest find there was dried-up food. French fries, to be exact."

Greg sighed. "Bummer. I thought sure we had the guy."

She put a hand on his shoulder. "We'll catch him eventually." She understood Greg's disappointment. She was feeling a lot of that herself, especially with how long they'd been trying to solve these murders.

Tomlinson leaned back in his chair. "Where are you on contacting Lysandra's former friends?"

"I've found and talked with six of them, and a seventh is deceased. Two of the ones I spoke with think they might have some pictures but will have to search for them. None of the women remember any details. I think most of these girls did more partying than studying."

Lexi propped her elbows on the arm of the chair and intertwined her fingers over her stomach. "Anyway, I've got two more to talk to. I feel we're right in our assumption that the killer is one of the guys they played tricks on. And Lysandra's Gary is my top pick." Of course, that might not be his name. Lysandra wasn't sure.

"Keep me posted."

"I will. I'm hoping one of these last two women will come up with some good pictures. Lysandra has a great one of the guy, pink tutu and all." She released a small chuckle. "Unfortunately, it's from the back."

She rose from the chair, ready to follow Greg out the door, when Tomlinson's voice stopped her.

"Simmons, I hope you're planning to take the night off."

She smiled back at him. He'd accused her more than once of being like a bloodhound on a scent, driving herself relentlessly, refusing to let up.

"I am. Alan and I are going to dinner."

He nodded, his widening smile confirming his approval. "Glad to hear that. I'd love to see you two work through whatever's come between you."

Heat crept up her neck and into her cheeks. Had Alan discussed their personal life with Tomlinson?

The man was going to have to learn to keep his mouth shut.

Her sergeant smiled, as if he'd read her thoughts. "No one told me anything. No one needed to. I can see it in your eyes every time you mention him. And I hear it in his voice every time he talks about you. Let it go, Lexi. Life's too short to not embrace a chance at love when it comes our way."

She nodded, then escaped down the hall. That was easy for him to say. He'd been happily married for thirty years. Most of the people she knew weren't that lucky.

Like her parents. They must have been wildly in love at some point. But whatever zeal they had experienced in their early years had cooled to mere tolerance once she appeared on the scene. By the time she was a teenager, even the tolerance was gone. Her mom harped at her dad constantly, and her dad simply shut down.

No, there were worse things than being alone.

When she rounded the corner, Greg was waiting for her. She lifted her brows. "Did you need to see me?"

"I was wondering if there was anything I could help you with. I know I'm not in homicide yet, but I hope to get there eventually. I'd love to get some investigative experience. I'd even be willing to do it on my own time."

She continued to move toward the exit. "Thanks, but at this point, I think I'm good. I'm just trying to track down the last of the sorority sisters."

"I'd be happy to help you make some of those phone calls."

"Right now, I'm mostly waiting on return calls. Beyond that, it's Kaminski's deal. But maybe Tomlinson will let you ride along when they meet with some of Lysandra's friends."

He frowned. "I still think it's a bummer that he took you off the case."

"Yeah, me, too."

She stepped from the building. After thanking her, Greg walked to his patrol car, which was parked a few spaces away from her SUV. He waved and flashed her another smile, then slid into the driver's seat.

Even though she hadn't been thrilled when Tomlinson had first paired them up, she had to admit she liked Greg. He was enthusiastic and persistent, the type to jump in with both feet and not give up until he'd accomplished what he'd set his mind to, traits she possessed herself. She'd already put in a plug for him with Tomlinson and would likely put in a few more. When that detective position did finally open up, maybe he'd be the one to get it.

As she climbed into her SUV, thoughts of Greg slid away. In just under an hour, Alan would arrive at her house to pick her up for their date. A quiver passed through her stomach and her heart beat a little faster.

She'd told him she wanted to take things slow. He'd agreed he would. She planned to hold him to that promise. She wasn't ready to rush into anything. No snap decisions. When it came to relationships, *cautious* was her middle name.

She turned the key and the engine roared to life. No, not *cautious*. A better descriptor would be *untouchable*. At least since her relationship with Alan had ended.

For the past seven years, avoiding entanglements

had been easy. For three of those years, she'd been busy with school. Then she'd thrown herself into her work. One didn't make it into homicide in less than four years by being a slacker.

But how much of her busyness had been an excuse, a way to guard her heart? Did she really want to continue walking that predictable but lonely path? Could she find the courage to veer away from the comfortable and familiar?

Maybe, for once, she should just relax, drop her guard and see where things led.

Lexi stepped out the door of Harry's Old Place, her fingers entwined with Alan's. A faint breeze whispered through the trees, bringing cooling relief to what would otherwise have been a stuffy evening.

She and Alan had just finished a delicious meal. Everything had been perfect. Harry's, overlooking Winter Haven's Lake Ned, was famous for its fresh fish. The relaxed, rustic atmosphere had been just what Lexi had needed. All through the meal, their conversation had consisted of lighthearted banter and lots of reminiscing, but not one word about the case. It had been a nice reprieve.

She stopped at the passenger side of Alan's Mustang and waited for him to open the door. "Thank you for a wonderful evening. I'm glad we made it a date, instead of a business meeting."

He smiled down at her. "Me, too."

She slid into the seat and waited for him to get in on the driver's side before continuing the conversation they'd begun inside the restaurant. "Who are the bad boys of Harmony Grove now?" According to Alan, the troublemakers they'd grown up with had finally straightened out. Or were in prison.

Alan cranked the car, and its low rumble vibrated through her seat. He'd bought the '68 Mustang shortly before they'd started dating, and he and his dad had worked on restoring it together. It was hard to imagine him in anything other than that or his cruiser.

He backed from the space. "When mischief happens now, Duncan Alcott is usually at the center of it."

"He's got it pretty rough at home." At least he had seven years ago. According to her mom, nothing had changed.

"I know. So far, it's been minor stuff. You know, skipping school, vandalism, getting into his dad's liquor stash. The problem is, he's an instigator."

"And you're trying to keep him from corrupting the other kids." She smiled over at him. The epitome of the humble public servant, he took a personal interest in all of Harmony Grove's citizens, especially its troubled youth.

Alan nodded. "I'm holding out hope for him, though. A month or so ago, a new family moved to Harmony Grove. Their sixteen-year-old daughter has caught his eye. She's a good girl, and I think she's made him her project. Nothing like a pretty girl to turn a guy's world upside down."

His tone was heavy with meaning. He was no longer thinking about the newcomer. He was thinking about her. Lexi's stomach made a funny little flip before settling into a puddle of warmth.

He had certainly turned *her* world upside down.

Several times. The first was when she'd fallen for him all those years ago. She'd fallen hard. Head over heels.

Now he was doing it again, turning her world upside down in an entirely different way—upending all her resolutions, weaving his way through the walls she'd put around her heart. In the wake of hours spent working side by side, culminating in a romantic dinner out, all her reasons for maintaining her independence suddenly seemed lame.

When Alan braked to a stop behind her Mazda fifteen minutes later, she wasn't ready for the evening to end. "It's probably too late for a movie, and we already had dessert at Harry's. So I don't have an excuse to invite you in."

He grinned over at her. "I think I need to say hi to the cats. I mean, they haven't seen me in what, four days?"

She returned his smile. "Then you're definitely overdue."

Evidently Suki thought so, too. As soon as they stepped inside, she was in the entry, weaving between their legs and hollering up at them.

"Didn't you feed them before we left?"

"Of course I did. Those aren't hunger cries. She's letting us know she didn't appreciate being neglected for almost three hours."

"A little demanding, isn't she?" Alan picked her up and held her against his chest, sliding his fingers through her silky fur. "She purrs almost as loud as she meows."

He followed her into the living room and put the cat back on the floor. "When can we do this again?"

"What, Harry's?" She grinned up at him.

"Harry's two or three times a week might be a little pricey. I was thinking more along the lines of a movie. Tomorrow night, maybe?"

"Two dates in one weekend?"

"I'll make it three if you'll agree to Sunday, too."

She shook her head, still grinning. "What's that going to do to your playboy reputation? All your other lady friends are going to feel neglected."

He stepped toward her and rested both hands on her shoulders. "There's only one lady I care about. And she's standing right in front of me."

His features held an earnestness that caught her off guard, and her own teasing smile slid away. She had wanted to take things slow. But with him looking at her that way, she was ready to throw away all her resolutions and once again fall head over heels in love.

She moistened her lips. A kiss would be the perfect end to a perfect evening. Alan was thinking the same thing. She could see it in his eyes.

He leaned closer, slowly enough to give her ample opportunity to avoid his kiss. But she didn't turn away. Instead, she slid her arms around his neck and tilted her face upward, welcoming his advance. A moment later, his lips met hers, gently at first, then with more pressure. She had wondered if the spark would still be there. She needn't have worried. It was there and then some, as if it had been held on a slow simmer for all those years, ready to ignite when the conditions were right.

Tonight, they were right.

Love surged up from within, so powerful it almost made her dizzy. Maybe it had been there all along, buried in some remote corner of her heart, kept under lock and key. Now she could no longer deny it. She loved Alan, and regardless of what she might have to give up, she no longer wanted to live her life without him.

All too soon, he ended the kiss and stepped back to put some distance between them. "Tomorrow night then?"

She forced a casual smile. He didn't seem nearly as affected as she was. "Tomorrow night."

"And Sunday?"

"We'll see. You might be tired of me by then."

"Never." He moved to the door, then turned to face her. "Are you sure you won't let me stay? I'll sleep on the couch. You won't even know I'm here."

"I'll be fine. I won't open the door, and if someone is stupid enough to try to break in, I'll be waiting in the bedroom with my thirty-eight."

She swung open the door and watched him walk out.

"Lock the door behind me."

She should have known he wouldn't even step off the porch without making sure she was locked safely inside. She closed the door and twisted the deadbolt.

Several minutes later, her cell phone rang. Instead of a name or number, "Blocked" displayed on the upper portion of the screen. Her stomach tightened. She pressed the phone to her ear and breathed a tentative, "Hello?"

"Alexis." The hoarse whisper raised the hair on the back of her neck and sent goosebumps cascading over her skin.

"Who is this?"

The caller continued in the same hoarse tone,

making the voice impossible to identify. "I've warned you before. I'm warning you one last time. Back off or you're next. Don't think you can evade me. I know where you live."

The phone clicked dead. A chill swept over her and a knot of fear settled in her gut. How had he found her?

He hadn't. He was bluffing. He'd taken her name and number from one of the flyers that she and Alan had passed out. She was nothing but a name on a piece of paper. He couldn't know where she lived.

Five women had been murdered, with another living in fear. All six deserved justice. She wasn't going to let some idle threats keep her from doing her part to give it to them, as small as that part might be.

At least the call hadn't come in until Alan had left. She had no intention of telling him about it, either. If she did, it would only end badly.

But maybe she needed to tell him. She'd chosen a career in law enforcement. This wasn't the first time she'd faced danger, and it wouldn't be the last. If they hoped to have any kind of relationship, he was going to have to accept what she did and the risks that went with it.

If he couldn't, they would have to part ways.

She would rather it be sooner than later.

FIFTEEN

———◆———

A LAN EASED TO a stop in the Hope Community Church parking lot, two spaces over from an ancient faded blue Impala.

Duncan Alcott at church? *No way.*

But in Harmony Grove, the blue bomb was one of a kind. Maybe even in all of Polk County.

He turned off the car and opened his door to the gong of the church bell. The sky was cloudless, the sun midway to its peak, promising another warm spring day. Parishioners filed into the small brick building topped by a white steeple.

Halfway to the covered porch, he glanced back at the Impala. The driver still sat inside, slouched down as if he didn't want to be seen.

Alan turned around and walked toward the vehicle. With an SUV parked between them, he hadn't noticed Duncan before. Now that he had, he couldn't in all good conscience go in and enjoy the service knowing Duncan would be outside, probably breaking into cars.

Duncan watched him approach but didn't roll down the window until Alan tapped on it.

"Morning, Duncan. What are you doing?"

"I'm waiting for someone."

"You're waiting in the church parking lot." He didn't try to keep the skepticism out of his voice.

"No way am I going in there by myself."

Alan lifted his brows. "You're here to attend services?"

"What else would I be here for?"

He wasn't going to answer that. At least not out loud. "All right, then. I'll see you inside."

He turned to head back toward the front of the church and had to wait for a silver Lexus to pass. A familiar figure sat in the back seat, face framed in the window, waving enthusiastically. It was Juliette Nolan, the same girl he'd caught in the tree with Duncan. She was probably the reason Duncan would be sitting in church on a Sunday morning instead of roaming the streets looking for trouble.

A glance back at the Impala confirmed his suspicions. Duncan was getting out of the car.

When Alan walked into the church, Roger Tandy met him at the door. At somewhere just shy of sixty, he was a fixture there, had taught a Sunday School class for every age group at one point or another and had held several positions on the board. Now he was an usher and made sure that no one got into Hope Community Church without a bulletin, a firm handshake and a welcoming smile.

Alan moved up the aisle and scanned those seated until he found Shane and his wife, Jessica, then took a seat at the end of the row. For the past month he'd avoided sitting with any of the hopeful single ladies. He'd also pretty well given up his social life, too, except for what involved Lexi. But that was all right.

Since she'd come back into his life, he hadn't wanted to see anyone else.

He'd just gotten comfortable and was enjoying the prerecorded warm-up to worship when a tentative tap on the shoulder drew his attention.

"May I join you?"

When he looked up, Lexi was staring down at him. His heart stuttered. She was beautiful. Her hair was loose, flowing around her face like golden silk, and her lips, touched with pink gloss, were curved in a shy smile.

"Of course." He stood and guided her into the space between him and Shane.

It was obviously the day for unexpected guests. In the row opposite theirs, Duncan Alcott sat nestled between the new girl and her father, looking as if breathing might somehow bring down the wrath of God. Hopefully, Lexi would be a little more comfortable.

She settled in next to him. "Yeah, I'm here. I can tell that all this is important to you. I figure if there's going to be anything between us, I'd better check it out."

"I'm glad you did." He'd invited her last night, after a movie and a walk in the park. She hadn't given him much hope she would come. But here she was, an answer to his prayers. Actually, he'd had a lot of those lately.

The worship band stepped onto the platform. Once in position, they began to play and sing, and everyone rose to their feet. As the songs progressed from one to the next, Lexi followed the lyrics displayed on the screen at the front. Her lips moved, but whatever came out was too soft for him to hear.

Even Duncan attempted to sing along. Alan had cast some quick glances in that direction and found him much like Lexi, eyes glued to the screen. More than likely, his participation was for the sole purpose of trying to impress his new girlfriend. Or more importantly, her father. Regardless of his reasons, Duncan Alcott sitting in church was a huge step in the right direction.

When the band exited the platform, Pastor Tom took his place behind the Plexiglas podium. Well into the sermon, Alan cast another glance at Lexi. She didn't look bored. In fact, she appeared engaged. Up on the screen was Romans 8:28, that oft-quoted verse about how God causes all things to work together for the good of His people.

The pastor stepped out from behind the podium. "The presence of darkness doesn't negate the power of light. Light drives out darkness, but it doesn't eliminate it entirely. This verse doesn't say that God causes all things to be good. Instead, he orchestrates everything to work together for good in our lives if we love Him and walk the paths He's laid out for us." He paused. "In case you're wondering, *everything* includes the good, the bad *and* the ugly."

He walked back to the podium. "God has a plan for your life. The devil has a scheme. The devil's scheme is always to try to knock you out of God's plan. Let God use the trials in your life to draw you closer to Him. If you do, whatever you're facing, you'll come out stronger on the other side."

When he'd finished his message, he signaled for the worship band to return to the platform. Lexi sang the closing song with everyone else but didn't respond to Pastor Tom's appeal to come to the altar and do business with God. Alan didn't expect any different. Lexi would take what she'd heard and mull it over. She wasn't the type to make snap decisions.

When the service was over, Alan led her toward the door. Another twenty minutes passed before they emerged into the sunshine. Fully two-thirds of the membership of Hope greeted them. One thing was certain: they were a friendly bunch.

"What did you think?"

She nodded. "I liked it. I think I'll be back."

"Good." If he could have hand-picked the sermon topic today, he couldn't have done any better. It was something he'd experienced on numerous occasions himself—hearing exactly what he'd needed at a given time in his life.

He scanned the parking lot for the gold Mazda and found it near the back. "How about lunch?"

"Okay, but this time it's on me. I've got a bunch of homemade chili simmering in the Crock-Pot."

"Mmm, sounds yummy." He remembered her chili. She'd been a good cook even back when they'd been together.

She pressed the key fob and the locks clicked open. "I'll see you at my place in about twenty minutes."

Before she could get into the car, a sound stopped her, the barely-perceptible buzz of a phone set on vibrate. She stiffened, and concern flashed across her features. When she looked at the screen, the tension fled her body. She released a pent-up breath. "Oh, it's Mom."

He watched her while she explained that no, she

wouldn't be there today, that she had already made plans. She repeated the words, along with a promise to stop by tomorrow evening after work. After a couple of sighs and eyerolls, she adopted a more emphatic tone and apparently got her point across.

When she ended the call, Alan eyed her with suspicion. "Since when are you relieved to see that it's your mom calling?"

She shrugged and slid into the seat. "You just never know."

"Yeah, I do know. You'd rather take a sales call than a call from your mother." He narrowed his eyes. "What are you not telling me?"

She hesitated, as if trying to decide how, or whether, to answer him. Finally, she sighed. "I got a call from the killer. Or at least someone posing as the killer."

Heat shot through his veins, and he struggled to keep his voice at a reasonable volume. "Were you going to tell me about this at some point?"

"Yes, I was. I just hadn't gotten around to it yet. It only happened Friday night."

Friday night. They were together all evening Saturday and she'd failed to mention it. But chastising her would only make her clam up.

He gritted his teeth. "What did he say?"

"He said he warned me before, and that if I don't back off, I'm next. He said he knows where I live."

Alan clenched his fists, fighting for control. When he finally allowed himself to speak, the words came out sharper than he intended. "Are you ready now to go stay with your mom?"

She crossed her arms in a gesture of stubbornness. "I'd rather fight fire-breathing dragons."

"Then stay with me. I have a guest room."

"Look, he doesn't know where I live. He's bluffing." The confidence she'd probably hoped to put behind the words wasn't there. She was afraid, and it showed in her eyes.

"Then how did he get your phone number?"

"The flyers we passed out. They've got my name and cell number at the bottom." She pulled in a stabilizing breath. "Someone's messing with me. If it really is the killer, he's grasping at straws. I'm not the only one working on this. There are ten of us. Granted, I was lead on three of the five murders, but eliminating me isn't going to make the investigation stop. Threatening me probably gives him a sense of power, but it's easy, because my name and number are out there."

If she argued her points strongly enough, she might convince herself, but she'd never convince him the danger wasn't real. He reached into the car to squeeze her shoulder. "Please go stay with someone. Don't take unnecessary chances. You don't have anything to prove."

She jerked away from him, then twisted in the seat. "Is that what you think, that I'm trying to prove something? Look, Alan, this is my job. There's risk. As a police officer yourself, you should understand that better than anyone."

He did understand. He took those risks, too. But watching the woman he loved put herself in danger was a different story. "I'm worried about you."

"I appreciate that. But I'm well-trained and I'm careful. You're going to have to trust me." She uncrossed her arms and gripped the steering wheel.

When she looked back up at him, her eyes were filled with sadness. "If you can't cope with what I do, then maybe we need to end our relationship right here."

Pain stabbed through him at her words. No, he couldn't lose her again. He would do whatever it took to make it work. "I walked away once. I'm not making that mistake again."

She slid her gaze away from him to stare out the front windshield. "You're not the only one who walked away."

No, they had both made mistakes. Now they were getting a second chance. He just had to come to grips with the dangers she faced every day and the fact that he wouldn't always be there to protect her.

"All right." He heaved a sigh of resignation.

Things were much simpler when she had planned to be a business major.

◆

Lexi walked toward the briefing room feeling almost weightless. Life was good. She'd spent most of her weekend with Alan, each hour reminding her of all the reasons she'd fallen in love with him to begin with. In all that time, he hadn't brought up his concerns for her safety once. Maybe he was coming to terms with the danger inherent in her job.

If all that wasn't reason enough to celebrate, yesterday evening after Alan left, she'd made some more phone calls and had hit the jackpot. She'd found Ashley Rittman, another one of Lysandra's sorority sisters. Ashley had photos from that period of her life, lots of them. Tonight, she was tied up but promised that tomorrow night she'd be happy to pull out every album she possessed. With all those pictures, there were bound to be one or two of Gary.

Lexi released a contented sigh. If they could obtain actual photos to circulate, it would only be a matter of time until someone recognized the killer and called in a tip. They were so close.

Yes, life was good. Gratitude swelled inside and she sent a silent *thank you* heavenward. Alan was rubbing off on her. She wasn't complaining. She'd spent so many years blaming God for the bad things in her life that it was only fair to credit Him with the good. That didn't mean she was ready to go all religious. She knew the way. She had attended church enough times as a child. But she didn't commit to something until she was ready to give it a hundred percent.

She headed down the hall and several detectives filed into the briefing room ahead of her. When the meeting was over, she would suggest that Tomlinson allow Greg to accompany whoever would be making contact with Ashley Rittman tomorrow night. Greg would be leaving for his Jeep event the next day but would probably jump at the chance to be involved.

She walked into the room and took a seat next to Kaminski. She'd called him last night to fill him in on the latest, after she'd placed an excited call to Alan, then to Tomlinson.

The sergeant took his place at the front of the room and delivered a brief rundown of the events of the past few days. "Last night, Simmons located one of Lysandra Tucker's former sorority sisters. The name's Ashley Rittman, lives down south. According to Simmons, she had some pretty interesting stories. These girls always looked for some incoming freshman who had gullible written all over him. Then they went to work scheming. Rittman remembers all these guys, although she doesn't specifically recall the name Gary. She says she's terrible with names. But the pink tutu was unforgettable."

Tomlinson paused as some snickers rippled through the room. "Rittman claims to have great shots of all the guys they played tricks on. As far as I'm concerned, every one of them is a suspect. But based on what Tucker said, this Gary character is in the number one slot. Kaminski, I want you to meet with Rittman. She's not available until tomorrow evening. She lives way down in Bonita Springs, but it sounds like it'll be well worth the drive."

Tomlinson's gaze shifted to Lexi. "Good job, Simmons."

Lexi gave him a sharp nod, pride swelling inside. A job well done. Maybe there would finally be justice for Kayla and the other women who'd been murdered. It was what Lexi lived for, what kept her coming back for more, enduring the sometimes-grueling schedule, putting herself in the middle of people whose lives had been torn apart by tragedy.

When he dismissed everyone, Lexi held back. After the others had filed out, she approached Tomlinson.

"Thanks for the recognition."

"It's well-deserved."

"I have a favor to ask."

"The answer is no."

"You haven't even heard my request."

"You're going to ask me to allow you to interview Ashley Rittman. The answer is no. I'm sending Kaminski."

She crossed her arms. "That wasn't what I was going to ask. If it's all right with Kaminski, I was wondering if you would let Greg tag along. If he's going to end up in homicide in the not-too-distant future, it would be good experience for him. It would also mean a lot to him. He was pretty disappointed when the Moorehead arrest didn't turn out as he'd hoped. I think he wants to get this guy as badly as I do."

"I'll check with Kaminski, see if he'd mind his company."

"Thanks, Sarge."

Approaching footsteps sounded in the hall then stopped. A second later, there was a soft knock on the door jamb. Greg stood in the opening, smiling. "I was hoping to catch you when the meeting was over. Any breakthroughs?"

"Actually, yes. Last night, I made contact with an Ashley Rittman. She was one of the sorority sisters, but unlike the others, she kept pictures of all these guys."

A smile spread across Greg's face. "That's awesome news. Congratulations!"

"Thanks. We're meeting with her tomorrow night. We'll find out then whether it's as much of a breakthrough as we hope."

"Is she local?"

"She's in Lee County, Bonita Springs, so it'll be about a two-and-a-half-hour drive."

"Would you like company?"

"I won't be the one going." She glanced at Tomlinson but knew better than to even ask. "Kaminski will. I already asked Sarge if you could tag along, though. I thought it would be good for you to be involved in the final part of the investigation. He said it was fine with him if it was all right with Kaminski."

"I'd love to. But I think you should do this last interview." He turned his attention to Tomlinson. "This is our big break, and Lexi's been with this thing from the beginning. It seems only fair."

Tomlinson fixed narrowed eyes on her. "Did you put him up to this?"

"No." They responded in unison. Greg continued. "I'm sticking up for her on my own. She's been awesome to work with. She's a good detective and a great mentor."

She offered him an appreciative smile. It was nice of him to go to bat for her, even though she didn't expect it to do any good.

Tomlinson shook his head. "Greg, you can go, as long as it's all right with Kaminski, but Lexi stays. Until this guy is locked away, she remains behind the scenes."

Greg nodded. "All right. But if you'll consider changing your mind, I promise I won't let anything happen to her." He smiled. "I'll be her personal bodyguard."

When she walked from the room, Greg followed. "Thanks for suggesting that I go along."

"And thanks for sticking up for me."

"I hope Tomlinson reconsiders. You've worked so hard, you deserve this."

"It's all right." It really was. Granted, she was disappointed that the sergeant had taken the investigation out of her hands, but what mattered was the end result—a ruthless killer being taken off the streets. She stopped at the opening to her cubicle. "Fingers crossed that everything goes as we hope. After six long months, it looks like we might finally be ready to bring this guy to justice."

He smiled. "That's what this job is all about, isn't it? Justice."

———◆———

Lexi slouched against the back of the couch, feet propped on the coffee table and a distorted image frozen on the television screen. She'd been halfway through her movie when Alan had called. Her phone was still on silent from an afternoon meeting, but she'd seen the screen light up in her peripheral vision. Once they finished their conversation, she'd turn the ringtone back on.

If Alan had a reason for calling, he hadn't told her yet what it was. So far, it had all been small talk.

"I miss you."

She smiled at his lost-puppy-dog tone. "We were just together yesterday."

"That was yesterday. This is today. After three straight days of seeing you, I think I'm going through withdrawal."

"You know, you're getting dangerously close to pathetic territory."

"Hey, I can't help it if I'm crazy about you."

"You know what? I'm glad…even if you are pathetic." As much as she teased him, she'd been pretty pathetic all day herself.

"What are you up to other than watching a movie, which I so rudely interrupted?"

"Tonight, that's it. Then tomorrow night, there's a

slim chance that I'll be going to see Ashley Rittman."

"A slim chance?"

"More like microscopic. Greg is trying to talk Tomlinson into letting me go talk to her, but Tomlinson is pretty adamant. I suggested that when Kaminski goes, they allow Greg to ride along. Greg wants to solve this thing as badly as I do." She sighed and switched the phone to her other ear. "He was pretty convinced the killer was Wendell Moorehead. His enthusiasm and determination are definitely there. He just needs a little direction."

"If anyone can give it to him, you can."

The doorbell rang, cutting off her response. A hollow coldness spread throughout her body, holding her frozen in the chair as surely as if she had been bound. Despite the presence of all three of her cats, her solitude was more pronounced than ever.

"Was that the doorbell I just heard?" The fear in Alan's voice reflected her own.

"Yeah."

"Don't open the door. Call 911. I'll be there as fast as I can. Whatever you do, don't open the door."

She swallowed hard and pushed her body into gear. It could be a neighbor needing to borrow something. She glanced at her watch. At ten o'clock at night? Not likely.

"I need to at least look through the peephole before I get the police out here." The last thing she wanted was for a neighbor to be detained trying to borrow a roll of toilet paper.

"Just call 911." His tone was filled with urgency. "In view of the threats you've gotten, you shouldn't go anywhere near that door."

"If it's the killer, he's not going to shoot me through the door. That's not his M.O." She stepped into the entry and moved slowly forward, then dropped her voice to a whisper. "Stay on the phone with me."

She moved closer. Six feet to go. Her visitor was just on the other side of the door. But he wouldn't know she was there. The porch light was on and the entry light was off.

Four feet. Shooting through the door wasn't his M.O. But she wasn't just another potential victim. She'd been warned. Would he shoot her just to get her out of the way? Not if he didn't know where she was.

Her hand went to her hip. Her pistol wasn't there. She'd removed the holster the same time she'd changed out of her suit. But she didn't need her weapon at the moment. All she was going to do was look.

Two feet. The bell rang again and she stifled a startled shriek. She pressed her hand to her mouth and willed her heart rate to slow.

Finally, she leaned in toward the door. Peepholes were one way. And with the light off inside, there wouldn't even be a shadow. She pressed her face to the door. No police uniform.

The last of the tension fled her body. "It's just Greg."

"Why would Greg show up on your doorstep at ten o'clock at night?" Her relief obviously didn't transfer to Alan. Suspicion was heavy in his tone.

"Maybe Tomlinson gave in." She was still whispering.

"He could call to tell you that."

"You don't know Greg. *Enthusiastic* doesn't begin

to describe him. He'd be exactly the type to insist on giving good news in person."

"At ten at night."

"I wouldn't think anything of *you* showing up at ten at night."

"That's different."

"Trust me. If he has anything in mind other than the case, he'll find out really fast that I'm taken." The possibility that he was there for any kind of romantic purpose was highly unlikely. He'd made it clear that he was quite happy, just him and his dog. Alan had nothing to worry about.

"I'll call you back." She disconnected the call before he could protest further and slid the phone into her back pocket. Alan would just have to stew for a few minutes. Whatever Greg's reason for coming, he wouldn't be there long.

She opened the door about twelve inches. Greg stood on her porch, a Jeep in the driveway behind him.

"You *are* here." The smile he gave her didn't quite reach his eyes. "I was beginning to wonder if you were home. Can I come in?"

A wave of uneasiness swept over her and she wasn't sure why. Maybe she should have grabbed her weapon after all. No, that was ridiculous. He was a coworker.

"It's pretty late. What did you need?"

"I had some things to talk to you about, things related to the case."

Her uneasiness intensified. He was turned just enough that she couldn't see his right hand. Was it coincidence, or was the angle intentional?

"How about if we discuss this tomorrow?"

"I was really hoping to talk to you tonight."

He took a step closer and she tried to slam the door. Just shy of closing, it suddenly exploded inward. A scream rose in her throat but never made it to her mouth. With lightning speed, Greg burst through the opening, spun her against him and pressed something over her face.

A sweet-smelling white cloth.

Her heart slammed against her ribcage, and her world tilted. Greg was the killer. How could she have missed that?

She clasped her hands and thrust her arms forward and up, breaking his hold. In one smooth motion she spun and kneed him in the groin.

She didn't wait to assess the damage. A grunt and a muttered curse followed her as she flew into the living room. He should have known better than to accost a woman trained in self-defense.

Now if she could just get to the back door.

The vase in the entry crashed to the tile floor and heavy footsteps pounded behind her. The next second, rough hands against her shoulder blades sent her hurtling forward, facedown on the carpet. Before she knew what had happened, he had flipped her onto her back and straddled her, arms pinned beneath his knees. The cloth once again came down across her face, and no matter how she bucked and twisted, she couldn't break free.

She held her breath, still fighting with every ounce of strength she had left. If she could just throw him off her, she would stand a chance. Not a big one, but better than what she had while pinned to the floor. But he was too strong and too heavy.

Her lungs burned, the urge to inhale overshadowing all else, until she finally gulped in those coveted breaths of air. But they were tainted. Sickeningly sweet. The room seemed to stretch and blur, shifting slowly to one side, then the other, as Greg's face came in and out of focus.

Suki watched from the end of the hall. Lexi couldn't see her, but she could hear her, yowling in the low, plaintive cry of the Siamese. Midnight and Itsy were probably hiding. What would happen to them when she was gone?

She should have listened to Alan. All the times he'd pleaded with her to stay somewhere else and she'd stubbornly refused. Now what he feared most was coming to pass. He would be devastated. *I'm sorry, sweetheart. I love you.*

The grogginess intensified and the cat's cries grew farther and farther away. Nausea swept over her, wave after wave, until she would almost welcome the sweet comfort of oblivion.

Her eyes no longer wanted to stay open. The room faded into the distance. Greg did, too. He was wearing a grimace. Or maybe it was a smile. She wasn't sure.

Her eyelids drifted shut and refused to open.

SIXTEEN

———

A LAN SAT IN his recliner clicking through the channels. The thought of Greg being with Lexi shouldn't bother him. But it did. What business did he have showing up at her house at ten o'clock at night? Sure, they worked together. But something about it didn't sit right with him.

He was pretty sure Greg was single. Lexi hadn't come right out and said so, but that was the impression he'd gotten. And Lexi was an attractive woman. Maybe if he knew the guy, it would be different. But he'd never met him. He was just a name, a faceless man in a uniform. Right now, he was alone with Lexi. At her house. Late at night.

He laid down the remote and picked up his phone. After staring at the screen for several moments, he put it back on the end table.

No, she said she would call as soon as Greg left. It had only been ten minutes. If he called her back now, he would come across as a jealous boyfriend. Maybe that was what he was, because the thought of the other man hanging out alone with her at her house bothered him a lot more than it should.

He rose from the recliner and paced the living

room. The problem was, the dread that had swamped him the instant he heard her doorbell ring hadn't fully dissipated. He forced himself to relax. She was safer with Greg than alone. Greg was a cop, possibly armed, even though he was off duty. In fact, he probably *was* armed, knowing the danger Lexi was in.

He sank back onto the couch and once again picked up the remote. If nothing had sparked his interest during ten minutes of channel surfing, it probably wouldn't now, either, but at least it gave him something to do. He advanced to the next channel. It was a reality TV show with a stupid premise and lots of over-acting. He clicked the *up* arrow again.

Lord, please protect her.

This one was a movie, but since he was coming into the middle of it, it wasn't going to make much sense. Even less in his current frame of mind. With Lexi constantly intruding into his thoughts, he had the attention span of a goldfish.

God, help me to put her in your hands and leave her there.

The next channel selection offered a commercial for a popular pickup truck. He pressed the power button, cutting off the announcer midstream while he speed-read through the terms and conditions.

Lexi was safe. She wasn't alone. She had someone with her, albeit temporarily, which was what he'd been pushing for during the past couple of weeks. He should be relieved.

He checked the clock on his phone for what must have been the twelfth time, then dropped it back on the coffee table. Twenty minutes. She should have called by now, if for nothing more than to tell him everything was fine and she and Greg were having a powwow. She knew how concerned he was. The least she could do was let him know she was safe. Instead, the two of them were probably sitting on her couch, chatting, laughing and joking while he worried himself sick.

A few more minutes ticked by. Maybe Greg was hitting on her, refusing to take no for an answer. Alan snatched up the phone and redialed her number. She would think he was acting like a jealous boyfriend. Greg would, too. So be it. He had to make sure she wasn't in some kind of trouble.

The phone rang once, twice. "Come on, Lexi, pick up." A third ring. He clutched the phone more tightly. She often left it on vibrate, forgetting to turn the ring volume back up after a meeting. If that was the case, unless the phone was close by, she wouldn't know he was calling. Whether she'd adjusted the notification volume in the settings or it had been a factory default, her phone's vibration was something that was felt more than heard.

After the fourth ring, her message came on and he disconnected the call. He laid down the phone and resumed his pacing. He'd been trying to convince himself for the past twenty-five minutes that everything was fine. If that was the case, why the crushing sense of dread? Why the persistent feeling that something was horribly wrong?

He froze mid-step, his blood turning to ice in his veins.

What if the killer isn't someone impersonating *a cop? What if he* is *a cop?*

What if the killer was Greg?

He grabbed his keys, pistol and Bluetooth earpiece and ran for the door, dialing Tomlinson as he went. Judging from the slurred, "Hello?" the sergeant had been sleeping. Hopefully the man would wake up fast, because Alan didn't have the time or patience to ease into the conversation. He backed from the driveway and sped away, leaving a long path of rubber and probably several annoyed neighbors.

"What kind of car does Greg drive?"

"Greg who?" Tomlinson's words were still laced with the remnants of sleep.

"The deputy who's been working with Lexi."

"Lanning."

"Yes, what does he drive?"

"A Jeep."

"Does he have a second vehicle?"

"I don't know. The Jeep is the only vehicle he's mentioned. Why? What's going on?" Tomlinson sounded fully awake now.

"I'm on my way to Lexi's. I think the killer might be Greg."

A heavy silence passed before Tomlinson spoke. "Are you sure?"

"Not a hundred percent. But I was on the phone with her and Greg showed up at her house. She was going to call me as soon as he left. That was almost a half hour ago."

"Have you tried to call her?"

"She's not answering."

"I'll put out an APB on the Jeep and the white Camry. And I'll send units to Lexi's. I'm also going to see what vehicles are registered to Greg. Call me as soon as you get to Lexi's."

"I will. And call me with anything you learn."

By the time he pulled onto Lexi's street, sirens sounded in the distance, screaming ever closer. Soon two Auburndale P.D. cruisers followed him into her drive, sirens silenced but lights still flashing.

Alan jumped from the car and ran toward the house.

"Freeze!"

The command stopped him in his tracks and he turned slowly, hands raised. Two pistols were trained on him.

"Alan White, Harmony Grove P.D. I initiated the call."

Both guns went back into their holsters and the officers approached.

"We were told you were on the way. We didn't expect you to beat us here."

He pounded hard on the door. He wouldn't touch the bell. Greg knew enough to use a knuckle or a gloved hand, so there probably weren't any prints, but he wasn't taking a chance. His knock went unanswered.

One of the officers disappeared around the side of the house. The other walked to his car and returned with a pair of latex gloves. After trying the door, he dropped his hand.

"Locked."

Locked up tight and lights off.

Just as with the other victims.

"Do you have a key?"

He shook his head. They hadn't gotten that far yet. In fact, they were just getting started. *Lord, please don't let me lose her already.*

He stood back and thrust forward with one foot.

The door exploded inward, the strike plate side of the jamb splintered. Across the entry, a vase lay shattered on the tiled floor, evidence of a struggle.

The kitchen was untouched. The living room was, too. Suki sat in the middle of the floor, mouth open in a mournful cry that shredded his already frayed nerves. Itsy waited in the hall, watching him with wide green eyes. Midnight was probably too freaked out to show himself. If only cats could talk.

While the officer headed down the hall, Alan scooped up Suki then Itsy and closed them up in the first bedroom. He would close the other doors, too, and hope Midnight was secure. Lexi would want her cats to be safe when she returned. *If* she returned.

No, he wasn't going to think like that. He continued down the hall, almost reaching its end as the other officer exited the master bedroom. "Looks like she's gone."

He swallowed hard. As soon as he'd seen the shattered vase, that had been what he'd expected. When his cell phone rang, his heart leaped.

The caller was Tomlinson. "Are you at her house?"

"Yeah. I'm inside now. She's gone."

A heavy sigh came through the phone. "I guessed as much. I got the info on the vehicles, and it's not good."

Alan tried to steel himself for what he was going to hear.

"There are two vehicles registered to Greg. One is a 2016 Jeep. The other is a 2007 Toyota Camry, white."

His mouth went dry. If there had been any doubt, the slightest chance that this was all a misunderstanding,

Tomlinson's words shattered that possibility in an instant.

"We'll find her, Alan. We've got law enforcement from all agencies combing the county."

Alan swallowed the lump in his throat. "I was on the phone with her when Greg arrived. I tried to keep her from opening the door, but she wouldn't listen. Once she knew it was Greg at her door, she disconnected the call."

He drew in a sharp breath. Her phone. She'd had it in her hand when Greg rang the bell. Had she taken the time to lay it aside? Or had she slipped it into her pocket?

"I'll call you right back." He rushed through the words. "Lexi might have her phone with her."

He ran down the hall and into the living room. Her purse was lying on the end table. He dumped its contents onto the couch and checked each of the pockets. No phone. After glancing around the room, he bolted into the entry. The phone wasn't there, either. A search of the porch and driveway revealed the same.

He called Tomlinson back. "I can't find her phone anywhere. I think she might have it with her."

"We'll use the GPS to track her. If you guys hadn't been conversing at the time…"

He left the thought unfinished, but Alan couldn't stop the unspoken words from forming in his mind. If they hadn't been conversing, her phone would still be at the house, and finding where Greg had taken her would be almost impossible. In fact, if not for that conversation, no one would even know she was in danger.

But they'd lost too much time. Why had he waited so long to try to call her? Between those twenty-five minutes he'd spent at home, the drive from Harmony Grove to Auburndale and the time it took to enter and check her house, Greg had had her for a good hour.

Alan pressed his lips together. Lexi had her phone, and they had time to locate her. Knowing the way this guy worked, he wouldn't kill her right away. He'd wait until she revived. Then he would hit her and begin his photo shoot, bruising and bloodying her up a little more between each shot. The thought drove a red-hot poker through his heart.

He sucked in a stabilizing breath. "Let me know as soon as you get a fix on her signal."

"Will do. What are you going to do in the meantime?"

"I'm going to question the neighbors, see if they saw anything." It wasn't likely. The houses were all dark. Apparently, none of the commotion had disturbed the occupants—not the sirens, now silenced, nor the blue lights, which were still flashing. He didn't expect to learn anything, but talking to the neighbors would pass the time and maybe help him keep his sanity while he waited for news.

As he ended the call with Tomlinson, the police officer passed him in the living room on his way out. There was nothing more for him to do. The same for his partner outside.

Alan pocketed his phone and headed toward the house on the right. His stomach churned, and a shaky weakness filled his limbs.

Lexi had her phone. He would remind himself of

that fact as many times as it took. Soon they would have a fix on her location. Dozens of highly-trained law enforcement personnel would swoop in and do whatever they had to do to bring her out safely.

Unless Greg had already discovered her phone and disposed of it. Without the help of GPS, they would never find her in time.

No, he wasn't going to dwell on that scenario. He would keep praying and believing that Lexi had managed to hold onto her phone.

If she hadn't, he would still keep praying and beg God for a miracle.

Lexi squeezed her eyes shut, trying to block out the pain throbbing through her head. If this was what it felt like to wake up after a night of wild partying, she didn't see the appeal. No amount of fun was worth this.

But she hadn't had any of that kind of fun. She'd never been a partying girl. So why did she feel so rotten?

Her hip hurt. Her upper arm did, too. She was lying on something. She tried to shift her position and a moan escaped through her nose.

Sounds nearby filtered through her confusion—the rustle of clothing and the crack of twigs. Her eyes fluttered open. She wasn't home in bed. In fact, she was outside. Pine needles lay all around, providing little cushion for what were likely exposed roots.

"Well, well, well."

The familiar male voice sent awareness crashing down on her, as violent as a landslide. Her chest and throat tightened, and the rapid, jagged breaths she managed were woefully insufficient to provide the oxygen she needed. The killer was Greg.

But how was that even possible? He didn't drive a Camry. He drove a Jeep. In two days, he was leaving to attend the Jeep Jamboree in Tennessee. He'd told her all about it. She'd seen the vehicle herself, sitting in her drive.

And Greg hadn't attended Florida State. He'd graduated from UCF. Orlando, not Tallahassee, nowhere near one another.

And the suspect's name wasn't Greg. It was Gary.

None of her mental arguments did anything to change her situation. She'd been attacked, drugged and kidnapped and was now lying somewhere in the woods, and it was Greg who was standing over her.

She'd been wrong. They'd all been wrong. Lysandra had said his name was Gary, but she'd also said she wasn't sure. Gary…Greg. Both four-letter "G" names. She'd been close.

As far as where he'd gotten his degree, Lexi hadn't seen his diploma. She'd taken his word for it.

And the vehicle…no one could mistake a Jeep for a Camry. But just because he had a Jeep, that didn't rule out the possibility of his owning a second vehicle.

She'd made some serious mistakes. Her biggest mistake of all was not listening to Alan.

"I'm glad you finally decided to come around. It's no fun without you."

She tried to sit up, but couldn't move her arms. Her hands were tied behind her back, the ropes cutting into her wrists. Her ankles were restrained, too, and something covered her mouth, likely duct tape. Just like the others. A violent shudder ripped through her, and her mind stalled out. She was going to be victim number six.

No, she wouldn't go down without a fight. She curled her hands into fists and struggled to hold the panic at bay. If she had any chance of surviving the night, she would have to keep her head.

Greg leaned over her and she shrank away from him. Instead of hitting or kicking her, though, he pulled her to a seated position. She looked around, trying to determine her location. A half-moon shone from a sparsely clouded sky. Trees stood all around, mostly scrub oaks and pines. There was nothing to distinguish the place from any other stretch of woods in Florida.

He stepped back and moved slowly around her, like a lion circling its prey. He was dressed in jeans and a red polo shirt, and a camera hung around his neck. The uniform he wore with the other victims hadn't been necessary. She'd let him in without it.

How could she have been so gullible? She was trained. She had good instincts. Coworker or not, his showing up on her doorstep at ten p.m. should have raised red flags. How could she have interacted with him repeatedly over the past two weeks and never suspected anything? She'd been careless, blind and stupid. And she might end up paying for it with her life.

Stop it! Berating herself was accomplishing nothing. She needed to focus her efforts on staying alive.

"You just had to keep pushing, didn't you? It's really a shame, because I like you." He continued to circle her. "But you couldn't just let it go. I was ready to call it even. I was only halfway through my list, but after almost getting caught at Jennifer Rushdan's house, I decided to consider the price paid. I can do that, you know. I have the authority to mete out the punishment, and I have the authority to offer pardon, to declare the debt paid. That's what the uniform is all about. Justice."

Dread trickled over her at his words, so eerily reminiscent of the ones he had spoken at the station. He'd said that the job was all about justice. She'd agreed. That was when she'd believed his definition of justice was the same as hers.

He stopped pacing to stand over her, blocking the moon from view and intensifying her sense of vulnerability. "It would have been all over. No one else needed to die. I even gave you the perfect out, someone to pin the crimes on and declare the case solved."

He gave her the perfect out? What was he talking about? He hadn't had much to do with Wendell's arrest.

Realization slammed into her. Greg had nothing to do with the arrest, but he was involved in the investigation, which gave him the opportunity to plant the chloroform. That was why it had taken him so long to get back after picking up lunch and dropping off Jeff—he'd made a trip home first.

He'd even verified that the crime scene folks hadn't processed the kitchen yet. Then after lunch, he'd volunteered to clean up their mess while she retrieved the crime scene tape. Those few minutes she'd left him alone in the kitchen had given him plenty of time to tuck the little brown bottle under the sink. She hadn't questioned any of it.

There'd been another clue she'd missed. She'd wondered why the killer didn't just do away with the black Lab that found Denise rather than allowing the dog to lead his owner to her. It was because he was an animal lover, specifically a dog lover.

Greg had told her he was crazy about his German shepherd. And he'd been worried about whether Wendell's dog would be cared for. Those details had gone right past her.

Greg paced back and forth in front of her. "I gave you every opportunity to back off. I even warned you. Twice. And you ignored me." He looked over at her, shaking his head, his expression scolding. "Not a wise decision. Because look where it got you."

Yeah, bound and gagged. Helpless. A wave of despair threatened to engulf her, and she fought to hold it back, clinging to a sliver of hope. Alan knew she was with Greg. When she didn't call him back, he would have tried to call her. How long would he have waited? When she didn't answer, would he have figured out that Greg was the killer? Or would he have assumed she was still busy or had left her phone on silent after a meeting and hadn't noticed the call come through?

Greg stepped back and lifted the camera to his face. The flash blinded her and she flinched.

"It's all good, though. I'm getting to kill two birds with one stone." He gave her a devious grin. "Pardon the pun."

He moved to the side of her and she followed him with her gaze.

"Look straight ahead. I'm trying to get a side shot."

She continued to stare at him. He was expecting her to pose for his photo shoot? He was nuts. He snapped the picture anyway and resumed his pacing.

"As I was saying, it's all working out beautifully. Good things come to him who plans." He smiled at his twist of the well-known proverb. "Not only will I get you off my back, but I'll have the satisfaction of once again seeing justice done. Nothing gives me greater joy. It's why I went into law enforcement. To see wrongs atoned for. Tonight, you're paying for Lysandra's sins. I'll make sure she knows it, too. It's much more satisfying when the guilty party has met the sacrificial lamb." He tipped his head back and spread his arms. "Justice. Oh, sweet justice."

Lexi tried to repress a shudder but wasn't successful. A chill swept over her, seeping into her bones. His warped sense of right and wrong wasn't justice. He was a vigilante. No, he was worse, because he preyed on the innocent.

When he looked back down at her, his smile faded instantly. He narrowed his eyes and took a threatening step closer. "Don't look at me like I'm crazy, because I'm not. This has been done all through the ages— the innocent sacrificed so someone else can live. You know the stories. The people offering a young virgin to the dragon so the village can have peace and protection. Children being sacrificed to appease the gods. That principle is even at the foundation of Christianity—Jesus Christ dying for the sins of the world."

He snapped a third picture and continued to talk. "What's really nice, though, is that, thanks to your expert sleuthing, all these women are learning that others have died for their actions. They'll carry that knowledge all the way to their graves. That's the sweetest revenge of all."

He leaned over her again, but this time he drew back a fist and slammed it into her left cheek. The blow came so suddenly, she didn't have a chance to prepare. It knocked her to the side and she rolled onto her back. Pain throbbed through the side of her face and faded spots of light danced in the sky above her.

It was starting. The abuse each of the other victims had experienced. The gruesome photo shoot. Then strangulation. And more photos. But she wouldn't be there to experience them.

God, please help me.

She struggled to quell the rising panic. If Alan suspected she was in danger, he would have called Tomlinson. They would all be looking for her— Tomlinson, Kaminski, law enforcement personnel she worked with and those she didn't. Every one of them would do everything in their power to find her before it was too late.

But no one knew where to look. She didn't even know where she was. The wall of despair rolled closer.

"Sit up." His tone held an icy edge.

When she didn't respond immediately, he rewarded her with a boot in the ribs. A half moan, half grunt filled her mouth then escaped through her nose.

"I said sit up."

She struggled to comply. He circled behind her to put two hands under her arms and drag her backward. Something caught for a second, an item in her back pocket. Once he had propped her against a tree, she slid her bound hands over the curve of her bottom, where they met a hard rectangular object. Her breath caught in her throat. Greg hadn't taken her phone.

Since it was on silent, he probably didn't even know she had it. And he wouldn't feel a need to check. Bound and gagged, she wouldn't have an opportunity to use it. The possibility of the phone's GPS giving away her location wouldn't concern him, either. By the time anyone discovered her missing and authorities organized a search for her, he'd be long gone.

Alan was her only hope. *Sweetheart, help me.* She didn't believe in mental telepathy, but she'd heard of people sensing that a loved one was in danger. *God, please somehow let him know.*

Greg stepped back to study her, then raised the camera to take another picture. "That's a start. But we've definitely got some work to do."

When he approached her again, she braced herself for the second blow. It didn't help. Her head slammed backward into the tree and pain exploded across her mind. Almost immediately the side of her lower lip filled with heat and began to swell against the tape, throbbing with each beat of her heart. The metallic taste of blood filled her mouth. Clouds drifted over the moon, and her vision blurred.

He moved away to amble back and forth in front of her, posture relaxed. "Kaminski's appointment tomorrow evening won't be necessary. I'll have things taken care of well before then."

She blinked several times, trying to clear her thoughts. His words made little sense. She was floating on a sea of pain, her mind refusing to grasp the simplest concept. Appointment? What was he talking about?

"Did you know there's only one Ashley Rittman in all of Bonita Springs?"

Confusion gave way to clarity. Someone needed to warn Ashley.

"Thanks for giving me the city, by the way. That made my job a lot easier. But it's put us in a bit of a time crunch. I've got to fit in a little pre-visit before daylight. When Kaminski and I show up tomorrow night, we'll be shocked to find poor Ashley's body. The pictures she told you she has will be disappointing, though. There won't be a single one featuring a guy in a pink tutu."

He glared down at her. "Do you have any idea what that was like? No, of course you don't. Trust me, it was humiliating. But I'm sure you and the other detectives have gotten a real kick out of it. I heard you snicker when you mentioned the pink tutu to Tomlinson. Ten years later and I'm still being laughed at."

He leaned over her, clenching and unclenching his fists, cold fury emanating from him. She tried to prepare herself for another blow, but it didn't come. Instead, he straightened and looked past her. When he spoke again, his voice held more pain than anger.

"You beautiful, spoiled, popular women. Always playing games, using your wiles to draw us in. Then once you have us wrapped around your little finger, thinking we can't live without you, you cast us aside without a single regret."

Lexi stared up at him, trying to follow his train of thought. *Cast us aside?* Who was he talking about?

Lysandra and her friends? Or was he now thinking about the wife who dumped him nine months ago? Was his wife's betrayal what had pushed him over the edge, sending him on a killing spree to finally seek vengeance for an event that happened a decade ago?

He stepped back. "Now it's your turn to be put in your place."

After snapping another picture, he studied the camera display. He would probably be happy with the result. Her left cheek was already swelling. That warm, puffy sensation was there every time she blinked.

Finally, he let the camera dangle against his chest. "Those beauty-queen looks of yours are fading fast. This is much more satisfying."

He moved closer and her pulse jumped to double time. Although she tried to twist away, the third blow landed solidly on her right cheek, sending renewed pain flooding through her. Darkness encroached from all sides, creeping inward before once again retreating.

How long would Greg stretch out this ordeal? An hour? Two? The longer he toyed with her, the greater the chance that someone would find her.

But he'd already said he was in a time crunch. If he hoped to make it to Bonita Springs, kill Ashley, remove any incriminating photos, and still make it back to Polk County by daylight, he'd have to finish his business here by midnight.

What time was it now? He'd shown up at her place around ten, but she had no idea how long she'd been out after he'd drugged her. She likely had another hour max, maybe only ten or fifteen minutes.

He snapped three more pictures, then pulled something from his back pocket. Her blood froze in her veins. It was a coiled bungee cord, one of those black rubber ones. He unrolled it and gripped the metal hooks at its two ends, stretching and releasing the cord in a steady rhythm. He moved closer, one tiny step at a time, continuing the motion—pull... relax...pull...relax...

Her heart pounded out a staccato rhythm. *God, please. I'm not ready to die tonight. Please send help.*

She stared into the darkness and let the image of Alan's face fill her mind—his warm blue eyes, his teasing smile. Except if he had any idea of the danger she was in, he wouldn't be smiling. He'd be driving around, handsome face contorted with worry.

And praying.Yes, he would be doing a lot of praying. The thought gave her a small measure of comfort. For the first time, she understood the peace that Alan seemed to get from his faith.

When Greg moved closer, her body went rigid with tension. He stopped next to her extended legs, and leaned over her. "These final pictures are the most fun. Really unflattering. Have you ever seen anyone being strangled? Their face turns red, their eyes bug out—"

A rustle sounded nearby and he stopped midsentence, growing suddenly stiff with tension. It was probably just an armadillo or a possum. But after a dog had led someone to his last potential victim, Greg didn't appear ready to take a chance.

He dropped the bungee cord and pulled a pistol from an ankle holster. He hadn't used the gun the last time. It was a decision he probably regretted.

He could have killed the old man, then finished off Denise and not left a live witness.

But killing the old man would have involved killing the dog, something she now knew Greg would never do. Too bad she hadn't made the connection before.

"Don't go anywhere." He gave her a cheeky grin, obviously not considering escape a possibility.

He was underestimating her. As soon as he was out of sight, she drew her legs up and shifted her weight onto her knees. There was nothing she could do about her hands being tied. But if she could break free of the bindings on her legs, she would stand a chance.

She arched her back and gripped the rope, pulling hard to rotate the knot to the back, praying all the while. Once she had the knot where she could access it, she worked with shaking fingers, picking, pulling and grimacing as one then another nail broke off at the quick. Every rustle, every snap of a twig, sent panic spiraling through her. Greg was nearby, slipping silently between the trees, making sure they were alone. At any moment, he would return and finish her off.

The last of the knot loosened and came free. She struggled to her feet and stumbled through the underbrush, feet catching on vines that threatened to topple her onto her face. She had no idea which way safety lay. She didn't care, as long as each step carried her farther from Greg.

Now that she'd bought herself a few extra minutes, she stopped to pull her phone from her back pocket, careful not to drop it. As concerned as Alan had been for her safety, he likely already had the authorities searching for her. But she wouldn't leave it to chance.

Once she had a good grip on the device, she twisted to the side, pulling her hands into view. She could see the screen, just barely. After punching in the three numbers, she slid the phone back into her pocket, leaving the call in progress. She wouldn't have to say anything. Dispatch would assume the caller was incapacitated and send someone to investigate.

She resumed her slow jog, scarcely daring to breathe, but the thick underbrush and the dried leaves and twigs that littered the forest floor made stealth impossible. Greg's voice carried to her through the shadows, taunting, almost playful.

"Oh, Lysandra, where are you?"

She froze in her tracks. He was closer than she'd thought. She'd never be able to outrun him with her hands tied behind her back. Her best bet was to remain stock still.

And pray for a miracle.

SEVENTEEN

———◆———

ALAN SPED DOWN Berkley Road toward Highway 92, a feeling of lightness in his chest. He'd spoken with Tomlinson a few minutes ago and gotten what he hoped was good news. They had tracked Lexi's phone to a wooded area off of Recker Highway. Units had already been dispatched from Polk County, Winter Haven and Auburndale. And Polk County was getting a chopper in the air.

According to Tomlinson, the GPS signal was stationary. That meant Greg had chosen a place to carry out his plans for Lexi. Had she awoken from the dose of chloroform yet? He hoped not. Once she awoke, Greg would begin inflicting the pain depicted in the photos of the other victims. The thought tied his insides in knots.

He eased to a stop at the light and waited for the green arrow that would allow him to make his turn onto Highway 92. When the ringtone sounded on his phone, he snatched it from the cupholder. It was Tomlinson.

His hand shook as he pressed the phone to his ear. "You got something?"

"She called."

His pulse kicked into high gear. "She's all right?"

"We don't know yet. She didn't say anything, but the call came from her phone. She's moving."

The light changed, and he stepped on the gas, holding the phone with his shoulder while he prepared to shift from first to second gear. "What do you mean?"

"She's heading deeper into the woods. She's moving slowly, apparently on foot."

"That's encouraging. The fact that she succeeded in getting a call out means she somehow got away from Greg." She was nowhere near out of danger, but if she'd managed to escape, she'd bought herself some valuable time.

Tomlinson promised to keep him posted and ended the call. Shortly after Alan made his right turn onto Recker Highway, an Auburndale police cruiser flew past him, lights flashing and siren screaming. He resisted the urge to press the Mustang's accelerator to the floor and shoot off after it. He'd be there in a matter of minutes, without having to use excessive speed.

Tomlinson had given him the location when he'd called a few minutes ago—the large section of woods near where the extension of Main Street looped around. Alan knew the area. Just south of Main, a service road cut off of Recker and went back into the woods.

By the time he reached the area, more law enforcement had arrived, a sheriff's deputy and another Auburndale officer. The sirens had been silenced. A closed gate spanned the entrance to the service road, a chain looped around the post. Closer inspection showed the chain had been cut.

One of the officers pushed open the gate and the three cruisers sped down the dirt road, engulfed in a cloud of dust. Alan followed. They came to a stop where a green Jeep sat just off the road, against the woods.

When they had all exited their vehicles, the sheriff's deputy stepped forward. "Based on where we're picking up her GPS signal, she should be about a half mile away, approximately this direction." He lifted an arm, index finger extended. "More units will be arriving to give us a hand. Instead of charging in together, we want to spread out and surround them." He grew even more serious. "This one's one of ours."

Alan squinted at the man's name plate. Sergeant Bailey. He was older, probably mid-fifties, and carried himself with an air of confidence that Alan found reassuring.

Yes, she was one of theirs. Greg was, too.

Within minutes, more law enforcement had arrived, and Sergeant Bailey had divided them up and given them each sections of the large wooded area.

Alan jogged down the dirt road toward his assigned location. When he got to the bend that Bailey had pointed out on his map, he clicked on the flashlight and headed in. The undergrowth was thick. Florida's winters were too mild to kill the saplings, scrub and vines that occupied any natural areas. The tangled greenery hampered his movement and made stealth impossible. But he kept his flashlight beam aimed low and focused on trying not to sound like a Sasquatch lumbering through the woods.

Every minute or so he stopped to listen. If he couldn't

move silently, neither could Greg. Or Lexi. She had apparently managed to escape, at least temporarily. He clung to the hope that she was somewhere out there hiding while Greg searched.

Lord, please let us find her first.

A voice drifted to him, barely audible over the rustle of his own footsteps. He froze. The air was still. Whatever nightlife the forest possessed had hunkered down in silence. It was as if all of nature was holding its breath. Had he imagined what he'd thought he heard?

He had just lifted a foot to take another step when it came again. No, he hadn't imagined it. It was a male voice, higher pitched. He held his breath and listened.

"Oh, Lysandra. Where are you?"

His heart leaped. Lexi was alive, and she was still eluding Greg. Alan pressed the transmit button on the radio he'd clipped to his shirt collar and spoke in a hushed whisper. "I hear the suspect. I don't have a visual yet, but it sounds like he's in the southern part of block F."

Then he flew into action, pushing himself forward, ignoring the vines and brambles that clawed at him as he passed. Bailey would redirect the others. Soon that small section of woods would be crawling with law enforcement.

"Oh, Lysandra." The voice was closer now. "Where are you?"

The singsong tone sent goosebumps sweeping over him. It was all a game to Greg. Lexi's life meant nothing. Of course, Alan already knew that. Nothing meant anything to Greg except his vendetta. He was single-minded in his determination to right the wrongs of ten years ago, to carry out his perverted sense of justice.

The call came again, even closer. Alan was gaining on him.

"Lysandra, come out, come out, wherever you are. We're not finished yet. We still have one more photo to take."

One more photo. The words were like a punch in the chest.

Alan knew all about that photo. He had seen it with each of the other victims—the brownish-red line marring the creamy, white neck, lifeless eyes staring out from a swollen and discolored face.

That final photo wouldn't be taken until after Lexi was dead.

———

Lexi stood motionless, dragging in ragged, shallow breaths, trying to not make a sound. Greg was close. If she stayed where she was, he would likely find her. The woods weren't thick enough. If she ran, he'd hear her and be on her in moments.

"Come here, Lysandra. It's time for the last picture."

Tension spiked through her and she pressed her back against the tree. He couldn't be more than twenty or thirty feet away. Every sound ratcheted up her terror that much further—the thump of his footfalls, the rustle of limbs and brush as he moved, but most of all, that teasing, taunting tone.

"You're not laughing now, are you? You had your fun at my expense. Now the tables are turned. It's not so funny being on the receiving end, is it?"

She held her breath, every muscle coiled and ready to spring.

"Where are you? Ready or not, here I come."

Greg continued his taunts, enjoying his macabre game of hide-and-seek. They filled the air around her, the embodiment of evil, chilling her all the way to her core. She pressed herself more tightly against the tree at her back.

Then there was another sound, faint and deep, the distant rumbling of a helicopter. Her knees almost buckled. Her frantic 911 call had gotten through. Or maybe Alan was behind the massive search. It didn't matter who. All that mattered was that they were coming for her. The chopper was in the air, but there would be dozens of law enforcement on the ground. All she had to do was hang on until they arrived.

She peered around the tree behind her. A light flashed through the woods, sweeping back and forth. Greg had a flashlight and he was headed her way.

The panic she had struggled to keep at bay exploded, and she stumbled from her hiding place. Immediately, heavy footsteps pounded behind her, moving ever closer. She emerged in a clearing and, with an unobstructed path in front of her, broke into a full run. But Greg was faster. He was gaining on her, and there was nowhere to hide.

She was almost to the middle of the clearing when he gave her a hard shove and sent her hurtling forward. She twisted, instinctively trying to protect her face, and landed hard on her right shoulder. Pain shot the entire length of her body.

He grabbed her upper arms and forced her into a seated position, her back to him. The next instant, the cord was wrapped around her neck.

"You thought you could outsmart me." His tone was low, his breath warm against her ear. The cord tightened. "You're much more resourceful than the others were, but even you aren't any match for me. That's because justice is on my side."

She struggled to breathe through a constricted airway and slammed her head backward. The blow made contact, possibly with his jaw. His nose would have been better.

The cord jerked even tighter, shutting off her windpipe completely. The pressure built, heating her face and swelling the arteries in her neck. She twisted and bucked and slammed her head repeatedly into Greg's chest, but nothing she tried broke the hold he had on her.

She was going to die. She had her whole life ahead of her, a life that was to include Alan, but she was going to die. Why hadn't she listened? Why did she have to be so stubborn?

She lifted her eyes to gaze above the treetops on the other side of the clearing. The sky stretched into infinity, stars strewn across the cold, dark expanse. God was up there somewhere. He could see her. He was watching the entire scenario play out. For once, she didn't blame Him. She had no one to blame but herself.

God, forgive me.

The edges of her vision darkened, her angle of sight growing narrower and narrower. Soon she would black out, and it would all be over.

Her ears filled with the throbbing of her own heart, then settled into a faint ring and finally a rumble that grew louder and louder until she could feel it in her chest. A wide beam of light circled the clearing. The cord suddenly loosened and fell from her neck, and she gulped in several frantic breaths.

The rumble was deafening now, the light blinding. It surrounded her, bathing her in virtual daylight.

The chopper. They had found her. Alan was probably somewhere nearby.

Relief flooded her, mixed with a sort of euphoria. *Thank you, Lord.* She would never take anything for granted again. And she would give credit where credit was due. *Thank you, thank you, thank you.*

Greg hauled her to her feet and dragged her toward the woods.

No! She wasn't going back into the woods. She had to stay where they could see her. Already the chopper was descending. The door swung open and a commanding voice came to them through a megaphone.

"Stay where you are. You're surrounded."

Greg ignored the command and continued to drag her toward the woods. She stomped hard on his instep then kicked at his knee. The first blow met with a grunt and curse. He twisted and deflected the second.

Neither seemed to slow him down. He bent and threw her over his shoulder as effortlessly as he would toss around a sack of potatoes. Ten more feet and they would disappear into the woods.

She reared back and twisted, hoping to throw him off balance. As she lifted her head, a figure emerged from the tree line a short distance away and ran forward, weapon drawn.

"Freeze."

It was Alan. Greg spun and, still carrying her, pulled his pistol from the back of his waistband and fired two shots. A scream charged up her throat, but Alan had dropped and rolled and disappeared back into the trees.

"Give it up, Greg." The words were Alan's. He hadn't gone far. "Half of Polk County's police force is in these woods right now."

Greg hesitated, likely trying to decide if the other officer was bluffing. Lexi didn't know herself. After several moments of indecision, Greg fired three shots in Alan's direction, then bolted into the woods.

As Lexi bounced painfully on his shoulder, she sent more prayers heavenward, but these were for Alan rather than herself. *God, please protect him. Please don't let him be hurt.* If Greg would have hit him, he would have cried out. At least, he would have made some type of sound—a grunt, a moan, something.

Then someone was crashing through the woods behind her. She raised herself up to look, and a tree limb swatted her in the back of the head. She winced and strained into the darkness. Someone was there, closing in on them. *God, please let it be Alan.* She drew in a sharp breath. Yes, it was, and he wasn't more than twenty feet away.

Greg skidded to a stop and slipped behind a tree, pistol raised. He fired five more shots, and a high-pitched wail rent the night.

No! No, no, no! Muffled screams reached her, screams she suddenly realized were her own. Alan had been hit. Greg was once again bounding through the woods, but now there was no one to help her.

Another shot rang out, and Greg stumbled. His grip loosened and the next second, Lexi was sailing through the air, the ground rising up to meet her. She somewhat broke her fall with one foot and landed hard on her left side. Pain shot through her shoulder and a muffled groan made its way up her throat. Greg was sitting on the ground next to her, moaning.

What had just happened? She struggled to her feet and looked down at Greg. His pistol was aimed at her chest.

Something moved in her peripheral vision, and a figure flew out of the darkness and slammed into Greg. The weapon discharged, but the shot went wild. Greg's attacker had him pinned to the ground and was trying to wrestle the pistol away from him. When he'd succeeded, he raised his head to look at her, and her knees buckled.

Alan? He appeared unhurt. So who had screamed?

Rustling seemed to come from all around them. Two officers converged on them. Several more came at them from various directions. They really were surrounded.

She didn't see what happened next. Because suddenly Alan was on his knees beside her, wrapping her in his arms and peppering her face with kisses. He lifted her onto his lap and whispered her name again and again, interspersed with I-love-yous and more kisses. Finally, he pulled away and reached for the tape.

"I'm sorry. This is going to sting."

He ripped it loose with a grimace then studied her. The chopper moved in and hovered some distance above them, its roar almost deafening. Tree branches whipped violently in the rotor wash, casting dancing patterns in the sharp white light that shone around them.

Alan lifted his hand to stroke her cheek. His touch was gentle, but there was a tic in his jaw and a hardness in his eyes. When he spoke, his voice was raised to carry over the whine of the engine and slap of the whirling blades. "He hurt you."

She attempted a weak smile. With her busted and swelling lips, it probably wasn't a pretty sight. "I'm all right."

A few feet away, two law enforcement personnel had cuffed Greg and were helping him to his feet. Yes, she was fine. Better than fine. What were a few bruises when Alan was holding her and Greg was in custody? The nightmare was over.

She looked Alan up and down. "You're okay?" Her volume matched his. "I heard you scream. I thought you'd been hit, and I feared the worst."

The chopper lifted, moved in a large circle, then retreated into the night. Its sound faded to a distant rumble.

"Sorry to scare you like that. I wanted Greg to think he'd taken me out so he'd let down his guard."

"The shot I heard?"

"I got him in the leg. I didn't fire sooner because I didn't have a clear shot. I also didn't want to risk hitting you."

"If you hadn't gotten here when you did…" A shudder shook her shoulders. "He had the cord around my neck and…"

Alan didn't let her finish. He pulled her into a careful embrace and gently claimed her mouth with his own. Then he was kissing her cheeks and her forehead and her hair and mumbling about how he was never going to let her out of his sight again. She buried her face in his muscular chest and breathed in his familiar scent.

Finally, she pulled away to look up at him with a teasing smile. "Would you mind untying me, please? Unless you think I'm easier to control tied up."

He laughed, all the tension and worry and fear draining from him. He stood, then helped her to her feet. Once he'd released her, he turned her to face him, holding both of her hands in his.

"I don't ever want to try to control you. I love you and respect you too much to try to turn you into something you're not."

"In this case, I should have listened to you. I almost got myself killed. I almost got *you* killed. I'm sorry." She squeezed his hands. "Thanks for having my back. I owe you my life."

"I'll always have your back. Forever, if you'll let me." He put an arm around her and pulled her against his side.

Forever? As in the rest of her life? She looked up at him, searching for the meaning behind his words.

Before he could say anything further, a figure came into her peripheral vision, and she turned to see Tomlinson hurrying toward her, weaving between the trees. Judging from the ground he was covering, the younger cops didn't have anything on him. Alan watched him approach but still didn't release her.

The sergeant halted in front of them. "Are you all right?" Deep lines of worry marked his face, making him look ten years older.

"I am now." She drew in a shaky breath. "I still can't believe it was Greg."

Tomlinson frowned. "Me neither. I totally had him pegged wrong. I told you before, his record was exemplary. His enthusiasm was refreshing, his determination impressive. He was smart, ambitious, an analytical thinker, just the type of guy we look for."

Lexi nodded. "In retrospect, there were a few red flags. I didn't tell you that when we arrested Moorehead, Greg was worried about whether Moorehead's dog would be cared for in his absence. We knew the killer was likely an animal lover since he didn't kill the dog that found Denise."

She pressed a hand to her cheek. Some ice would feel good about now. "Greg was also focused on justice. We all are, but somehow, it was different with him. Several times when we were working together, he made comments about justice, how that's why we do what we do and why he became a cop. He used the position to mete out his perverted form of justice."

A sudden chill swept over her, in spite of the balmy night, and Alan pulled her more tightly against him. She snuggled into his warmth, letting some of that masculine strength buoy her.

Tomlinson heaved a sigh. "But why now? After lying low for ten years, why suddenly decide to take revenge?"

Her gaze shifted to three figures moving away from them—the two uniformed deputies with a slouched, shuffling Greg between them. He would be going away for a long time. He might even get the death penalty.

She had liked him, had enjoyed her brief time of working with him. Pity stirred inside, unexpected and unwanted. Had he always been made fun of? Was he that skinny, geeky kid on the playground that the others tormented, the last one chosen for the team, always put down, always alone?

Her eyes again met Tomlinson's. "I don't know. But the day we picked up Wendell Moorehead, Greg mentioned that his wife left him nine months ago, ran off with his best friend. Maybe that was what triggered all this. Maybe he got tired of feeling powerless and decided to take control. The timing is right. The first murder happened two or three months later."

Tomlinson shook his head. "I'm still having a hard time coming to terms with this."

His frown deepened. So did the furrows marking his face. He obviously had liked Greg, too. Some of his frustration was probably due to the fact that the killer had been right under his nose and he hadn't seen it. He'd been right under all of their noses.

She gave him an encouraging smile. "Don't beat yourself up. I worked with him, too, more closely than you did. I didn't see it, either. I totally missed the clue with the dog, and when he said he got his degree from UCF, I didn't question that, either."

Tomlinson frowned. "He *did* get his degree from UCF. That was six years ago, so he would have started four years before that. Maybe he began attending Florida State, then after this happened, decided he couldn't bear the humiliation and transferred."

She drew her brows together. There was still one

thing that didn't make sense. "Where does the Camry fit into all this? Greg has a Jeep."

"He also has a Camry, his second vehicle. That was something I didn't learn till tonight."

She nodded. "There were clues. We just didn't see them. I guess I was so focused on someone *impersonating* a cop, I never considered that it could be someone who *was* a cop."

Some of the tension left Tomlinson's features, and he gave her the first hint of a smile that she'd seen since he arrived. "You know what they say—hindsight is always twenty-twenty." He tilted his head to the right. "There's an ambulance waiting if you want to go to the hospital. It might not be a bad idea to get checked out. We'll take your report tomorrow."

She turned in the direction Tomlinson had indicated but couldn't see anything through the trees. The ambulance was probably somewhere out there, sitting silently alongside the road, lights flashing. Fatigue washed over her, bone-numbing weariness at the thought of extending the night another two or three hours. No, she would pass on the emergency room visit.

"I'm all right. I just want to go home."

He lifted his eyebrows, concern etched into the lines of his face. "You're sure?"

"Positive."

He gave a sharp nod. "Okay. Take your time coming in tomorrow. I don't want to see you before noon."

"No argument there." She turned tired eyes up to Alan. His protective arm across her shoulder hadn't moved during the entire exchange with Tomlinson. Now he used it to direct her into the woods and toward his car.

As Alan helped her into the leather bucket seat, she stifled a groan. Everything was starting to hurt. Besides the damage to her head and face, Greg's kick had seriously bruised some ribs. Before she could reach for the seatbelt, Alan leaned into the car to stretch it across her body and fasten it.

As he circled around to the driver's side, she let her head fall back. She would probably be asleep before they got to the outskirts of… She didn't even know where she was. But Alan knew, and he was going to take care of her. That was all that mattered.

The engine roared to life, and the car began to move, but she didn't open her eyes. As sleep drifted ever closer, she struggled to hold it back. They had a lot of talking to do. If not tonight, then soon. They were now finished working together, at least professionally. But they had decisions to make. And a lot of years to regain. They needed to evaluate their relationship. And decide where to go next.

She needed to tell him she loved him.

And find out what he meant by forever.

EIGHTEEN

———

LEXI BREATHED THE fresh, clean air, soaking in the peace and tranquility that Harmony Grove's park offered. Alan's hand tightened around hers in a confirming squeeze. He apparently felt it, too. No one could ignore the beauty of nature's late-afternoon show.

The sun was finishing its descent, painting the sky in broad strokes of orange, gold, pink and lavender. The glasslike surface of the lake reflected the spectacular display. Tiny fish created ever-widening ripples, snacking on the water bugs lighting there, and a pair of mallard ducks moved silently along the water's edge. Darkness would fall soon, but the promise of impending night no longer held an unspoken threat.

Alan gave her hand another squeeze. "Are you doing all right?"

"I'm okay."

She smiled up at him, trying not to grimace. Ice packs had helped with the swelling, and carefully-applied makeup went a long way toward hiding the bruises. In another week or two, the physical damage would be mostly mended. It would be a while before she felt emotionally whole again.

The nightmares probably wouldn't cease anytime soon, either. Last night, every time she fell into a deep sleep, she was back in the woods with her hands tied behind her back and a killer standing over her.

This afternoon, Sheriff Judd had held a press conference, letting the public know that the serial killer who had terrorized the young women of Polk County for the past six months had finally been apprehended. The story would be all over the news by tonight. Lexi had already filled her mother in on the details. She'd called her right after breakfast. Her mother had been shaken. They'd talked for fifteen minutes, and for once, her mother hadn't made the conversation all about herself.

Lexi had promised Tomlinson that she wouldn't go into the station before noon, and she'd remained true to her word. She'd shown up at one, taken care of her reports, then left again. Then she'd stopped by her mom's house to throw her mom's clothes in the wash. When she'd arrived, a load was already spinning in the dryer. Her mom's ankle was still wrapped, and the crutches were within easy reach, but she was actually up doing something for herself.

Lexi had mentally prepared for the pity party, the subtle control tactics. But they never came. Instead, her mom greeted her with a smile and a big hug. For the first time ever, she seemed to look on Lexi as an independent adult, with a life separate from her own. Too bad Lexi had almost had to die before that happened. Hopefully the results would be permanent.

After leaving her mother's house, she'd met Alan for a romantic dinner out, followed by a romantic walk in the park. Now she was content, in love and pleasantly full.

Alan drew to a stop in front of the same bench they'd sat on several days ago. "How about a break?"

A break sounded good. A walk did, too. Any activity had appeal as long as she was with Alan. She sank onto the wooden slats next to him and rested her head against his shoulder. They'd just settled in when her ringtone sounded. She slid her phone from her back pocket.

"It's Tomlinson." She swiped the screen and greeted her supervisor.

"How are you feeling?"

"I'm well, all things considered."

For the next several minutes, she listened as he filled her in on information he'd learned that afternoon. When he'd finished, she thanked him. "I'll pass the info along to Alan."

"Are you with him?"

"I am."

"I thought you might be." There was a smile in his tone.

She told him goodbye and pocketed her phone.

"News?"

She nodded. "We learned some interesting things. First, Tomlinson was right in his supposition about Greg transferring from Florida State to UCF. He spent only three weeks at Florida State. The incident that started all this happened only a week or two into the school year. He didn't make it long after that."

"I can hardly blame him."

"I know. Makes you feel sorry for him, doesn't it? Anyhow, we got a warrant to search his house. We already knew he had a nice camera. It was hanging from a strap around his neck when they arrested him. But when they searched his house, they found that he'd set up a dark room in one corner of his garage, with all the equipment—developing tank, reels, chemicals, you name it. He apparently wanted something higher quality than what he could print from his computer but didn't want to entrust the developing of his pictures to a film lab."

"That was probably smart on his part. If someone would have seen any of those photos, it would have raised some very uncomfortable questions."

"Tomlinson said there wasn't anything at the house that definitively linked him to any of the murders. No film, no pictures kept as trophies, nothing. When Greg kidnapped me last night, he told me that he'd decided not to kill anyone else after almost getting caught with Jen. All five of those cases would have eventually gone cold and remained unsolved. Instead, each of those families is going to have closure." That in itself made everything she'd gone through last night worth it. She was at least alive. Five other young women weren't.

Alan squeezed her hand. "When I realized that Greg was the killer and that he had taken you, I was afraid I had lost you. I can't tell you what I felt right then."

"I know. I always try to be optimistic and never give up, but I have to confess, there were several times I was pretty sure I was a goner."

He released her hand to wrap an arm around her and pull her closer still. "I love you, Lexi. I don't ever want to let you go. But I don't want to smother you, either."

"I love you, too. And right now, a little bit of smothering doesn't feel so bad."

For several minutes they sat in silence, watching the colors melt away as the final remnants of day faded.

"Do you know what's significant about this spot?" Alan's tone held a hint of teasing.

"This is where you first kissed me." She grinned over at him. "Remember, *I'm* the one who told *you*. You had forgotten."

"But I remember it well now. The full moon, the stars spread across the sky, the few straggling couples who weren't ready to call it a night and go home."

Warmth spread through her, bringing with it a smile. He remembered more than she thought he had.

"I wondered what you would do if I kissed you. I was afraid I might be rushing things. But if I remember right, you were quite receptive."

Yes, his memory had served him well. They'd been dating for two weeks, and she was beginning to think he would never kiss her.

He released a contented sigh. "This is definitely a special place. But I think it needs some more significance."

She leaned away to look up at him. "More significant than a first kiss? The earliest stirrings of true love? How are you going to manage that?" She tried for a teasing tone, actually accomplished it, in spite of her heart doing a frantic dance inside her chest.

There was nothing teasing about the way he was looking at her. "When I told you I would have your back forever if you'd let me, I meant it."

He took both of her hands in his, and her heart

throbbed harder. When he slid off the bench to drop to one knee, it almost stopped. She'd guessed this was where the conversation was headed, but that didn't make it any easier. Now that the decision was imminent, she wasn't sure she was ready.

"Lexi, I'd like to ask you to marry me. If this is too soon, that's all right. I've waited for seven years. What's another few months?"

She drew in a calming breath and fixed her gaze on the opposite shore. Alan was asking her to marry him. Again. The first time, she'd panicked. Giving up her independence had seemed too big of a price to pay. It was still a big price, but so was living her life without him.

When she met his eyes, he was looking up at her with adoration. Patience and understanding, too. He knew her struggles and was willing to wait until she was ready.

Emotion flooded her, love for this man who devoted his life to serving others, who cared so deeply it hurt, who put her on a pedestal and kept her there. She'd blown it once. Now she was getting a second chance.

No, she didn't want to wait. "After seven years, I think we've waited long enough. Yes, I'll marry you tomorrow if you want."

He rose and pulled her up with him. Laughing, he wrapped her in a hug, his breath warm in her hair. "You might need a little longer than that to plan a wedding."

"Okay, two weeks."

He lifted her off the ground and spun her around. Giddiness swept through her, and her laughter spilled out, carried away on the gentle night breeze. She was marrying Alan. And she was doing it without hesitation or regret. So what if she was giving up a small piece of her independence? He was, too.

After setting her back on her feet, he tenderly replayed that long-ago kiss. But this one held all the pent-up emotion of seven years of longing. Those Memorial Day fireworks that preceded the first kiss exploded across her imagination. She melted into his arms and surrendered completely.

Yes, she was sacrificing some of her independence, but the thought was no longer scary. Some sacrifices were worth it. This one certainly was.

Independence for love.

She couldn't think of a better trade.

THE END

ACKNOWLEDGMENTS

Thank you to my family and friends for your encouragement and support.

My sister Kim for your skill in helping me solve plot problems when I've written myself into a corner

My critique partners, Sabrina Jarema and Karen Fleming, for helping me make my stories the best they can be

My mother-in-law, Martha Post, for all the hours you spend editing and critiquing my books

My husband Chris for keeping me fed and well-supplied with chocolate when I'm burning the midnight oil.

And thanks to all of you who read my stories. You are the reason I write.

ALSO BY CAROL J. POST

Harmony Grove Series:
Flee the Darkness
Shatter the Silence
Pay the Price
Survive the Night

———

Cedar Key Series:
Deadly Getaway (novella)
Shattered Haven
Hidden Identity
Mistletoe Justice
Buried Memories
Reunited by Danger

———

Murphy Series:
Fatal Recall
Lethal Legacy
Bodyguard for Christmas

———

Trust My Heart
Dangerous Relations (The Baby Protectors)
Trailing a Killer (K-9 Search and Rescue)

ABOUT THE AUTHOR

Carol J. Post is an award-winning inspirational romance and romantic suspense author who splits her time between sunshiny Central Florida and the mountains of North Carolina. She's also a popular speaker, presenting workshops on a variety of craft topics. Besides writing, she works alongside her music minister husband singing and playing the piano. She also enjoys sailing, hiking, camping—almost anything outdoors. Her two grown daughters and grandkids live too far away for her liking, so she now pours all that nurturing into taking care of two sassy black cats.

Thank you for reading *Pay the Price*. Please let other readers know what you thought of it by posting a review.

For exclusive content, news and fun contests, sign up for Carol's newsletter by clicking on the link below:

https://caroljpost.com/newsletter/

<small>CONNECT WITH CAROL ONLINE:</small>

http://www.CarolJPost.com

Twitter:

http://twitter.com/@caroljpost

Facebook:

http://www.facebook.com/caroljpost.author

Goodreads:

*http://www.goodreads.com/author/show/6459748.
Carol_J_Post*